# High Velocity

FREYA BARKER

HIGH VELOCITY

Copyright © 2025 Freya Barker

**All rights reserved.**

No part of this publication may be reproduced, distributed, or transmitted in any form or by any means, including photocopying, recording, or by other electronic or mechanical methods, without the prior written permission of the author or publisher, except in the case of brief quotations embodied in used critical reviews and certain other non-commercial uses as permitted by copyright law. For permission requests, write to the author, mentioning in the subject line: "Reproduction Request" at the following address: freyabarker.writes@gmail.com

This book is a work of fiction and any resemblance to any place, person or persons, living or dead, any event, occurrence, or incident is purely coincidental. The characters, places, and story lines are created and thought up from the author's imagination or are used fictitiously.

9781988733975

Cover Design: Freya Barker
Editing: Karen Hrdlicka
Proofing: Joanne Thompson
Cover Image: Jean Woodfin—JW Photography
Cover Model: Brandon Thyfault

FREYA BARKER

When the FBI sidelines Special Agent Stephanie Kramer over health concerns, she sees her hard-won dream career go down the drain. Suddenly adrift and without purpose, she jumps at the chance when a friend offers for her to stay in their trailer by a quiet, secluded creek near Libby, Montana. As much as she tries to enjoy the tranquil settings, it's not long before local wildlife—and the man chasing it—invade her sanctuary. When it appears the job she's trying to leave behind is following her to Libby, the illusion of her solitary retreat is shattered.

After that last special ops assignment cost Jackson Hart his leg, he's had a hell of a time getting back on his proverbial feet. Being hired as a member of the High Mountain Trackers team went a long way to reclaiming his sense of identity. He's back in the saddle and adapting to a pared-down, mostly solitary existence. So the sudden jolt to his gut, when he encounters the blond federal agent he remembers well, is a harsh reminder of what is missing from his life.

Still, as much as they try to avoid the other, they seem destined to cross paths. Whether it is the intimidation of a local predator, or the threat of a former nemesis, it becomes clear they stand stronger together.

# One

*Stephanie*

Thank God for the small wood stove, I'd be freezing otherwise.

Of course, the downside is I have to go outside from time to time to grab some more firewood.

Not so bad during the day, when the temperatures venture into the fifties, but at night—when they dip below freezing—it's still a shock to the system. Hopefully, by the time May comes along, I won't need those extra blankets at night.

Not that I'm sleeping much, I spend most of my nights rewatching episodes of *House*. I'm almost through season seven, which leaves me with just one more season to go. I hope my sleep improves before I run out of episodes, otherwise I'll surely go nuts. The days are already hard enough to get through.

I can't believe I've been hiding out here for close to two weeks already. In some ways it doesn't feel quite that long, and yet, it seems like I left Kalispell ages ago. Maybe it's just that I'm determined to bury the events leading up to my departure deep. Nothing I particularly care to be reminded of, but my mind won't let me forget.

Then to add insult to injury, I was forced to take a leave of absence to *sort myself out*. My boss's words, not mine, but they were delivered in the hospital by my bedside, where I was recovering from what appeared to be a cardiac event.

It wasn't. According to the doctor, what I'd suffered was an anxiety attack. However, they did discover my blood pressure was concerningly high and I was put on medication for that.

When Don Bellinger—my boss at the Kalispell FBI office—walked into the hospital room the next morning, the serious expression on his face made it clear he didn't come bearing good news. He explained the health scare had been the last in a culmination of reasons he felt it was better for me to take some time off. It hadn't been a question, it was clearly an order, and it couldn't have hit me harder.

The FBI is my life. It has been for the past twelve years, and I don't know anything else. Other than going to the gym regularly, I don't really have anything but my work to keep me occupied. Which is why my life feels like an endless void now that I've been sidelined.

After only one week stuck in my apartment in Kalispell, I'd been climbing the walls. A random phone call from Janey—who I'd remained friends with after she'd found herself at the center of not one, but two intertwined cases I was working on last summer in Libby—gave me the idea a change of scenery might be better for me.

I don't really have many friends outside of my colleagues, mostly because work takes up all of my time, but I connected with Janey. Probably because we're not all that different. She's a veterinarian, but she's also a bit of a workaholic. Anyway, I ended up spilling the beans. I told her the entire sordid story and she immediately offered me a place to stay and lay low for a while.

That's how I ended up in JD Watike's trailer on the banks of Libby Creek.

JD is Janey's man, and although they now live together at her place on the other side of the highway, he still has this trailer sitting on his pretty patch of land. I can see why he wouldn't want to let it go, it's a beautiful spot. It definitely offers a better view than I had from my second-story apartment in Kalispell.

It's also lonely though, something I never thought I'd feel. Other than Janey meeting me here with boxes of groceries when I arrived, I haven't seen anyone. Besides the occasional sighting of wildlife, that is. However, I don't know that I'm ready to face people just yet. I've spent enough time in Libby over the past years since I was transferred to the Kalispell office, I don't think I'd be able to avoid bumping into someone I know. I'm feeling a bit too brittle, still.

Unfortunately, after two weeks here my groceries have dwindled to the point of a limp stalk of celery, a quarter onion, the butt end of my last loaf of bread, and half a jar of peanut butter. Not exactly the sum of a meal. I'm not going to have any choice but to hit up a grocery store once the sun is up, which should be in another half hour or so.

With the quilt wrapped around my shoulders, I get up, shove my feet in my Crocs, grab the bucket by the back door, and slide it open to get to the firewood I chopped and stacked on the deck yesterday afternoon. It actually felt good, doing something physical after weeks of inactivity, staring into space like a couch potato. It was a decent workout I'm still feeling in my arms and shoulders. I groan as I fill my bucket and lift it up.

A rustle draws my attention just as I'm about to step back inside. Swinging around, I squint into the morning's deep shadows, trying to focus in on what I heard. As I scan the faintly visible tree line on the far side of the creek, I hear it again and my eyes snap in the direction of the sound.

Even with only the first faint hint of dawn in the sky, I have no trouble recognizing the large shape of a bear at the edge of the water on the other side of the creek. I can just see him off to my right where the creek bends out of sight. His front legs are in the water as he bends down for a drink, not paying me any attention. This is his domain, after all, and he's at the top of the food chain.

Then suddenly his large head snaps up and he appears focused on something on this side of the creek. I can't see what might've spooked him, but I jump when I hear the snap of a rifle shot.

Instinct has me drop the quilt and the bucket, and I duck inside, where my gun is sitting on the kitchen counter. When I slip back out, brandishing my weapon, I notice the bear is down. A splash of water has me glance to the far right, but I can't see anything. Trees block my view of the creek as it meanders its way south. Careful not to make any noise, I move to the edge of the deck and step down, keeping my eyes peeled and my gun aimed at the spot where I heard the splash.

I stop in my tracks when I see a figure appear, crossing the icy waters of the creek.

*Jackson*

. . .

From what I hear, sightings had been piling up this past week.

This isn't an unusual issue for April in these mountains. The animals come out of hibernation and are generally starving for food and water. With a rising population in recent years, food has become more scarce and some of the bolder animals venture closer to populated areas, where they can find alternate sources. It's been a growing concern for fish and game wardens because of the danger to the public.

Last week, April fifteenth, the spring hunt on bear opened, and I've been keeping an eye on this big guy for days now. He was seen on trail cameras along the creek and has rampaged a few hunting shacks along the way, slowly moving closer to civilization.

I'd set up a few cameras of my own, hoping he'd eventually show up here, and this morning he did. I've been tracking him since the first watery signs of dawn.

This isn't my land, it's my friend JD's, but since he moved in with Janey, he doesn't seem half as interested to join me hunting. I don't blame him; I probably wouldn't want to get out of bed at the ass crack of dawn if I had a fantastic woman like Janey warming my sheets either.

But I don't mind being out here by myself. When it's just me and nature, I don't feel my limitations half as much as when I'm around able-bodied people. Don't get me wrong, I get around pretty well on my prosthesis—most people probably wouldn't even notice much more than a slight limp—but I am all too aware my right leg is missing.

They say it becomes second nature at some point, but the fact is about fifteen percent of the body I was born with is missing, which isn't that easy to adjust to. Every time I catch a glimpse of myself coming out of the shower, I'm still startled at my own reflection. This mental image I have of my former intact body persists, and I'm shocked each time to find part of it gone. Even in my dreams, I still have my right leg.

I went through a really dark phase for a while, especially right after my official medical discharge came through. Special ops had been my dream and I worked my ass off to get there. The training was brutal, my position on my team hard-earned, and our operations were dangerous, but I loved every goddamn minute of my years in service. I was good at my job too; as a sniper I could pick off a moving target at a thousand yards.

But in the end, my excellent marksmanship was irrelevant. We were on our way back to base when we ran into an ambush. Grenades from a Russian GM-94 were launched into the lead vehicle I was in. I don't remember much more than one minute I was looking forward to a shower and a hot meal back at base, and the next there was a scream, right before a blinding flash of light and a loud explosion filled the Humvee. The last thing I remember is the acrid smell of burning flesh.

A sound from across the creek drags me from my slippery slide down memory lane. Lifting my rifle to my shoulder, I squint through my night-vision scope to see the large lumbering shape of the bear moving out of the trees toward the water.

I wait a moment, allowing him to step into the creek for a drink, as I take in a breath and let it out slowly, grounding myself. I place the reticle of my scope right behind the bear's front shoulder, just as the animal raises its large head, blocking my side shot. From across the creek, I swear the animal is looking right at me, but I can't let it unnerve me. If this was just another bear or any other hunt, I might hesitate to pull the trigger, but this bear clearly has no fear and could pose a serious danger to the public.

Determined, I reset my scope, my target now low, between the bear's eyes at the bridge of his snout. The animal still hasn't moved a muscle when I slowly depress the trigger. The crack of the rifle reverberates loudly in the early morning silence, and the bear drops down instantly.

It's not until I start wading across the creek I detect the smell of a wood fire. Odd, there's not much out here except for JD's vacant trailer. I turn my head and find it just a few hundred yards from where I came out of the trees.

The first thing I notice is the faint glow of light through the small kitchen window and it stops me in my tracks. Next, I catch movement on the bank of the creek, and see the outline of a woman, her arms stretched out in front of her. She's holding a gun in her hands and it's aimed at me.

"You're on private property!" she yells.

Her voice sounds familiar, but at this distance I can't make out her face.

"I'm well aware," I call back, changing direction as I start moving toward her.

Whoever she is, I'm pretty sure she has no business being here or I would've known about it.

"Not another step," she warns me as I approach.

Now that I can see more of her, I have no trouble recognizing her voice. In fact, I'm surprised I didn't recognize her sooner. Although, in my defense, the last person I expected to find camped out here in JD's trailer is Special Agent Stephanie Kramer.

"Easy...it's just me."

I pull off the camo-print balaclava I covered my face with, and see her expression change as she recognizes me.

She immediately lowers her gun, but keeps it in her hand by her side, aimed at the ground.

"Jackson. What the hell are you doing here?"

"I should ask you that question," I return. "I live a few miles down the road and this is my friend's land, but you're quite a bit farther from home."

I notice her eyes drifting over my shoulder toward the dead bear. I get the sense she's not eager to share.

Too bad.

"Are you here on another case?" I push. "Does JD know you're using his place?"

Her eyes come back to mine and her shoulders slump visibly.

"Yes, he does, and can you just forget you saw me?"

It sounds more like a plea than a question, and either way, it's a laughable request. Like I'd be able to forget, I've had a hard enough time forcing thoughts of her from my head when she was safely tucked away in Kalispell. There is no way I'd be able to ignore the fact she's camping out right under my nose.

I'm also going to need a serious talk with my so-called friend, who is clearly keeping shit from me.

"Not a chance in hell," I tell her honestly. "So you may as well clue me in. Are you here for work?"

Her gaze drifts again, but this time she answers with a shake of her head.

"I'm on a break. Call it a vacation. I just needed some peace and quiet."

Something doesn't quite ring true. The Stephanie Kramer I met last year does not take breaks or vacations. She struck me as a bit of a workaholic, someone who doesn't have any quit in her and gives her all to the job. I recognized the drive. It's the same one I used to have. I have a strong sense she's not telling me the whole story.

"And you picked Libby?"

She shrugs. "That was Janey's suggestion. She offered JD's trailer which, she assured me, was sitting empty anyway. She was right, this place is peaceful and quiet. At least it was until this morning."

The last is said in a somewhat accusatory tone. It's a challenge I chose to ignore.

"Why did you shoot him?"

"Spring hunt opened last week and this guy was getting a little too comfortable around the more populated areas. Two birds with one stone."

Her eyes are still fixed on the bear's carcass, giving me a chance to take in her appearance in the pale light of dawn. She looks haggard—almost gaunt—with dark circles under her eyes, and I wonder if maybe she's ill. The messy bun, worn sweats, and ridiculous pink Crocs she's wearing are a far cry from the pony-tailed, buttoned-up, suit-wearing agent I know.

Something more is definitely going on and I am determined to find out what.

"I'm so sorry."

I wave off Janey's repeat apology.

I'd finally braved the grocery store in town, only to bump into her in the produce section. After this morning's encounter with Jackson at the creek, it suddenly seemed moot to try and keep my presence in town a secret. It wasn't going to last forever anyway.

I could sense he was curious and to avoid the close scrutiny from those somber brown eyes, I left him to deal with his bear and retreated inside. There, like the coward I am, I watched him from the safety of the small bathroom window.

Jackson is a bit of an enigma. He seems moody, a bit sharp-edged at times, but then there are these odd moments when he suddenly looks inexplicably fragile. Yet, there is nothing vulnerable about his tall, powerful body, despite his artificial limb.

Yes, I did my research when I was here last year. In part because I do my due diligence in every case I work, but I also looked into Jackson in particular because there was something intriguing about him. He seemed a bit uncomfortable in his skin, and looked almost out of place in small-town Montana. What I uncovered about him gave me some insight.

Twelve years in the armed forces with an honorable, medical discharge after he lost his right leg in what was described as a roadside incident. No further details or location, which is why I figured he was likely special ops. It fits.

All of this happened two years ago, so it's not a surprise he's still adjusting. Both to civilian life, and living with part of him missing. Although, you'd hardly be able to tell from the way he moves. His body is strong and his strides are long and almost graceful, despite the slight hesitation when he plants his right foot.

Still, for all his physical power and grit, there is something brittle about him. I saw it again this morning.

"It's fine," I tell Janey, while examining an avocado for ripeness. "I'm sure he had more reason to be shocked to see me there than the other way around."

The avocado passes muster and is placed in my cart with the rest of my groceries. I'm loading up for at least another week or two.

"I plumb forgot about the start of hunting season," Janey comments as she makes her way around the produce bins. "JD didn't mention anything either. It's a good hunting spot. Last fall, the two of them took down an elk on that stretch of land just east of the creek. We still have some meat left in the freezer, if you'd like some."

Growing up, I can't remember ever eating game meat, although my father supposedly went out on regular hunting trips. I only discovered later he was hunting animals of the two-legged variety. I've tried it since and enjoy a good elk steak or venison strap, but I've never actually cooked the meat myself.

"I love it, but to be honest, I wouldn't know how to prepare it."

Janey follows me as I circle around to the fruit and toss a few Honeycrisp apples in a bag.

"JD could tell you. He usually does the meat on the grill or in the smoker, and I think I have a good recipe somewhere for a nice stew I can dig up."

I glance at her, suddenly curious.

"Hunting doesn't bother you? I mean, being a vet and all?"

She grins and shakes her head.

"Not in the least, as long as it's for food. I'd rather eat that than those impersonal packaged pieces of meat you find in the cooler. It's too easy to forget that was an animal once, raised and kept under generally poor conditions for the sole purpose of ending up on a Styrofoam tray in a grocery store. At least the animals hunted for food had a fair chance and a free life."

I glance over at the meat section where all the packages are neatly lined up, unrecognizable as having once been a living, breathing creature, and I at once feel guilty for all the years I've thoughtlessly grabbed an anonymous protein for my dinner.

Janey's rationale definitely puts the bloody tableau I finally turned my back on this morning—as Jackson processed the bear on the other side of the creek—in a different perspective. What may have looked like a lot of messy work for some meat, suddenly seems the more fair and humane approach.

When I walk past the meat cooler without picking anything, Janey softly chuckles behind me.

"I'll drop some elk off this afternoon, and I'm sure Jackson will be happy to share some bear meat too."

I give her a thumbs-up and make my way through the aisles. I'm trying to stick to healthy food items, but when I get to the baking aisle, I find myself perusing the shelves, thinking maybe I can try some baking. I've read making your own sourdough bread can be gratifying. So I start by picking up a bag of flour and some yeast, but by the time I get to the cash register, my cart is almost full with other baking-related items.

Janey is through the checkout line faster than I am, but is waiting for me just outside the doors.

"I was thinking, why don't you come over for dinner tonight? JD can give you a quick tutorial on how to cook elk meat and I can find you that recipe. That is, if you feel up to it," she adds carefully.

I hesitate for a moment, wondering if maybe after my run-in with Jackson and this outing to Rosauers for groceries was enough for today. After my near solitary existence these past weeks, perhaps it's too much people exposure at once. Then again, it feels almost rude to refuse after what they've done for me.

"Sure. Yes," I reply clumsily, quickly adding, "I'd love to. I'll bring dessert."

Lord knows I bought enough baking ingredients to feed a family of six comfortably. At least I'll have an opportunity to share some of those calories, otherwise they'll just end up on my hips.

I load my groceries in my vehicle and wave at Janey a row over before climbing in behind the wheel. No sooner have I started my engine, when a call comes in over the CR-V's sound system my phone automatically hooks into. The screen on my dashboard lists a Michigan number I don't recognize, so I silence it and turn on the easy-listening playlist I found on Spotify.

If it's important, they'll leave a message.

*Jackson*

"That's great. Yeah, we're home, drop by any time."

It had taken me a good chunk of the day to process that bear, and haul all of it in parts across the creek. No way I was going to get it to my truck any other way, he was a big guy. So I opted to butcher him in place. I'd already given Buck Adams—our fish and game warden—a heads-up, and he showed up to take a look to make sure this was the same bear they'd been receiving complaints about. He confirmed it and, with his blessing, I got to work.

It's a messy job, but also very gratifying. There is some primal satisfaction in hunting and gathering to feed your clan. I could never eat all this meat by myself—heck, I wouldn't even have the room to store it in my cabin—so it gets divided. Some of it will go to the ranch house for Jonas, my mother, and Thomas. At least half goes to JD; not only did I shoot the bear on his land, but even when we hunt together, we always split the meat between us.

My share is already hanging in bags in the garage at the ranch, where I'll let it age for a couple of days before wrapping it up for the freezer. The other half is in the back of my truck waiting to be delivered. I've already taken a quick shower to wash the stench and the grime off me, and grabbed a quick bite to eat.

"I'm on my way," I tell JD as I walk to the door.

My dog, Ash, starts to whine, none too pleased I'm leaving him alone again. He's a border collie cross, smart as a whip, but very excitable. At not quite a year old, he's going to need a bit more training before I let him tag along on a hunt.

"You wanna come see Ginger?" I ask him as I tuck my phone in my pocket and grab my keys off the hook.

Ash is by my side like a shot, his tail wagging furiously. Ginger is Janey's dog—or I guess now both Janey and JD's —and Ash loves her, even though she's not that sure about him. He's a bit too rambunctious still, but she doesn't hesitate putting him in his place when he gets out of hand. Something that doesn't appear to bother Ash in the least.

He's already standing by the passenger side of my truck before I can close the door to my cabin.

"Heading out?" Thomas yells from his perch on the porch.

Thomas is technically my stepgrandfather. He's my mother's father-in-law. My dad died in combat when I was just thirteen. Ma was alone for a dozen or so years before she moved her horse rescue to Libby and bumped into a local rancher. That was Jonas, my stepdad, and Thomas is his father. Jonas doesn't have kids of his own, and even though I was already twenty-three when I met him, he has treated me like his son. Maybe it's because I was already older, but for some reason I've never called him Dad, although I do occasionally call Thomas, Grandpa. If only to see the smile it puts on the old man's face.

"Just dropping off the rest of the meat at JD's," I share.

"You tell that boy to smoke me some bear jerky. My

mouth needs something to do now his ma cut me off my cigars."

Ama, JD's mother, runs the ranch house and tries to keep Thomas—who she treats like he was her own father—on the straight and narrow. He's a bit of a handful, especially now that his mind is slowly starting to go. He's forgotten he's been cut off from his cigars for a while now.

"I'll pass it on," I tell him as I open the passenger door and let Ash jump up. "Later, Grandpa."

He raises one bony hand in acknowledgement before tucking it back under the blanket covering his lap. Then he leans his head back against his rocking chair and closes his eyes. He'll probably be asleep before I turn my truck down the driveway.

The garage door is already open when I get to Janey's place, and JD steps outside as I back my truck in. I have to maneuver past a small SUV I don't recognize. Impatient, Ash jumps over my lap the moment I open my door and is already assaulting JD for pets by the time I get to the back of my truck.

"Still can't curb his excitement, can he?" JD observes, scratching my mutt behind the ears.

"He's been cooped up inside for most of the day. He hasn't had much exercise."

"We'll throw him out back with Ginger in a bit, she'll give him a workout."

As I'm lowering the tailgate, my eye catches on that SUV.

"Whose is that?" I ask, even though I have a faint suspicion.

He narrows his eyes on me before confirming, "Someone I hear you had a run-in with this morning."

"Right. Stephanie Kramer." I climb into the bed of the

truck and grab the first bag of meat, tossing it at JD. "Any reason you never mentioned she's staying at your place?"

He lifts the bag onto a hook hanging from a chain attached to the rafters.

"Hey, tonight's the first I've seen of her myself. Janey talked to her, she told me Stephanie needed a quiet place to recover, and offered her my trailer."

My ears perked up at that.

"Recover?"

I'd wondered whether maybe she'd been ill. She didn't look well.

"She's had some health issues," he clarifies.

"What do you mean, health issues?"

That came out sharper than I intended and JD throws up both hands defensively.

"Brother, that's not mine to share."

Frustrated, I toss him another bag.

I don't understand where that need to know is coming from. I don't normally stick my nose in other people's business. In fact, I generally avoid getting sucked into someone else's issues, I have plenty of my own. Yet here I am, grinding my teeth because JD has information he won't share.

Information about Stephanie Kramer, to be more specific.

"Come in for a drink?" he offers when he's hung the third and final bag of meat.

"Yeah, sure." I hop down from the tailgate and pull the bear's pelt toward me. "Where do you want this?"

I don't have any use for a bear hide, but there are those who do. In the past, JD or one of his parents would take an animal's pelt, clean and cure it, and find someone who had use for one. Sometimes, they'd end up with their family or friends at the Flathead Reservation, or were used as part of the ceremonial garb worn at powwows. Sometimes, one would be donated to a school, a wildlife information center, or some other educational facility. I like the idea as few as possible of the animals' parts I shoot go to waste.

JD helps me carry the pelt—which probably weighs a good eighty pounds with the head still attached—to an old chest freezer in the far corner.

"I'll probably have a chance this weekend to frame it up," he comments when we tuck it inside. "Looks a good size."

"Yeah, he was a big boy. Bold as hell. Didn't even flinch when he caught sight of me."

JD kicks off his boots in the mudroom and I do the same before following him inside.

The women are sitting across from each other at the table. Stephanie looks up when we walk in, and Janey spins her head around.

"Jackson," she greets me with a smile. "Have you eaten? We have leftovers I can easily heat up."

I hold up a hand. "I ate. Thanks. Hey, Stephanie," I provoke when she stubbornly keeps her back turned.

"Jackson," she replies, with a quick flash of her face as she lifts her head for a second.

"Beer?" JD asks from behind me.

"Thanks."

I grab the bottle he hands me over my shoulder and walk around the table to sit down next to Janey, so I'm facing Stephanie. Except her eyes are on her hands, which are clasped together on the table in front of her.

Ash, who lumbered in behind us is doing the rounds, getting rubs from Janey, growls from Ginger. Then he discovers Stephanie, a new-to-him human he's eager to explore with nose and tongue. Her soft chuckle when he jumps with his front legs on her lap, so he can reach her face, has me smiling too.

"Sorry. His name is Ash and I'm trying to teach him manners," I volunteer

She raises her eyes and sends a faint smile.

"He's fine. I happen to like dogs."

Definitely a point in her favor.

"Also, I apologize for the early morning disturbance," I add.

"No problem. I was awake anyway." She abruptly gets up from the table. "Which is why I should probably get going."

"Wait," Janey stops her as she's already moving toward the door. "Let me grab you some elk."

Stephanie waits awkwardly by the door while Janey digs through her freezer drawer, and I take a sip of my beer during the loaded silence.

"Here you go," she says, joining Stephanie at the door and handing her a paper bag.

With a hug for Janey and a quick wave at us, she darts outside.

"What did you do to her?" JD wants to know from me when Janey returns to the kitchen.

"Me? Nothing."

Still, I can't help wonder if her hasty departure is directly connected to my arrival.

Is it possible she's running from me?

# Three

STEPHANIE

"Vallard."

I'm annoyed when my stomach gives a little twist hearing his voice. Taking in a deep breath, I get right down to business.

"Ben, it's Stephanie. I just got your message."

I don't tell him that irrational anxiety had me staring at the little red dot marking the voicemail icon on my phone half the morning, before I finally listened to it. That unknown Michigan number had been his, but I never checked my phone until early this morning while I was once again waiting for the sun to rise.

Another rough night.

Dinner had been amazing, and I'd enjoyed the human interaction. The conversation was laid-back, I even had a good chuckle at Janey's description of her new intern's first encounter with the back end of a pregnant donkey. JD also shared some funny anecdotes of life at the ranch in his calm voice. I didn't have to talk much and just listened, appreciating the fact I didn't feel I needed to work hard at being social. They didn't ask questions, didn't probe me about work, or how I was doing, and instead simply let me be.

Yeah, I'd really enjoyed the evening. That is, until Jackson walked into the house with that friendly pooch.

Not that he did anything wrong—he was just being friendly—but I could feel the keen scrutiny from those serious, brown eyes. Like earlier yesterday morning, he looked at me in a way that made me feel exposed to the core, leaving me with no place to hide.

So, I ran, for the second time in one day.

All that to say, I had a restless night, my mind rarely still long enough to get some decent sleep, and that strange Michigan number was all but forgotten until I saw the evidence of a message on my screen this morning.

*Ben Vallard.*

He didn't need to introduce himself, even though he did so on the message. I don't think I could forget the slightly raspy quality of his voice if I wanted to. It's actually the first thing that drew me to him all those years ago when I was a rookie agent, walking into the Traverse City, Michigan office for the first time.

God, I'd been so green. So excited I'd been assigned to the office where my father spent most of his career. This was every dream coming true...until I fucked it up.

"Hey, Steph, how the hell are ya?"

Well, if that isn't an empty question. If there's one thing I'm sure about, it's Ben has no interest whatsoever in knowing how I am.

"Fine." I brush him off, not bothering to return the interest. "Why are you calling me, Ben? All you say in your message is that you need help on a case."

His chuckle grates on me, and so do the words that follow.

"I see we're getting right down to business. No catching up on old times?"

I close my eyes against the rush of anger, and breathe in through the nose and out through my mouth in an attempt to curb my temper.

"What do you need, Ben? And how did you get this number?"

This is my personal cell. I handed over my Bureau-issued phone along with my badge and service weapon to SAC Bellinger when he put me on leave.

"Come on...give me some credit," he taunts. "It took me five minutes to find after someone at your office told me you were on hiatus. What does that even mean?" he adds.

I glance out at the creek. The water looks higher than it did yesterday, and I'm pretty sure it's flowing faster. It must be the start of the winter runoff now the days are getting warmer.

Whatever he thinks he needs me for, he'll have to find another way. The building volume of water in the creek functions as a visual reminder of the rising blood pressure in my veins that got me here in the first place. Already I can feel my heart pumping harder.

"What it means is you'll need to find someone else to help you on your case," I tell him with determination.

"Ah, but I have a feeling you would want to be in on this one. I'm sure you remember Mitchel Laine?"

Damn right I remember him. My first collar twelve years ago. I was twenty-four and feeling pretty damn good about bringing down the man who had robbed a series of bank branches in smaller towns across several states. He'd repeatedly and brutally pistol-whipped an elderly teller at a bank in Manistee, Michigan, when she couldn't get the vault open, leaving her with a shattered jaw and a fractured skull. Almost two years after I caught up with him, that miserable punk was sentenced to fifteen years in jail. I didn't think it was enough at the time.

"What about him? He should be safely behind bars for at least another five years or so."

"Sadly, no. He was released on good behavior three months ago. Overcrowding and a turn to Jesus granted him early parole."

"You've gotta be kidding me?"

It's a slap in the face to law enforcement who spill sweat, blood, and tears catching these animals, only to have them released because of administrative inadequacies or limited capacity. Especially since in a lot of these cases, we have to spill more sweat, blood, and tears to get those same assholes back behind bars when they offend again, which a lot of them do.

"Not even a little," Vallard returns, sounding grim. "He was released and never even showed up for the first visit with his parole officer. I'm pretty sure he's responsible for a couple of bank heists; one in Monmouth, Illinois, one in Fort Dodge, Iowa. Similar MO; small branches, same kind of language used, ball cap, facial hair which is likely fake."

I remember that's what threw off investigators for so long last time, he'd change his appearance just enough. He'd go from a black mustache and goatee with a beanie, to a full beard and ball cap between robberies. He also traveled, crossing state lines and never hitting the same region twice. It took a while to pick up a pattern with the crimes taking place in different jurisdictions.

"Bigger towns though. He used to stick to populations

under ten thousand. The ones you mentioned are well over."

The theory had been, he picked the small towns, hoping for a more inexperienced and perhaps understaffed sheriff's department or police force. Not that he ever copped to that, he never admitted to anything.

"He's escalating. Two days ago, a Great Plains Bank branch near the Aberdeen airport in South Dakota was hit," Ben relays in a serious tone. "Two civilians and an off-duty police officer were shot. The police officer is still in critical condition. Suspect took off running through a back door. His fake beard, ball cap, and navy hoodie were found in a dumpster in an alley on the next block over."

"*Jesus*," I hiss.

If this is Mitchel Laine's doing, he definitely has escalated.

Despite my earlier determination, I feel myself getting sucked in, and I hate myself for asking, "What makes you so sure it's him?"

"For the past five years, Laine has been corresponding with a woman named Tracy Elliston. She's a twenty-nine-year-old hairdresser from Troy, Montana," he explains.

I see now why he contacted me; Kalispell would be the closest FBI office to Troy, which also happens to be only thirty miles or so from where I am now. Although Ben doesn't need to know that.

"You think he's on his way to meet up with this woman."

"All you have to do is draw a line on the map to see that's where he's heading," Vallard points out. "Unless he's already there."

It does appear that way.

Dammit, this is hard. Every instinct in me wants to take

this on, but I've had to hand in my badge and weapon, and I don't think Bellinger would be too happy if I defied his orders.

If I started messing around in an active investigation without the necessary credentials, I could risk losing my badge altogether.

"I'm sorry, I can't help you."

Before he can get a word in edgewise, I end the call and power down my phone.

~

*Jackson*

"Got a call from the game warden's office."

Dan, Fletch, JD, Bo, Wolff, and I were working around the ranch when Jonas put out a call for everyone to meet him at the ranch house. I guess because of the size of the group, we ended up gathering in the kitchen, where Ama already had a fresh pot of coffee on the go.

Jonas waited for all of us to be present before getting into the reason for this impromptu meeting.

"A hunter radioed in from up on Quartz Mountain. He and a friend were on the trail of a bear when he stopped to take a whiz, while his hunting buddy had gone ahead. When he tried to catch up with his friend, he couldn't find him. The guy had disappeared. He'd been looking for over an hour before calling it in. He thinks his buddy—the name is Juan Pérez—may have tried to cross a stream of runoff water in their path, slipped, and got swept away. According to Buck, it's probably one of the tributaries feeding into West Fork Quartz Creek which is currently near cresting its banks with all the snowmelt coming down from the mountains."

"Yeah, I heard a few areas on the north side of town are already dealing with some flooding," Fletch contributes.

Spring flooding is not uncommon but, with the rapid temperature rise these past few days, it's shaping up to be a particularly bad year.

I shake my head when Ama comes by with the coffeepot for refills. These days even that first cup of coffee makes my gut hurt. I don't know if I'm getting old at thirty-eight, or whether drugs burned a hole in my stomach. I don't take them anymore—some of those medications I was prescribed while I was recovering were pretty heavy duty—but the damage could already have been done.

Whatever the case may be, I'm not in the mood to examine either possibility too closely at the moment. Sounds like we have more important things on the go.

"Yeah, the rivers and creeks in the valley are starting to crest as well. It'll likely be a bad year for flooding," Jonas echoes my earlier thoughts. "At any rate, the guy could be halfway down to the Kootenay River by now. Adams wants us to meet him at the cutoff to forestry road NF-4654," he gets us back on track. "Fletch, if you don't mind covering the ranch?"

Fletch nods in acknowledgement. He's been dealing with arthritis for a few years now, making it difficult to be effective on these potentially long searches. Even on a healthy body, a couple of hours in the saddle can be a challenge. The man knows his limitations, the last thing he wants to do is risk slowing down or holding up a search when time is often of the essence.

Sully limits himself to operating the drone and manning base camp communications. Not even Jonas himself goes out much anymore. James and Bo are the only ones of the old guard who still regularly make up part of the tracking team.

Bo is in pretty good shape for his age, plus he's our field medic, which often comes in handy. As for James, not only is he still the best tracker we have—although JD is a close second to his father—but I suspect we'll have to pry him off his horse when he dies in the saddle.

It's mostly up to the younger guard these days, which Jonas confirms when he continues assigning tasks.

"JD, Bo, Dan, and Wolff, gear up; you guys are going out there. Pack the gear, and load up the horses." Then he turns to me. "Son, I'll need you to fly the Matrice and run communications. Sully and James should be back from their run to Missoula by tonight, so if we haven't found him yet, we'll switch things up a bit for tomorrow."

Of course I'd prefer to be in the field with the others, but I'm learning to accept every part of an operation is important. Arguably, managing communications and providing intel gathered with the drone to the men in the field could be considered crucial to the team.

I'm good on horseback, my stamina is at par with the others. However, when working in this rugged terrain, there are plenty of times the team has to dismount and lead their horses through some rough spots. That's where my limitations come in, because traversing rough terrain on my prosthetic leg is tough, and as much as I'd like to claim my equality to the others, the simple truth is I'm not. Not when it comes to agility.

Hence, I'm not surprised I was assigned to man base camp, but that doesn't mean it doesn't sting a little.

"I'm gonna help you set up, but then I have to get back here. I promised your mother I'd take her to that new

Brazilian barbecue restaurant in town for our anniversary," Jonas announces, clapping his hand on my shoulder as we walk down the porch steps. "Personally, I don't know what's so special about Brazilian barbecue versus good old American barbecue. As far as I can tell, a good piece of meat is tasty no matter what flag they fly over the grill they cook it on."

I don't think I'll share I heard they have a couple of guys walking around Gaucho—the name of the new restaurant —with a guitar and an accordion, serenading the guests. Ma would kill me if I spoiled her fun.

"Congrats on the anniversary," I tell him instead. "How long has it been?"

"Fourteen years married and almost fifteen together, Son. Best fifteen years of my life, bar none."

I remember having had some apprehension at first. I was twenty-three at the time and pretty protective of my mother. Or maybe I was a bit protective of my role as the man in her life. Either way, I had my reservations about Jonas initially but that didn't last long. Even for me, the man had been hard to resist.

First of all, it was obvious how deeply he cared about my mother, even in the early days of their relationship. Secondly, he was straight-up with me from the start as to what his intentions were. And, of course, last and definitely not least, he was former special ops which—at the time—was the dream career I'd been afraid to talk to my mother about. I didn't think she'd be receptive to the added risk since she'd already sacrificed a husband to the military.

It had taken her a while to adjust when I first enlisted, following in my father's footsteps, but at least she knew where I was at any given time. That wouldn't be the case if I was part of a special ops team and we ended up getting sent off on some assignment.

I'd been able to talk to Jonas about those concerns, and he'd been helpful in dealing with Ma when I broke the news to her.

At the time, I didn't think I needed or even wanted another father figure, but nevertheless, I'm grateful for the role he's played in my life since. He was a rock for my mother, and for me, in some of our darkest times. He was pivotal in dragging my ass back from the brink two years ago when I was drowning in what I perceived as the insurmountable magnitude of the loss my missing leg represented. He assured me the worth of a man was not the sum of his limbs, but the weight of his actions...and then showed me the way to becoming that man.

For the past fifteen years, he's been a great father to me without receiving any credit. It's about time he did.

I'm a step behind him when we reach the shed where we store the equipment.

"I'm happy for you both, Dad."

I know he heard me when he abruptly stops, but he doesn't turn around. A moment later he expels a deep breath before he disappears into the shadows of the shed.

Taking a second longer to collect myself, I follow him inside.

# Four



STEPHANIE

The sound of the birds waking up welcomes me when I slide open the door to the deck to watch the sunrise.

The temperature has been steadily rising, and this morning a spring jacket and my hot coffee are enough to keep me warm. With my travel mug in hand, I wander down to the creek, which is swollen with melt waters but so far staying within the bounds of its banks.

I fill my lungs with the crisp morning air and feel a smile tugging at my lips. I'm starting to see what drew JD to this spot, it's so beautiful here. It's taken me a while to be able to fully appreciate it.

Since dinner at Janey's last Friday, I've been actively trying to get out of the house at least once a day. Nothing big, just grabbing a fancy coffee and a pastry at Bean There, or picking up a few odds and ends at the pharmacy. Enough to at least see, if not interact with, other human beings.

I didn't recognize myself on Friday, scurrying off to the

relative safety of solitude when Jackson walked into Janey's kitchen with JD. I'm not that person, I'm an experienced federal agent, for crying out loud. Jackson spells trouble for me, but I don't run away from trouble, I face it. That's who I am.

But I'd been hiding for weeks, and although I may have been healing physically, I could feel my courage and mental strength eroding. I realized what a coward I was becoming when I ran from Jackson that night.

So I've been pushing myself out of the safe cocoon the trailer has become. Yesterday's outing was to the UPS store in Libby to collect up a package I ordered, and I picked up a burrito at a roadside stand on the way home.

This morning my plan is to unpack the hand-knitting kit I ordered online and get a start on my new project. I'd seen an ad on Instagram when I was mindlessly scrolling, and loved the look of the bold texture of the blanket in the picture. It didn't look too complicated when I did a little research and found a YouTube tutorial on how to make one. I clicked on the product link in the description.

It'll be good to get my hands busy with something other than baking, which I bought ingredients for last week. I've been doing a little of it every day, but unfortunately, there is no one but me to eat it and I can feel my ass growing.

But first I want to greet the morning and drink my coffee surrounded by all this beauty. I want to learn to be in the moment. Too much of my adult existence has been spent in my head, plotting and contemplating tomorrow instead of appreciating today. That constant feeling of trying to catch up to something elusive, but never quite catching up.

Here, right now, I let myself hear, see, smell, feel, and appreciate the clean air in my lungs, the steady beat of my heart, and the taste of that kick-ass new coffee I bought on my tongue.

I feel good. Energized.

Not so much a few hours later, when I try to free my hands from the tangle of knots I managed to create for the umpteenth time.

Easy, my foot! On the video they showed a five-year-old hand-knitting to illustrate *anyone can do it.* Sure, anyone but this thirty-six-year-old, college-educated, decorated federal agent. I have no idea what I'm doing wrong.

Frustrated, I reach for my phone to call a friend.

"Do you know how to knit? Because it's not working for me."

Janey bursts out laughing on the other end of the line.

"I'm sorry," she immediately apologizes. "You caught me off guard with that. You've taken up knitting?"

"Well, I need something to do with my time and my hands," I respond a tad defensively. "Besides, I like the look of those big, chunky blankets, so I ordered a kit, but I keep getting tangled."

"Oh, hand-knitting? I've always wanted to try that. The principle is the same as with needles."

"Which I've never done in my life either," I clarify.

"Right. Growing up the only child of a farmer, I had the benefit of being groomed by both my mother and father. Dad made sure I knew my way around livestock, and Mom taught me all the necessary traits a good farm wife would need. I think it was a bit of a disappointment when I didn't follow in either of their steps, but at least I did pick up a few handy skills. Including knitting," she adds.

The picture she paints of her childhood evokes a long-buried ache in my chest. My mother died when I was twelve, leaving my grief-stricken father to care for my older brother,

David, and me. Not that he was around much, we were mostly left to our own devices while he drowned himself in his work. Admittedly, raising kids alone was not the easiest thing in his line of work; he was an FBI agent.

Sadly, the only thing my father instilled in me was a burning need to gain his approval. Hence my career choice. Any actual life skills I have either my mother imparted on me before she died, or were self-taught. Knitting definitely did not make that list.

My fingers stroke the soft, lush yarn in my hands, as I push down the surge of bitterness. I should know by now it does me no good to dwell too much on things I can't fucking change anyway.

"Can you help?" I ask Janey.

"I'm about to go into surgery and have a few visits this afternoon, but why don't I pick us up some dinner in town and drop by after? JD is working anyway. He's hardly been home since the team was called out on that search this past Friday."

"What search?"

Normally, I stay on top of what goes on around me and in the world at large, but I've been living in a bit of a bubble these past weeks. The world could be on fire, but unless it was raging outside my window, I'd be completely oblivious.

"You haven't heard? Missing hunter," she explains.

"Wow, and they've been searching for five days already?"

That seems like a long time.

"Yeah, apparently there is a lot of pressure to find this guy, dead or alive. His name is Juan Pérez, and he's the son of Diego Pérez—"

"The Argentinian ambassador?" I guess, interrupting.

"One and the same," Janey confirms. "Although, that part hasn't been made public knowledge yet."

I can see how that might put the pressure on. *Yikes.*

The few cases I've worked on involving high profile individuals were an exercise in diplomacy. Something I haven't exactly been blessed with an abundance of. Hard to concentrate on the job at hand when every step you take and every decision you make are under a tremendous amount of scrutiny.

I bet the High Mountain Trackers team wishes they were dealing with an average Joe Blow.

"Wow. That's gotta be tough. What if they don't find him?"

"It's a distinct possibility. For all they know he could've been washed out into the Kootenai River somewhere, heading for Canada."

The Kootenai River has the unique feature it both starts and ends in Canada. It rises somewhere in the Canadian Rockies before dipping south into northern Montana. Then it heads back north, cutting through a corner of Idaho before ending back up across the border in British Columbia. Right around Libby is where the river curves and changes from a southern flow to a western, and finally a northern one.

"Well, I hope they find him, although after five days, the likelihood he'll be alive when they do is slim," I suggest.

"Oh, I know. Anyway, I should get going. So dinner, what do you feel like?" Janey changes the subject.

"I'm good with anything."

"Pizza, ribs, burgers, Mexican, or Japanese?"

"Oh, Japanese. I haven't had sushi in ages."

"Done. My patient is here, but text me your preferences."

∾

"Go home. Get a good night's sleep."

Jonas looks rough. I wouldn't want to be in his shoes for the world.

He, along with the game warden and the sheriff, have been the ones to be fielding the pressure from a variety of national and international government agencies. I would definitely not have the patience for that.

It's clear the powers that be were not happy with his decision to give the team a twelve-hour break before we move our base camp to a lower elevation. The fact is, our horses need a break, and so do we. For the last three days, under the rising urgency, we've worked in teams of two, trying to cover as much ground in as little time as possible.

At this point, the entire team—myself, Jonas, and Sully included—have been out on horseback, alternating with the others to make sure someone was always covering communications and manning the drone. The problem is, with only four or so hours of rest between shifts for days on end, it's not only our effectiveness that is suffering, it's the horses' concentration that starts to falter as well.

That's why, after Wolff's horse, Judge, slipped on a rock earlier this afternoon and he had to walk the lame animal back to base camp, Jonas made the executive decision to impose a longer rest. I'm sure Judge is going to need more than twelve hours, plus a checkup from Janey, but for the rest of us that should be enough to get reenergized.

Truth is, the chance of finding Juan Pérez alive is highly unlikely at this juncture. But that's not something either the man's family or the hovering government agencies want to hear, which is understandable. Until we recover his body, they'll cling on to every last shred of hope.

My stump is sore when I lead Banner into the horse trailer. I've taken off my prosthetic leg whenever I had a stationary shift at base camp, but the last one was thirty-two or so hours ago, and that's too long to be wearing my leg without any breaks.

The skin tends to start getting red and raw inside the silicone sleeve that holds the socket of the leg in place. After that blisters can form, and that could be complicated by an infection. If you don't look after your stump properly, you can easily get yourself in trouble. I learned that lesson the hard way and have no desire to go there again.

"Jonas," I call out when I see him heading for the communications tent Sully is starting to dismantle. "Tomorrow morning, can I have first shift in the tent? My leg is sore."

I get a thumbs-up.

I don't have to explain, he's had a firsthand look at the effects of ignoring the signs before. It's taken some time for him to trust I don't push myself too hard. He's made it clear if I'm the one who wants to be treated like everyone else, I have to be responsible for piping up when there is an issue. After what I put him and my mother through a few years ago, it was a challenge to earn his trust, so I'm not about to risk losing it again. Jonas may give you a second chance, but he's not the kind of man who'd be handing out thirds.

"What are you doing for dinner?" JD asks when he hops into my passenger seat when we're done packing up.

"I don't know. I'll see what I have left in my fridge, or else grab something at the ranch. Why?"

I ease my truck into the convoy down the mountain as

soon as the horse trailer Dan is towing behind the ranch truck passes.

"Just got off the phone with Janey. She's on her way to grab some sushi in town. I'm about to put my order in, are you interested?"

My mouth is already watering. After days of eating easy canned food or MREs, I crave the crunch of something fresh in my mouth. But I really need to get this leg off.

"Sounds amazing, but I should be getting home."

I can feel him looking at me so I glance over.

"What?"

He shrugs. "Oh nothing. I was hoping you could drop me off at my trailer on the way to the ranch."

That has my attention.

"The trailer?"

"Yeah," he says casually. "Janey was gonna have dinner with Stephanie, so I'm meeting her there. She's planning on checking in on Judge after dinner anyway, so I would've hitched a ride back to the ranch with her after to pick up my truck. But that's okay, I can—"

Despite my better judgment, I find myself cutting him off.

"I'll take an assorted sushi and tempura platter and a side order of teriyaki ribs. If I'm gonna drop you off anyway, I might as well eat while I'm there."

It's a pathetically transparent excuse and I know it. So does he; from the corner of my eye the hint of a grin appears on his otherwise stoic face, which I try to ignore.

*Bastard.*

# Five



STEPHANIE

I'm out on the back deck, enjoying the setting sun, when I hear the crunch of tires on the gravel driveway.

Assuming it's Janey, I jump to my feet.

I left the sad results of my continued efforts this afternoon on the couch when frustration finally drove me outside. My laptop is open on the coffee table where I watched about two hours of tutorials, and still I ended up with mysterious knots and even a fist-sized hole in my knitting.

I can't wait for Janey to show me what I'm doing wrong.

Ginger is the first to barge in when I make it to the front door and open it. Janey follows behind, carrying two massive paper bags.

"What's all that?"

"Dinner," she explains, slipping past me to set the bags on the kitchen counter.

Ginger is sticking close, her nose sniffing the air.

"That's a boatload of food for the two of us," I point out.

"It's not just for us," she clarifies, a guilty look on her face. "JD called just as I was leaving to pick it up. The search was halted for the next twelve hours to give everyone a rest, so he was about to head home. I haven't seen JD in a few days and I have to head over to the ranch to look at an injured horse after dinner, so I told him to come here and eat with us. I hope you don't mind."

"Of course not. We'll wait to eat until he gets here."

Janey has already spotted my butchered handiwork and is moving toward it when she corrects me.

"*They* get here. Jackson is with him."

I was just grabbing some plates from the cupboard, when my hands freeze midair. My body reacts to that piece of news with a racing heart. For a moment I'm worried I'm having a panic attack, but then I realize I'm feeling a different kind of anxiety, one of anticipation.

There's something mildly threatening but also exciting about the thought of Jackson in my space. I think it's because of the way he looks at me with such intense focus. It makes me feel uneasy, a little vulnerable, but also seen.

"Is it too much?" Janey's soft question drags me from my thoughts. "I can call JD and tell him to—"

"No, it's fine," I rush to assure her, squaring my shoulders.

Cowering in a corner is not my style, and that's what I feel I've been doing for a while now. Enough of that. I'm not a fan of these beaten-down victim vibes I apparently give off.

After pulling out an extra plate, I join Janey, who is plucking at my creation.

"Is it bad?" I ask.

She tries to hold back a snort but almost chokes on the effort.

"Uh...it's definitely not salvageable."

Brutal, but honest.

I take it on the chin, but let out a strangled squeak when she starts unravelling my stitches.

"I'm sorry, but it has to be done," she states as she deftly rolls the untangled loops of yarn back on the skein. "We have some time before the guys get here to make a fresh start. Come sit next to me, we'll do it together."

For the next twenty minutes, she patiently guides me through every stitch, making quiet corrections when I fuck up, until I get the hang of it. By the time a soft knock sounds on the door, I barely even need to think about what my hands are doing.

"I'll get it. Don't stop until you get to the end of this row," Janey instructs me as she gets to her feet.

I try to focus on what I'm doing, but it's hard when I'm acutely aware of the two additional bodies entering what has become my safe space. I glance over to see Ginger greet both men with enthusiasm. Determined to make it to the end of the row, I don't even acknowledge their presence, but doggedly plod on while Janey engages them in conversation in the kitchen.

When I reach the end of my row, I secure the last loop with a clothes pin so it doesn't unravel itself, and blow out a sigh of relief as I put it aside. Then I get to my feet and turn my attention to the kitchen. I find three pairs of eyes fixed on me, looking amused. Jackson is the first to speak.

"What are you making?"

"A blanket," I return, doing my best to sound normal, even though I feel a little flustered. "I was making a dog's breakfast out of it, so Janey showed me how. I'm new to knitting."

"Aren't you supposed to do that with needles?" he probes.

"Would have to be some pretty massive needles to handle yarn that thick," JD pipes up. "It's called hand-knitting. Ma did a few of those."

Janey, who has been unpacking the paper bags and setting out the food and some on plates the counter, claps her hands.

"Come on, guys. Let's eat. I've got a lame horse waiting at the ranch."

We fill our plates and sit down at the small kitchen table. It's a little tight, but we manage.

I'm suddenly starving and dive into my sushi, quietly listening to Janey interrogate the guys about the search for the Argentinian ambassador's son.

"Did Jillian come out with the dogs?" she asks.

"For two days," Jackson responds. "Not even a hint of a scent."

"Weird. You'd think there'd be at least some trace left behind. So what's next?"

JD is the first to answer that question. "Next, we set up camp farther downstream. Given there is no detectable scent for Jillian's dogs to pick up on, we're now convinced he was swept away by the water."

He goes on to explain how they'll set up their communications tent just west of town, where the creek meets up with the Kootenai River, and will backtrack north to search.

"We think he may be hung up in the creek somewhere. You get clusters of fallen branches and downed trees in the creek during the melt. Wouldn't be the first time a body gets tangled up in those."

"So, this is a recovery operation now?" I question, sitting back to give my full stomach a little space.

"Yes. That's the assumption," Jackson confirms.

Janey shoves her chair back and gets to her feet. JD follows suit.

"So sorry to dine and dash, but I should really go see to Wolff's horse."

She starts collecting the remnants of dinner when I firmly stop her.

"Go, I've got these," I urge her.

"I don't wanna leave you with the mess."

"You were responsible for dinner, so cleanup is mine."

Jackson—who hadn't budged from his spot—abruptly gets up as well, volunteering, "I'll give you a hand."

Before I have a chance to object, JD says his goodbyes while Janey collects her dog. I watch the three of them disappear out the front door.

When I turn back to the kitchen, Jackson is still standing by the table, his eyes fixed on me.

"Do I make you uneasy?"

*Jackson*

I have a hard time getting a proper read on her.

Last year she was confident, capable, determined; all qualities that attracted me to her. What I'm seeing now is insecurity and vulnerability, but the determination is still there. Oddly enough, I find myself equally attracted to this version of her.

Of course, it's always possible she was all of these things

all along, layered on top of each other. Something happened to peel some of those stronger traits back to reveal her softer underbelly. The difference between last year and now is, she doesn't have her job to shield her.

"Why would you say that?" she answers my question with a question of her own.

A common evasion technique I've used myself on occasion.

"Do I? Make you uneasy?"

She stares at me for a moment, definitely uncomfortable under my scrutiny, when she suddenly drops her eyes to the floor.

"A little," she admits in a soft voice, before adding more forcefully, "I think it has more to do with me than you though."

I gently push. "How so?"

She shrugs, moving past me to the sink and turning on the faucet to wash the dishes. I grab a towel from the hook and step up beside her. She darts me a quick glance and sighs.

"I had a bit of a health scare a little over a month ago and ended up in the hospital. It wasn't as bad as it initially looked," she rushes to clarify. "But, apparently, serious enough for my boss to pull me off the job until things have stabilized."

That confirms what I'd suspected when I first saw her over a week ago.

"What happened?"

She hands me the first dripping plate before answering.

"We'd just chased down a suspect and I was putting him into cuffs, when my chest got tight and I suddenly couldn't breathe. I thought I was having a heart attack. Next thing I know, I'm in an ambulance, hooked up to monitors as I'm being rushed to the hospital, and scared out of my brain."

I know I must've made some sound, when her head turns and those hazel eyes lock on me.

"I lost my mom when I was twelve. One minute she was at the stove, cooking us Sunday morning breakfast, and the next she was on the ground; dead of a massive heart attack at barely forty."

*"Fucking hell,"* I mutter under my breath.

"Anyway…" She turns her attention back to the dirty dishes. "That's what was going through my mind at the time. It turned out it wasn't a heart attack but a panic attack. I was also diagnosed with hypertension and was put on medication for both. Then, to top it off, I was placed on indefinite leave. It's all been a bit much to wrap my head around, so if I seem a bit uneasy, it's probably because I feel like I'm still trying to adjust."

Her head is down and I can't see her eyes, but I could hear the barely contained emotion in her voice. I reach over and put my hand on her neck, squeezing gently.

"That's tough. I'm sorry that happened to you."

I understand only too well what it feels like to wake up in a hospital and have everything in your life changed, including your sense of self.

She shrugs her shoulders, and I'm not quite sure whether it is in response to my empathy or my hand on her neck, but I remove it anyway. Shouldn't have my hands where they're not wanted.

A moment later I break that rule already, when she says, "I shouldn't complain. It could've been a hell of a lot worse."

I toss the towel on the counter and grab her shoulders, turning her to face me.

"Don't do that," I urge her, crouching down so I can look her straight in the eyes. "Don't belittle what you're feeling, or what you're dealing with. It's a lot, trying to get a grip on a reality that is abruptly changed. Trust me, I know what that's like, and I can tell you that trying to muscle your way through can come back to bite you."

I have no idea if she knows I tried to end things when I was struggling two years ago, but her eyes well up with tears.

"Dammit," she mutters, blinking furiously to keep them at bay. "This is why I try to avoid you. I can't hide; you see too much."

I chuckle at that admission and drop my hands from her shoulders.

"Only because I've been in your shoes. Turns out we have more in common than I thought."

When I turn to grab the towel and finish drying the dishes, I inadvertently put my weight on the right side. A sharp hiss escapes me when a stab of burning pain shoots through my stump and I grab on to the edge of the counter for support.

"What is it?" Stephanie asks, immediately concerned. "Is it your leg? Do you need to sit down?"

Even though I don't necessarily advertise it; the fact I'm an amputee isn't exactly a secret. I shouldn't be surprised she instinctively draws the link.

"Actually, I should probably head home," I share, not really wanting to leave.

I'd prefer sticking around, exploring this newfound connection. Now that I have a better understanding of what happened to her, I can offer her my support, a listening ear, a strong shoulder.

It's been a while since I've felt a sense of purpose. Since I've had the ability to make a difference.

"Of course," she immediately responds, her shoulders tight as she's already moving to the front door.

I feel like I owe her an explanation.

"If my stump wasn't raw from wearing this damn prosthesis too long, and I didn't have to be back out in the field by 6.00 a.m. tomorrow morning, I'd be sticking around if you'd let me."

She swings her head around, a smile pulling at her lips when she finds me right behind her. For a moment, she peers at me through squinted eyes, as if she's trying to gauge my intentions. I stare right back, letting her look her fill. From somewhere inside the trailer a phone starts ringing, breaking the spell.

"Do you need to get that?"

She shakes her head, even as she glances over my shoulder. "If it's important they'll leave a message."

She steps aside as I reach past her to open the door. As I step outside, I lean over to drop a kiss on her cheek.

"Go answer," I prompt her. "I'll be in touch when I can."

She's already darting toward the kitchen when I pull the door shut.

It only takes five minutes to get from the trailer to the ranch where I park the truck in front of my cabin. I curse a blue streak under my breath as I get out and start hobbling toward my front door.

"Honey, is that you?"

I groan at the sound of my mother's voice, which stops me as I'm about to step inside. Glancing over at the porch, I see her hurrying down the steps, her silver braid flying. My mother doesn't know what slowing down means, not even at sixty.

She's still spry on her feet, and still works with horses every day. She gets called in far and wide to handle some of the most difficult, even meanest, horses out there. Most of the time, these animals turned mean as a result of some kind of abuse, and Ma is the best at patiently building trust with them. We jokingly call her the horse whisperer, but it's not far from the truth. She has a gift, even though she sometimes takes risks sharing it.

"Hey, Ma."

Despite her short stature, she gets right in my space, her hand reaching up to cup my cheek.

"Jonas mentioned your leg was bothering you, and when you weren't showing up, I got worried."

I suppress my mild irritation and plaster on a reassuring smile. It's my own fault my mother still checks in on me at my age. She's always been a worrier, ever since I followed in my father's footsteps and enlisted, and truthfully, I've given her every reason.

"My stump is raw, that's all. I just grabbed some dinner out and am heading for a shower and bed next."

She smiles up at me and nods.

"Okay, then. Don't push yourself too much."

I chuckle at that. "Pot meet kettle."

She punches my arm half-heartedly.

"Don't be a brat. Night, honey."

"Night, Ma."

Leaning down, I kiss her cheek. Her scent is familiar and invokes warm memories.

Unlike Stephanie's scent, which lingered in my nostrils and fed my imagination on the way home. The whiff of vanilla and something citrusy I caught is now forever associated with my mental image of her.

As innocent as kissing Stephanie's cheek may seem, I can tell you it's a vastly different experience from kissing my mother's, that's for sure.

# Six



Startled by the sound of a car horn behind me, I jerk my eyes to the rearview mirror.

A large pickup with a pissed-off guy behind the wheel, gesturing wildly, is riding my ass.

Great, I'm already pissing off the locals.

I didn't realize there was anyone behind me, I was too busy scanning the numbers on the mailboxes, slowing down each time I passed one.

Edging the wheels on the passenger side of my SUV as close to the ditch as I dare, I motion for the guy to pass me. I hold up my hand in apology and receive an extended middle finger in return.

Charming.

The address I was given is on the north side of the river in Troy, it's a more remote, wooded area I'm not familiar with. The houses are spread out, and sometimes not visible from the road or each other, a good portion of them no more than ramshackle trailer homes. I'm starting to wonder if, maybe, I should've let someone know where I was heading.

The only person who knows is Ben Vallard, and he's back in Michigan.

I wasn't going to get involved—I don't owe Vallard any favors—but he knew damn well, calling me to let me know the police officer Mitchel Laine shot had died that afternoon, he'd have me hooked.

I work hard on any case, regardless of who the victim or victims may be, but when it involves a fellow law enforcement officer, things get personal. Enough so I find myself looking for Tracy Elliston this morning.

Mitchel Laine's girlfriend.

I didn't jump in with both feet, mind you. Still, Ben explained he had to testify in one of his cases that went to trial in the coming days and wouldn't be able to get away. Then he mentioned he'd tried to get assistance from the Kalispell office but was told they were swamped. That was a direct hit, since the reason they're swamped is likely because I'm not there to do my job.

Ultimately, he had some valid concerns once news about the officer dying got out, Laine could well aim straight for the Canadian border. After all, Troy is less than eighty miles from the border. It wouldn't take much for him to disappear from our jurisdiction.

In the end, I caved and told him I'd look into it.

He was able to give me an address for the woman, 254 Waterfront Road, and the name of her employer, Cuts 'n Curls, a hair salon in town. But, as he pointed out, he couldn't guarantee that information was still correct.

I'd spent some time last night lying awake in bed, trying to come up with a credible cover. There's no way I'm going to invoke the FBI. Aside from the fact she'd clam up immediately, I don't want to risk my job by flaunting the Bureau without the badge to show for it.

This morning I'd looked up the hair salon online. No website, but they do have a Facebook page, which I scanned, finding a comment under a post from a woman who raved about the cut she got from Tracy. I made note of the customer's name and waited until nine to call the salon. When I asked for an appointment with Tracy, I was told she wouldn't be in until that afternoon and was booked up, but had space tomorrow.

My plan had been to go in—my hair could use a trim anyway—and see what I could find out. Most hairdressers are Chatty Cathys in my experience anyway. But since I couldn't get in until tomorrow, and I didn't want to waste today, I decided to have a look at the address Vallard gave me.

It wasn't until I turned down this road and happened to spot a for-rent sign on the mailbox of a dingy looking trailer a mile or so back, an enhanced plan formed.

Most of the number has flaked off the side of the brightly painted mailbox, but I'm just able to make it out. The driveway is little more than two ruts winding through the trees. I only get a glimpse of an equally bright-colored trailer from the road. Confident my cover will hold up; I turn on to the trail to take a closer look.

The house looks to be a double-wide trailer, and it's in better shape than either the mailbox or the driveway. Nothing is blooming yet, but I can see someone loves gardening. There are planters on either side of the steps going up to the house, and the small clearing in front of the house has a couple of flower beds, filled with dormant plants.

A gray Pontiac Vibe is parked on the right side of the trailer. I hope that means she's home.

No sooner have I turned off my engine, when the front door of the trailer swings open and a woman with glasses perched on the tip of her nose and a mass of vibrant red hair piled high on her head steps outside. If this is Tracy, she's changed quite a bit from the DMV image Ben sent through last night. She had blond hair and full makeup on in that picture.

"Can I help you?"

The question is friendly enough, but her tone has a sharp edge. This is not a woman to mess with.

"Yes, hi." I plaster on my best smile as I walk up. From closer up I recognize her features. This is definitely Tracy, unless she has a twin. "I believe you have a place listed for rent?"

"For rent?" she echoes.

I pull out a scrap of paper and pretend to read something, squinting my eyes.

"This is 254 Waterfront Road, isn't it?"

Her face registers confusion first, but then quickly relaxes.

"It is, but this isn't for rent. There's a trailer down the street a bit that is though. I think it's 234 Waterfront, you must've written down the wrong number."

I make it look like I'm scrutinizing the paper even closer before pressing a hand to my forehead.

"Oh my God, I feel so stupid. You're right. It's a three and not a five. How bad is it I can't even read my own writing anymore?"

The woman chuckles and lifts her glasses off her face, holding them up.

"Believe me, I know only too well. These days I have to wear reading glasses for everything except driving."

"I guess I have no choice, I'll have to invest in a pair," I return. "I was hoping to put it off for another, let's say, decade or two." I lift my hand. "I'm so sorry for bothering you. I'll go find 234."

"Not to worry."

She's already turned her back, pushing open the door, when she suddenly swings around, her eyes drifting to my CR-V.

"If I were you, I wouldn't bother with that place. I don't think it's for you, it's a bit of a dump and the owner is an asshole."

"Oh. Okay, thanks. I've got a few more places to look at anyway."

This time she disappears inside and I head back to my vehicle.

I didn't see any movement inside, and Tracy did not strike me as nervous, the way I would expect if she were harboring a fugitive and some stranger came knocking on her door. I don't think he's here, at least not now, but that doesn't mean he won't be at some point.

Still, I'm smiling when I turn back onto the road. My hook is set, and tomorrow when I coincidentally show up for my haircut, she and I will have lots to talk about.

*Jackson*

"How's the leg?"

I look up from the computer screen to see Jonas stepping into the tent. We'd just loaded up the horses early this morning and were about to take off, when he received a notification he was expected to attend some kind of task force meeting at nine thirty. He'd been none too pleased.

"Better."

I had to give my stump a little extra care last night before I rolled into bed. A good wash and some derma repair cream with vitamin E to do its thing overnight. Then this morning I put on a fresh, super-thin stump sock, and used a different prosthetic liner.

Still, I brought my crutch, and once we'd set up communications, and I was sitting at the monitor, I took my leg off to give the skin some air.

"What was that meeting about?" I ask him.

"A bunch of posturing and finger-pointing between agencies. The Argentinian government is not happy we haven't been able to locate the ambassador's son and feels not enough people are searching and more should be done. The reason they wanted me there was to explain why more searchers would not be helpful."

People don't realize this can be very unpredictable and treacherous terrain. Sending groups of inexperienced people on a search in these mountains is asking for trouble. We'd end up spending more time hauling out injuries or looking for missing volunteers than we'd be searching. It really is more trouble than it's worth.

"And?"

He shrugs. "They were temporarily satisfied with my suggestion to call the dog team out again."

"Jillian?"

"Yeah. But this time with Emo."

Jillian is my teammate Wolff's wife. She has a search-

and-rescue dog team, but also handles a cadaver dog, Emo, who is trained to find human remains.

"I assume you'd have told me if you caught anything with the drone?"

"Nothing particular," I share as I open the topographic map of the area on my screen. "I tracked the creek up the mountain and back down, and marked up the areas where I saw the collection of melt-off debris."

I point at a turn in the river, where I'd spotted a substantial obstruction had formed, forcing the water out of its bounds to get around.

"That's a big one. Let me find this section on the video from the Matrice, so you can see it yourself."

As I was watching the live feed and marking the areas of interest on the map, I also noted the time tag on the video, making it easier to find.

"There was something else that drew my attention. Keep an eye on the trees at the east side of the creek about fifty or so feet from the water," I point out as I cue up the tape to roll.

I lean out of the way, so Jonas has a clear view of the screen as the feed shows the drone's path over the creek. I can tell from his reaction he saw what I saw, before he opens his mouth.

His mumbled, "Grizzly," is followed by a healthy curse.

"Keep watching."

"*Shit*, are those cubs?"

On the screen two little dark blobs appear to bounce behind the bear.

"Yeah."

Bears give birth during hibernation, usually in January or February. They stay in the den with the mother until anytime between the end of March and May, when the warmer weather coaxes them out. The cubs trail along with their mother who, by this time, is ravenously hungry.

Food is generally abundant at this time, but grizzlies will eat anything; from plants and fruits to fish and any and all kinds of animals. They're opportunistic eaters, often foraging or hunting for whatever is in season, and in the spring it's not unusual for them to feed on roadkill or other dead animals they come across.

Or dead humans.

A female with cubs is not going to turn up her nose at an easy meal like that.

I fast forward the video feed to the drone's return trip to base camp. When I reach the same section in the creek, I let it play at normal speed. This time the grizzly looks to be rummaging in the debris that has piled up in the creek bend. Her cubs are just visible at the edge of the tree line. She lifts her head and appears to be looking right at the drone as the Matrice passes overhead.

"You think he's in there?" Jonas asks.

"I think something got her attention. Could be anything, but it probably warrants a closer look."

"It'll be tough getting close if there is something she's feeding on in that pile," Jonas suggests.

The bear will be protective of her food *and* of her cubs, so yeah, it won't be without risk.

"Send the drone up again," he orders. "I want to have a good look around. See how close of a visual we can get before we call the team back."

I supply the Matrice with fresh batteries and launch her from the clearing in front of the tent. Then, with the controller board in hand, I head back inside where the feed from the camera is up on the big screen.

As the crow flies, it takes the drone far less time than it

would on horseback to get to that particular bend in the creek. It's pretty rough terrain, and won't be easy to access on the ground. Unfortunately, because of the rapidly moving water, as well as the debris washing down, it's too dangerous to try and use the creek itself. We often use the path of water to get to places that are otherwise difficult to access, but that won't be an option now.

"First scan the area. See if you can spot the bear."

I steer the drone around, getting as low as I dare to the treetops without risking damage. The farther you get from the water, the denser the woods appear to be. With the camera angled straight down, you still only get glimpses of what is underneath.

I circle the area a few times, but we don't see the bear or her cubs.

"Probably hiding out in her den until she needs to feed again," Jonas comments. "Could be anywhere in that terrain."

I grunt in agreement as I change the path of the Matrice and angle the camera toward the debris clogging up the creek.

"There's a bit of a clearing right in that bend," I point out. "I should be able to do a few flyovers right above the water."

"Do it, but slowly."

This close to the water, I have to concentrate on flying, while Jonas scans the camera feed. On my first pass I approach from the south. Nothing jumps out at me, and Jonas doesn't ask me to slow or give him a closer look.

Things change when I approach from the north.

"What's that?" Jonas asks, pointing at something on the screen.

I immediately slow down my approach and leave the

drone hovering to get a better look. What looks like a scrap of green fabric appears stuck in some branches.

"Ball cap?" I ask, trying to identify what it is.

"Looks like it. He was supposed to be wearing one that color," Jonas refers to the description we were given.

"Yeah, but the likelihood is, he would've lost that when he first hit the water," I point out, playing devil's advocate. "Just because his hat got hung up here doesn't mean the rest of him did."

"Doesn't mean it didn't either," he returns.

"That's fair."

Jonas draws circles with his index finger. "Can you get around the pile to where we saw the bear? If there is something she was feeding on, we may be able to see."

As instructed, I slowly maneuver the drone around the perimeter, keeping the camera focused on the debris.

"There," he announces, pointing at something poking out from between a couple of tangled branches on the screen.

I carefully inch the drone closer to the spot he's indicating, but it takes me a few moments to realize what I'm looking at is one side of a torso, still partially covered in camo, protruding from the pile. The arm is missing, clearly ripped off.

Suddenly the feed jerks with erratic movement; the camera spins, showing a slice of sky, fur, some trees, and finally dirt when it comes to rest on the ground.

The last image is of a large snout sniffing at the drone before the feed is cut off.

"We're gonna need a new bird."

Jonas's response is predictable.

*"Fucking hell."*

# Seven

*Jackson*

"Tranquilizer darts?"

The tent is crowded. Jonas called the team back and we just finished replaying the video for them to see.

"I don't think that momma bear is gonna let you get close enough," I answer Dan's suggestion. "But even if you'd manage that, the accuracy on those dart rifles is questionable at best, and if you missed you'd have a really angry bear on your ass."

"Too risky," Jonas confirms. "Sully is on his way with the spare drone so we can monitor from the sky. We'll try to avoid a confrontation."

Unfortunately, the spare drone is cheap and clunky compared to the Matrice and doesn't hold that long of a charge, but it's better than nothing.

"Dan...you, Wolff, and JD, you'll be retrieving the body," Jonas continues. "Make sure you have all the neces-sary tools to cut him free from those branches. Bring a body bag, extra rope and, because you'll have to go through rough terrain both coming and going, you might want to consider bringing another horse to carry the extra weight."

It makes sense he's sending in those guys. They're in better physical shape, which is a good thing; they may need to run. It still sucks though, getting sidelined, especially since this kind of assignment—a challenging one with a sharp edge of danger—would've been right up my alley at one point in time.

"Judge is strong, he shouldn't have a problem carrying the extra load," Wolff suggests, referring to his horse.

Jonas shrugs. "If you're sure; you guys may be in a hurry to get out of there."

"Yeah, he can handle it."

"Still, it's going to be a dangerous proposition trying to steal the grizzly's food source out from under her nose, especially from a mom with—"

He stops talking abruptly at the sound of a vehicle approaching and pokes his head out of the tent.

*"God-fucking-dammit,"* he grinds out as he returns his attention to the team, clearly unhappy. "We've got company."

Company in the form of Buck Adams and the suit from the DOS, the U.S. Department of State, who appear to have been tipped off. I didn't catch the DOS guy's name, but my guess is he's more concerned about the political optics than the viability of a recovery effort.

Confirmation follows five minutes later when he proposes we straight out kill the bear to simplify the retrieval of Juan Pérez's body.

"This bear happens to be a grizzly, and they are a protected species," the game warden points out. "You can't just randomly shoot one."

"That's preposterous," the suit returns. "They're dangerous animals."

The collective eye roll from most everyone else in the tent is almost audible. Luckily Buck shows more patience than I would've had with the idiot. Who the fuck shows up at a base camp for a field search in a tie and loafers? That should tell you enough about the guy.

"I'm not going to debate the merits of the law with you," Buck calmly returns. "There has been plenty of discussion on this specific topic here in Montana recently. If you want, you can take it up with whoever creates the laws, but in the lower forty-eight states, the grizzly bear is protected under the Endangered Species Act. You can't shoot one unless it's in self-defense, or if it's attacking or killing your livestock. That's the law."

"With all due respect," Jonas interjects, thick with sarcasm. Not that anyone really believes he has even the smallest scrap of respect for the DOS rep anyway. "We start losing daylight in less than four hours. We're gonna need at least that, and a healthy dose of luck, to retrieve the body. So if you don't mind, I'd like to finish laying out our approach and get going. Unless you want parts of the ambassador's son to end up dinner and dessert for that grizzly as well?"

The guy—looking mildly green around the gills—wisely shakes his head.

"Okay, where were we?" Jonas's eyes turn on me. "Got your rifle in your truck?"

I nod. I always have my rifle in a gun safe mounted behind the front seats. The high velocity weapon is a reminder of my specialty in the armed forces. Jonas is the one who encouraged me after my discharge to keep my skills sharp. He pointed out there was no way to know when it might come in handy.

Guess today is the day.

"I want you to find a high spot with a good view on the body and surrounding area. Any sign of that bear, you know what to do. Your priority is keeping your team safe."

He didn't need to remind me of that—the team's safety is always a priority—but I suspect that last comment wasn't meant for me.

I'm grateful for the assignment though. My marksmanship is the one thing my missing limb has had no impact on, whatsoever.

I'm good.

An hour and a half later, I'm wedged securely in the fork of a tree, about fifteen feet off the ground, my cheek pressed against the butt of my rifle, and my eye lined up with the scope.

I'm about five hundred yards downstream from where the body is trapped in the pile of debris, at the edge of the creek. I can't see much detail with the naked eye, but I have a 12-25x scope on my rifle that allows me as clear a picture as if I were watching from only feet away.

Here I am in the zone, focused on my objective in a way that has time suspended. This is familiar territory for me, up in a tree or an elevation of some sort, patiently waiting for my cue. My breathing is steady, my heartbeat slows down, and I have no trouble ignoring the discomforts and aches of my body. My whole world is through the scope of my rifle.

This is where I shine.

I watch as the rest of the team cautiously approaches the narrow clearing.

*"Any visual?"* Dan's voice crackles in the receiver in my ear.

The tiny microphone is attached to the earpiece.

"Negative. You're clear."

At least they are for now. I track the trees constantly, back and forth along the creek bank.

*"Fuck me,"* I hear JD mutter. *"He's ripe."*

I listen to the guys talk as they start cutting away at the debris to try to get the body dislodged. Some of the comments are off-color, but we're on a private frequency, and sometimes dark humor is the preferred way to cope with a disturbing task like this one.

It's not until I see Dan free a large branch from the tangle, and pull it off to the side, I catch the slightest of movements in the trees to his right.

There's no time to even shout out a warning when the large grizzly comes charging out of the brush.

My finger is already depressing the trigger before my brain catches up with my eyes.

*Stephanie*

"What happened to you?"

I take in the parallel scratches running down the side of his face and into his neck.

"A little tussle with a bear," Jackson responds with a wry grin.

"A bear? My God..."

I step aside and wave him in. As he hangs his hat and coat on one of the hooks in the tight entrance, I grab the opportunity to take him in. His short, dark hair looks wet and has hints of auburn in the artificial light. He showered, but didn't shave; the stubble he sports on his strong jaw makes him even more attractive.

On top of that, he smells fabulous; of leather, something woodsy like pine, and a hint of allspice. Just a faint scent, but enough to make me want to bury my nose in his neck.

"It was only a little one. A cub," he clarifies.

"Yikes. Where was its momma?" I ask innocently, moving ahead to the kitchen, where I left a pot of four-bean chili simmering on the stove.

It was a bit chilly today, which inspired my choice for dinner. It also happens to be a meal that lends itself perfectly to leftovers, and tastes even better the next day. I made enough to last me a while.

Grabbing the large wooden spoon, I gently stir, scraping along the bottom to prevent the bits of shredded beef getting stuck. It's far from a traditional recipe and the chili purists among us would be horrified, but I love to add chunks of sweet potato and a tablespoon or so of dark cocoa to the mix. The slightly sweet flavor enhances the mild heat from the poblano peppers.

"What are you making?" Jackson's voice sounds behind me.

I step aside and let him peek into the pan, realizing he never actually answered my question about the bear. I'm curious about other things too, like for instance, what happened with the search, and what brought him to my doorstep again tonight?

"Chili. Smells good. Different."

There's a glint of something in his eyes when he looks at me with one eyebrow raised. Is he fishing for an invite?

"I've got plenty."

One corner of his mouth pulls up. "I see that. Were you expecting company?

"Not really. I just like making a big batch so I can have leftovers and freeze some for later. But you're welcome to stay for a bowl," I add quickly.

"Won't say no to that."

I point at the fridge. "Grab a beer while I get the garlic bread out of the oven. And maybe you can tell me about the bear cub and what brought you here tonight."

"Fair enough. You?" he asks, holding up one of the beers I picked up in case Janey and JD dropped by again.

At least that's what I've been telling myself, since I don't like mixing alcohol with the medication I'm on. I was only ever a social drinker anyway, and seeing that I rarely ever socialized, that didn't amount to much.

"I'm happy with my water." I point at the ridiculously large Yeti tumbler I've started lugging around.

Jackson takes his beer and sits down at the kitchen table, cracking the tab of his can with a hiss before taking a sip. I try not to look at him and instead, busy myself getting out bowls, a couple of spoons, and some napkins.

"We found the hunter," he says somberly.

I can tell by his tone the man had not been alive, which isn't really a surprise. I don't care what they say, but you never really get used to dealing with the aftermath of death. It's generally messy, and no matter how hard you try to shrug it off, or bury it under jokes, the images still haunt you.

"A grizzly with two cubs wasn't happy to give up her post-hibernation snack when we tried to recover the body. Now she's dead, and two cubs are without a mother."

I wince at the mental picture that conjures up before I

turn to face him, leaning my hip against the edge of the counter.

"That sucks. Where are the cubs now?"

"They're in a temporary shelter until the warden can arrange transportation to the rehabilitation center in Helena. He seems to think they're young enough, chances are good they'll be able to return to the wild eventually."

"That would be good."

I've heard about cases where these orphaned cubs end up in zoos, or end up being euthanized. Rehabilitating them to give them a fighting chance back out in their own environment is the much preferred route to take, if you ask me.

"Yeah," Jackson mutters, taking another sip as his eyes drift out the window.

The timer on the oven pings, alerting me the garlic bread should be done.

Five minutes later, I'm sitting across the table from Jackson, steaming bowls of chili in front of us and a warm slice of garlic bread on a napkin beside it.

"Dig in," I prompt him when I see him waiting for me.

"Looks great, but I want you to know I didn't come here looking to mooch a meal off you."

I put the chunk of bread I had halfway to my mouth back down.

"Okay. What did bring you here then?"

"Told you last night I'd be in touch, but I didn't realize until today, I don't have your number."

"I see." I grin at him. "Could've asked JD. He has it."

He makes a face I can't quite place before explaining, "I prefer asking you for your number. That way you can tell me to take a hike if you don't want me to have it."

I let that resonate for a moment, deciding I like what that conveys; respect.

"406-673-8422," I rattle off without taking my eyes off him. "Don't you need to write that down?" I ask when he doesn't move to take out his phone.

"No. I'll remember it."

I'm not sure whether it was those words or my chili that had my stomach happily gurgling throughout dinner. We didn't talk a whole lot, and when we did it was about general subjects. Nothing too deep or too personal. It's as if that one brief exchange about something as mundane as phone numbers suggested a level of involvement we both apparently need easing into.

That doesn't stop me from turning around and slipping my arms around his neck when he catches me in the kitchen, circling me with his arms as I put away the dishes. It's almost like it's second nature.

"I should head out," he announces for the second night in a row.

The faint lines at the outside corners of his eyes deepen when he smiles, and my stomach does a little flip.

"I don't want to overstay my welcome. I already scored a bonus meal when I was only looking for a phone number. I don't want to push my luck."

I'm very aware of his strong arms, holding my body pressed firmly against his, and my voice is a bit hoarse when I respond.

"I wasn't complaining."

"I know," he whispers, brushing my lips lightly with his before adding, "but if I stay, chances are good I'd be nodding off in no time after my long day, and I'd really like to get out of my prosthesis first."

"Feel free to take it off here. It doesn't bother me, if that's what you're worried about."

He kisses the tip of my nose.

"That's good to know for next time."

The words hold a certain promise, but I don't have much time to think about it before I'm distracted. This time when he kisses me, he plunders my mouth, displaying a level of skill that makes me forget my own name.

When he walks out the door a few minutes later, I make a mental note to pick up some condoms tomorrow.

Just in case.

Suddenly tired myself, I take my pills, turn off the lights, and head for the bathroom to brush my teeth. When I'm about to crawl into bed with my book, my phone pings with an incoming message.

That was just what I needed. Thank you.

# Eight

STEPHANIE

Cuts 'n Curls looks like pretty much any other hair salon.

A young girl smiles at me from behind a reception desk when I walk in, and directs me to a sitting area with three chairs, one of which is already occupied by a slightly older woman with a tired perm. She looks vaguely familiar in the way some people just do, and I can feel her scrutinizing me as I sit down.

"You're new."

I glance over at her and she looks back with a raised eyebrow, making it obvious she's waiting for an answer.

"This is my first time at the salon, yes."

I'm just guessing that's what she's referring to, since she didn't specify what I'm supposed to be *new* to.

"Clearly, but I meant new in town," she clarifies.

I wonder how she would keep track; Libby isn't that big, but the population is still roughly three thousand, which is a lot of people to memorize. One more or less can't be that obvious.

"I guess I am."

I could've brushed her off or told her I'm just visiting, but this is easier. Besides, it makes more sense if I'm supposed to be looking for a place to rent, which is what I told Mitchel Laine's girlfriend.

"I knew it," the woman smiles triumphantly. "I'm Betty. You came through my lane at Rosauers the other day. I'd never seen you there before. You were talking to that vet lady."

I try to recall the cashier who rang me through and suddenly the woman's face falls into place. The recognition is immediately followed by a rush of anxiety. It's not like me to forget faces, I don't miss details like that. In my line of work that could be dangerous.

"I remember you," I manage to tell her while struggling to control my breathing, which is threatening to run away on me.

"Stephanie, you're here for a trim?"

I swing my head around to find Tracy standing in the reception area, a puzzled expression on her face when she recognizes me.

"Oh. You're the one who was looking for a place to rent. You knocked on my door yesterday."

I hope I don't look like a deranged lunatic when I conjure up a surprised look.

"She's new in town," Betty pipes up helpfully.

I'm actually grateful, since I don't know if I'd be able to get a word out right now, my throat feels like it's closing up.

Tracy barely spares her a glance and motions for me to come. I force myself to follow her to the back of the salon where she points at one of the three washing stations.

"Sorry about her," Tracy mumbles as she guides my head back over the basin. "She's a tad nosy. If you want to know anything about anybody in town, she's a better resource than our local newspaper."

She turns on the faucet and starts to wet my hair with nice, warm water. I focus on the soothing motions of her fingers running through my hair, while she gives me the lowdown on Betty, who apparently turned into a busybody after her husband died way too young.

When she starts working shampoo into my hair with a firm scalp massage, I almost groan in pleasure, and by the time she wraps my head in a towel and encourages me to sit up, all tension has left my body. Any signs of anxiety are gone.

"Sorry again for disturbing you yesterday," I apologize, taking a seat at her station.

She waves it off. "Not a problem. Did you find the right trailer?"

"I did, and you were right, it looked like a dump so I turned right around without even getting out of the vehicle."

"Wise choice. Did you end up finding a place?"

"I did. In Libby, actually. Just a bit south of town. Also a trailer, but a nice one with a great view."

I was once told the best lie sticks as close to the truth as possible.

She carefully combs through my hair and looks at my reflection in the large mirror.

"How much did you want off? You've got some dead ends we should probably take care of."

She holds up a two-inch section of my hair.

"Yeah, something like that," I agree.

I resist the urge to start asking probing questions, which is what I'd normally do trying to get information, but I'm using a cover, which means I need to be patient until the information comes to me. I don't necessarily control the narrative, but if I'm lucky I may be able to guide it.

A bonus is Tracy likes to talk, and people who talk a lot generally share more than they intend to.

While she snips away with her scissors, she shares a bit about the run-ins she's had with the neighbor whose trailer was for rent. I don't have to say much, just an occasional commiserating grunt, but I listen carefully for any useful information.

"So, what brought you to this area?" she suddenly asks, before adding, "that is, assuming Betty is right and you are new here."

This is my opportunity to try and forge a connection.

"Let's just say, I needed to get out of Dodge," I share in a soft voice.

She leans down, meets my eyes in the mirror, and mimics my conspiratorial tone.

"Man trouble, or trouble of the legal variety?"

I pretend to look around to make sure no one can hear.

"A bit of both. I found out my boyfriend was cheating and hit him with a golf club. Knocked him out cold."

Tracy buys it hook, line, and sinker, bumping my shoulder with a wide grin on her face.

"Girl...good for you. That's one way to keep those assholes in line."

"Right. Except, now he's looking for me and so are the cops, neither of which bodes well for me. So I packed my bags and headed north."

Her hand lands on my shoulder, squeezing gently.

"You picked a pretty good area to hide out, trust me on that. A little off the beaten track, lots of room to disappear, and if things get too hot, you can be across the border in an hour and a half."

"I hope so." I feign a grimace. "I probably shouldn't have shared all this with the first person who is nice to me."

"Your secret is safe with me," Tracy assures me with a grin. "Just stay away from Betty, she'd have all your dirty laundry blasted across town before you could blink your eyes."

"So noted."

By the time I walk out of Cuts 'n Curls half an hour later, I'm not a whole lot wiser, but I have plans for lunch at Tracy's place tomorrow.

I'm feeling pretty good about myself.

*Jackson*

"Are you busy tonight?"

My mother pokes her head around the door of the tack room, where I'm just returning Banner's saddle.

We spent most of the day checking and mending fences, making sure the back fields are secure before we move some of the horses there for the warmer seasons now the snow has melted.

To be honest, I'd been looking forward to maybe taking Stephanie out for a bite to eat. Unfortunately, cell reception is spotty in that back section, so I wasn't able to check with her but, depending on what my mother wants, that may turn out to be a good thing.

"Why?"

She smiles at me in a way I know means she wants my help with something.

"I have to pick up a horse just across the Idaho border outside Moyie Springs and I could use a hand, but Jonas has a meeting in town at eight. He can come with me tomorrow, but it has to be tonight."

"Okay...what's the catch?"

Because I'm sure there's a reason she needs a hand with this one, when she goes out to pick up animals by herself all the time.

"The horse is in really bad shape. Neglected. I got a desperate call from a neighbor, who has tried to get the local sheriff to step in but has been unsuccessful."

That's not exactly a surprise, in larger communities those calls go to the humane society, who will come and investigate. However, in the less populated areas that responsibility falls on the shoulders of local law enforcement, and they often have bigger fish to fry. Especially since the laws protecting animals in both Idaho and Montana leave much to be desired. In most cases, it's considered a misdemeanor, letting the offenders off with no more than a slap on the wrist, and making it barely worth the while for law enforcement to come out.

It's ironic that in some aspects our wildlife receives more consideration and attention than our domesticated animals do.

"Apparently, the horse's owner lives in a trailer down the road from the caller," Ma continues, "and likes referring to himself as a sovereign citizen."

Great. We've got our share of those. Often individuals tout that label to justify snubbing the law, as if that would make them exempt.

"Lovely. And you plan to steal this man's horse?"

I move past her as I start making my way over to my cabin for a much-needed shower.

"Rescue," Ma stubbornly corrects me, trotting to keep up. "Besides, he's a sovereign citizen, what is he gonna do? Call the sheriff?"

"No, but he might feel justified shooting you," I point out sardonically.

"Which is exactly why I have to pick up the horse tonight," she explains, a little out of breath. "The neighbor told me he plays the slots at the River Inn Casino every Friday night."

I stop in my tracks and turn to look at her through narrowed eyes.

"Does Jonas know the circumstances?"

She instantly sends a furtive glance at the ranch house, so I highly doubt it.

I have a feeling he'd have a thing or two to say about Ma putting herself in danger. Not to mention animal cruelty may not warrant a closer look, but law enforcement would come down hard on horse theft, even if it was to save the animal from a certain death. Seems backward if you ask me, but that's how things are.

"He will...after," she mutters.

When it's too late for him to do anything about it.

I'm starting to wonder if Jonas actually has a meeting to go to, or whether that was simply an excuse to get me to go with her. Which, of course, I will because I know my mother; she'll just go on her own. She's more concerned about the horse than she is about her own hide.

"Fine. I'm taking a quick shower though," I add. "And pack me something to eat. You're driving."

I have a handgun tucked into the back of my jeans, just in case, when I meet her by her truck twenty minutes later. She already has the small, single-horse trailer hooked up behind it. Waiting on the console between the seats are a bottle of water and something wrapped in tinfoil.

"Chicken, rice, and black bean burritos," she clarifies when I get in.

Starved, I'm already shoving down the food before Ma pulls out of the driveway.

"Buckle," she snaps, shooting a pointed look my way.

I comply and grin at the memory of what was a daily battle between us when my mother used to drive me to school. I wasn't a particularly rebellious kid, I think, but I did use to give her a hard time about wearing my seat belt. I hated the feeling of being restricted. Still do, although these days age and wisdom have me usually buckling up without thinking.

"So what's with you and that FBI agent?"

Her question comes out of the blue and catches me off guard.

"Stephanie?"

Her name flies from my lips without thinking and that fact already betrays more than I'm ready to share. I may be nearing forty, but this is my mother; she has a knack of tapping into things I'm trying to keep close to my chest.

"That's right. Lovely name," she adds around a triumphant little grin. "Pretty blonde? I think I've seen her at the ranch a few times."

"Not since last year, you haven't," I point out, and it makes me wonder how Stephanie ended up on my mother's radar. "Did JD blab?"

She snorts. "JD? I don't think blab is a word I'd ever

associate with him. No," she assures me. "It was not JD. I helped Janey with vaccinations at the rescue yesterday. She mentioned Stephanie is staying in JD's trailer, and you were there a few nights ago. I think that was the night I was waiting on the porch for you. Then I heard from Jonas about what happened with the search yesterday, and was a little worried when you disappeared before I had a chance to check in with you."

I get why she might've worried, and feel instantly guilty I didn't shoot her a quick text to let her know I was fine. I need to do better; I owe her that.

"Didn't mean to worry you."

She smiles when she glances over. "Oh, I know. I figured —or at least hoped—you'd sought her out last night. Given her profession, she'd be someone who'd understand the kind of day you had," she clarifies.

Funny how that never occurred to me as a motivation for seeking Stephanie out, even though calm understanding is exactly what I got from her. That, and a serious hard-on that lasted all the way home. I'm finding even more reasons to like her, and there were plenty to start with.

Still, whatever is sparking between us can only be temporary. She has a job in Kalispell she'll be going back to. It may not seem that far, but both our work schedules are highly unpredictable. Trying to grab time to connect, when there's also at least an hour and a half drive separating us, is impossible. At least it would be in the long run.

"Yeah, I went to see her but, Ma, we're just friends."

She quickly hides the flash of disappointment I catch on her face, and I feel bad for the lie.

Because—perhaps against better judgment—friendly was the last thing I was feeling when I kissed Stephanie last night. Nor is the craving for another taste of her that has stuck with me all day.

But I don't want to give my mother false hope.

A few minutes later, when her attention seems firmly focused on driving, I slip my phone from my pocket, and pull up last night's return message from Stephanie.

> Same here.

I wasn't sure how to respond so I left it there last night, but now I suddenly feel the urge to check in with her.

> Out with my mother picking up rescue horse tonight, but are you up for dinner tomorrow?

Just a few seconds later those little dots start dancing on my screen, announcing an impending response. I tilt the phone away when I catch Ma trying to sneak a peek from the corner of her eye.

The dots disappear, only to start up again, and I wonder if she's trying to find a way to let me down easy. It sure looks like she's got a lot to say, but when the text finally comes through, the message is only one, single word.

Sure.

Before I can change my mind—or she hers—I type out another text.

Pick you up at 6?

# Nine

STEPHANIE

"I don't think this is wise."

I roll my eyes at my reflection as I try to get some mascara on my lashes.

"It's the best I can do without a badge," I remind Ben.

Of course he called for an update, just as I was getting ready to head out to Tracy's. The man must have a sixth sense.

"I just want to know if he's there."

"Exactly," I return. "And that's what I aim to find out. The girlfriend's place is a trailer, set way back from the road in the woods. There's no way to keep an eye on the place without getting noticed. Trust me, this is a faster and safer way to get the information."

"Well, I don't like it," he snaps stubbornly.

Now he's just pissing me off.

I toss my mascara in the sink, giving up my attempts at putting on makeup, and walk out of the bathroom.

"Need I remind you, you're the one who asked for my help?" I sit down on the edge of the bed and lace up my Chucks. "Too bad if you don't like the way I do it; last time I checked you weren't paying my salary."

That's met with silence on the other end. Smart man.

"Now if you don't mind," I continue. "I need to get going; I'm already late."

"Call me after," I can just hear him say as I end the call.

*"Asshole,"* I grumble, shoving my phone in my small cross-body purse.

Big bags are cumbersome, and although this little one doesn't hold a hell of a lot, it leaves my hands free. Besides, it fits everything I need, plus, I can run with it in case I have to get myself out of a situation fast. Hence the jeans and sneakers as well.

Of course, I'm hoping it won't come to that, but you never know. If Mitchel Laine happens to show up, there's always a chance he might recognize me. The last time he would've seen me would've probably been at his trial, but that was twelve years ago when I was a fresh-faced agent.

Since then, time has marked itself in the lines on my face and the glints of silver in my blond hair. I would've had my hair back in a tight ponytail and been wearing a suit. Today my hair is loose, showing off my new haircut, and I'm wearing a boho top over torn jeans and my pink Chucks. I don't look anything like an FBI agent.

I grab the small container of Mace off the counter in the kitchen and slip it into the small purse. Not much in terms of a weapon, but enough to get the upper hand in a fight, if ever it came to that.

As I get behind the wheel of my SUV, I suddenly feel a little uneasy about going. I'm so used to working with a team behind me, it didn't fully hit me until just now I'll be out there on my own. Hell, no one even knows where I'm going.

Damn Ben, for making me question myself.

As I feel anxiety build, I pull up a number on my dashboard display and dial. Then I back out of my parking spot in front of the trailer.

"Hey."

I have no idea what's happening to me; just the sound of his voice puts a sappy smile on my face, and the panicked feeling dissipates.

"Sorry to bug you..." I start, but I'm immediately cut off.

"You're not," Jackson assures me. "This is a welcome break from the piles of laundry I've ignored for weeks and decided to tackle this morning. Unless...you're not canceling on me, are you?"

"No, not canceling," I clarify.

"Good. So what are you up to?"

"I'm actually on my way to meet someone for lunch," I share, turning onto the highway toward town. "She's a hairdresser at the salon in Libby, but lives in a trailer at 254 Waterfront Road in Troy. She cut my hair yesterday and ended up inviting me."

He hums in response. Of course there isn't much for him to say, I'm aware I sound a bit random, but I'm unsure how much to share with him. If I tell him, is he going to freak out and go full protector mode on me? Then again, if I don't give him the background and something does end up going wrong on my end, he might walk into something he's not prepared for.

"I'm actually doing a favor for someone," I confess.

"A favor," he echoes, sounding a bit confused.

"Yes, for a colleague. He needs to know the whereabouts

of a suspect in a case he's working. He suspects his target may have come this way to meet up with his girlfriend."

"The girlfriend being your hairdresser?" Jackson concludes accurately.

"Right," I acknowledge, sharing with him how I ended up with an invitation to lunch today.

"Clever," he comments, before adding, "Could be risky."

He doesn't even know I have a history with said suspect. That bit of information I kept to myself.

"It's only lunch, and I'm just gathering information."

"And you'll be careful," he adds.

"Of course I will," I assure him, feeling my confidence return. "I'll tell you all about it tonight. Looking forward to it."

"As am I."

I carefully scan my surroundings as I make my way up the driveway to Tracy's place.

It's always a good idea to get the lay of the land; knowing where a possible threat could come from, or finding alternate routes out.

I check out the trailer itself too. I can only see the front of it and note the door is off-center, with only one window to the right of it, and four windows to the left. I'm guessing maybe a bedroom on the right side, and living space and maybe a second bedroom to the left.

I'm not a fan of walking into a space when I don't know what is behind me, but I guess that can't be helped.

"Hey again, come in," Tracy says, stepping out of the way to let me through.

Her trailer may look a bit worn and dated outside, but she's clearly put effort into making the inside into a welcoming home. The style is a bit too in-your-face for me —I personally prefer natural shades and materials—but the black steel, bright colors, and bold prints suit Tracy perfectly.

"Have a seat." She aims me at a small round dining table with four chairs. Then she dives into the stainless steel fridge and comes out with a pitcher. "Margarita?"

"I'll have a water, if you don't mind. The meds I'm on don't mix well with alcohol."

That, and I also want to make sure I keep my wits about me. Drinking in the middle of the day is not conducive to that.

While she fills me a glass of water at the sink, I give her space a scan, looking for evidence of someone else living here.

There had been no men's shoes or boots by the door when I walked in, and I can see only one set of dishes drying in the dish rack on the counter. But that doesn't necessarily mean anything.

"Hope you like lasagna," she says, sliding a glass of water in front of me while sitting down across the table with a generous serving of margarita for herself.

"Is that what I smell? Delicious."

"Good. It needs a little more time."

We spend the next few minutes chatting about inconsequential things when Tracy suddenly asks, "So who was the douchebag?"

It takes me a moment to clue in she is talking about the fictional boyfriend I hit over the head with a golf club.

It was only partially fiction though. I distinctly remember standing in the living room of my little apartment in Traverse City, Michigan, the Callaway Paradigm five iron I'd just bought as a birthday present clutched in my hand. The temptation to swing it at Ben Vallard's smug face so great, I could taste it.

Most of my anger stemmed from the fact I'd been too stupid to see what was painfully obvious to the rest of the world. Ben was a known player, making it a sport to *bag* as many female colleagues he came in contact with as possible. That I read more into our brief relationship was entirely on me.

As was the fact I spent almost half of my hard-earned paycheck on a stupidly expensive golf club for his birthday.

Over the years, nurturing the fantasy of actually following through and whaling on him with the iron, made the cover story I'm spinning for Tracy feel almost real. The only adjustment I have to make is to our jobs. In my story I'm a paralegal and Ben is a lawyer for the same firm.

My cover doesn't need to be airtight—this isn't an elaborate undercover sting—I just want the story I've been weaving over lunch to be believable until I can get some idea of Mitchel Laine's whereabouts.

"Men, I tell you," Tracy commiserates. "I've had some losers in my day."

Finally, she gives me an opening to explore.

I put down my fork and lean back in my chair.

"Sounds like you've given up on men," I observe casually.

"Probably should have," she returns, tossing back the rest of her third margarita. She's singlehandedly killed off about three-quarters of that pitcher. "Did for a while too."

"I'm hearing a *but*..."

She shoots a grin my way.

"Yeah, well...I've always been a sucker for a bad boy."

I force a chuckle. "Couldn't stay away?"

"Actually, technically I did, for about five years," she confesses, and I find myself leaning forward in anticipation. "I only met him in person recently."

*Bingo.*

I try not to let my excitement show. The timeline works, but I want some confirmation we're talking about Mitchel Laine and not some other guy.

"Oh, you met online or something? I haven't had much luck with those dating sites," I probe.

"I wasn't too keen on them myself, but I figured I'd give it another try. That was five years ago, and the first one I met on there was him."

"Wait, are you saying you've been talking to this guy for five years but you never met face-to-face?"

"Until recently, yeah." She gets up to empty the pitcher in her glass. "More water?" she asks me.

I shake my head. "I'm good, thanks."

When she sits down and sips her drink, I worry I'm going to have to push harder to get more information, but apparently, she's not yet done sharing.

"Also, we mostly wrote each other. Then after a while I gave him my phone number and he'd call whenever he could. Gave us a chance to really get to know each other."

Tracy comes across as someone who has her shit together, so it's hard for me to believe the dreamy look on her face was put there by the likes of Mitchel Laine.

"Wow. Military? Was he working overseas or something?"

I do my best to make the question sound casual, and keep a close eye on Tracy's reaction. Instead of looking at me suspiciously, she averts her gaze, looking almost embarrassed.

"Or something," she finally responds after waging a silent battle. Her eyes come up and meet mine when she adds, "He was incarcerated."

"Oh," I feign surprise. At least I hope I do, because inside I'm giving myself a mental fist pump.

"It's not like that," she immediately jumps to his defense. "He was framed."

If I had a dollar for every time I've heard that excuse, I'd buy myself an island in the South Pacific.

"He's such a gentleman, so sweet and attentive. There's no way he could've done any of the things they accused him of. He's been nothing but good to me."

She's trying so hard to convince me, I feel for Tracy, I do. Clearly Laine spent the past five years brainwashing her into buying his claim of innocence. By her own admission, she didn't have many good experiences with men before meeting him, and that manipulative bastard must've caught right on to that. He turned himself into everything she'd ever wanted.

I wondered, at first, if perhaps this girl had been an accomplice of sorts, but I don't think so. She didn't stand a chance; she has stars in her eyes, and I want to bet she has no clue what he's really been up to since his release.

"So when did you two finally meet?"

"The first time was a little over a week ago," she shares, taking a drink from her margarita and getting that dreamy look on her face again. "He's dropped by a few times since."

So he's not actually staying here, but he can't be too far.

"Oh wow, so he's local," I observe, but I notice something about my comment doesn't sit well with Tracy.

She suddenly seems flustered and gets to her feet, carrying her still half-full glass to the kitchen sink where she dumps it out. Then she turns around and leans against the counter, folding her arms in front of her.

"Keep it to yourself," she says, a hard edge to her voice. "All he wants is a fresh start, and he doesn't want to draw any attention. I shouldn't have said anything."

I lift my hands, palms out, as I stand up as well.

"I get it. Believe me, I do. Heck, I probably overshared as well," I quickly add, playing the role of being equally vulnerable. "But, like you told me yesterday, this is a good place to hide out, and I hope it offers a fresh start for both of us."

That seems to appease her, but I still quickly make my excuses, thank her for lunch, and head out. I don't get away before exchanging phone numbers though. I'd prefer not to have to continue the ruse—I got what I came for—but I can't exactly say no when she asks.

Trying not to be too obvious about scanning my surroundings, I make my way to my SUV. Tracy is standing in the doorway, watching as I do a three-point turn until I'm aimed in the direction of the road. I roll down my window and wave as I head down the driveway.

It's not until I reach the end of Waterfront Road and stop, I notice the dark pickup pulling up right behind me.

# Ten

JACKSON

The only vehicles parked in front of 254 Waterfront Road are a gray Pontiac Vibe and Stephanie's SUV.

I had to leave my truck a little farther up the road, not wanting to draw attention to myself, and ended up approaching the trailer on foot. Just close enough to where I could get a clear view of the place.

I have no intention of interfering in Stephanie's investigation, and am happy to keep my distance, but I didn't like the idea of her ending up in a situation where she might need backup and wouldn't have any.

In fact, I suspect she wasn't nearly as sure of herself as she made it sound, why else would she call and give me the address where she'd be? My gut told me to get my ass out here and keep a discreet eye out.

Which is why I've been about ten feet up a tree, perched on a thick enough branch to hold my weight, watching the place. Climbing with my prosthesis was more of a hindrance than a help, and I was tempted to take it off, but that would seriously slow me down on the ground if I had to move for some reason. Fortunately, my upper body strength is decent, and I have some experience getting up and down trees, so I managed.

The moment I see Stephanie stepping out the front door, I breathe out a sigh of relief and lower myself to the ground. Then I quickly make my way back to my truck, reaching it just as her SUV comes out of the driveway and pulls onto the road.

I keep my distance, but when her CR-V comes to a halt at the end of the road, I have a vehicle behind me and have no choice but to pull up right behind her.

As she pulls away from the stop sign, my phone rings and her name pops up on the screen on my dashboard.

"Are you following me?" is the first thing out of her mouth when I answer.

"Define following?" I evade, while trying to come up with an answer that doesn't make me look like some weird stalker.

"Jackson..." she threatens, and I decide the truth is probably the best option.

"In case you needed a safety net. I figured normally you'd have your team for backup, but they aren't here, and I had nothing better to do. At least nothing better than doing laundry, and I was already sick of that."

It's quiet, and I'm half-waiting for her to get pissed, but she surprises me by laughing softly.

"I swear, you cowboy types can't help yourselves, can you?"

"Not sure what you mean."

That's a lie, I have a pretty good idea. I've had a first-row seat to several of my teammates developing a protective streak for the right woman. I always thought it was kind of funny, given every last one of those women can take care of themselves, but I'm not laughing now.

"This alpha thing. You do realize I'm a trained and seasoned FBI agent, right?"

"I do," I concede before confessing, "and I'm sorry to tell you, it doesn't make a lick of difference. It must be a hormonal thing; a surplus of testosterone or something. It's animal instinct."

I grin when I hear her snort.

*Jesus*, how long has it been since I've casually joked around with anyone, let alone a woman? I used to be pretty lighthearted, loved to goof around, but I haven't been that person for some time now.

"Are you following me all the way home?" she asks.

I hadn't really thought about it, but that sounds like a fine idea.

"I guess I am."

"Good. You can—" Her voice suddenly falls away, but she's back the next moment. "Oh, I've got a call I have to take. See you at home."

Before I have a chance to respond, she ends the call.

I wonder if that is the colleague she mentioned on the other line. The one who asked her for a favor. Something about that doesn't sit right. If she is here in Libby to take a break—find some peace and quiet, as she indicated—then why would a colleague not ask someone else for a favor? Unless, of course, he has a special connection with Stephanie; something to make him think he has a right to lay claim to her personal time.

Does this guy know why she is hiding out in Libby with shadows in her eyes? Or worse yet, did he have something to do with putting them there?

Not normally a jealous person, it takes me a moment to realize that's why I'm grinding my teeth as I follow Stephanie back to the trailer. The thought she won't share with me what some other guy already knows makes me even more determined to find out what brought her here.

"So was your lunch informative?" I prompt her when we walk into the trailer twenty-or-so minutes later.

She dumps the small purse on the kitchen counter and toes her shoes off before answering.

"Very. He's in the area; she's seen the suspect several times and he is staying close by. She has no clue who she's dealing with."

Stephanie plops down on the couch and I take a seat beside her.

"He's dangerous?"

She glances at me from under her eyebrows.

"That'd be par for the course, with the FBI after him. He went away for armed robbery and aggravated assault for fifteen years, overcrowding and good behavior got him released in ten, he did not hesitate one single second to get right back where he left off—bank heists—except this time he went a little further and killed a police officer in the process."

"Nice guy," I observe.

"Right? I don't know how it is possible, but he somehow managed to get on a dating website five years ago where he met Tracy. He's been grooming her ever since. She believes he was wrongly convicted in the first place."

"Let me guess, he told her he was set up?"

"Something like that."

She abruptly gets to her feet and heads for the kettle sitting on the stove.

"I'm making tea. Want some? Or would you rather have a beer?"

"I'll have a tea."

Can't remember the last time I had a fucking cup of tea, but I don't feel like beer and I want an excuse to stick around longer.

"So what's gonna happen now?" I probe. "Does this mean you're back to work?"

I hate myself for pushing the moment I see her face fall.

"No. My boss would be pissed if he found out. Ben is coming here."

"Ben is the friend who asked you for the favor?"

"Hmm, not a friend, a colleague."

Interesting distinction.

"Why would the guy ask you to do something that could get you in trouble?" I want to know.

She shrugs and turns her back to grab a couple of mugs from the cupboard. "It's complicated."

This is where she shuts me down if I let her, so I get off the couch and walk right up behind her.

"*Un*complicate it for me."

She turns around slowly and looks right at me, hesitation in her eyes. I lift my hand and brush away a strand that is stuck to her eyelashes.

"Please?"

*Stephanie*

There's a part of me that wants nothing more than to spill everything to this man.

However, that would require making myself vulnerable. Not something I'm accustomed to or particularly comfortable with. The image I try to portray of a strong, capable, even-keeled person is one I honed for most of my life. First at home, my father and brother would never tolerate weakness after Mom died, and all the years I've worked for the Bureau since have made me a master at keeping up that unbreakable shield.

Oh, who am I kidding? Clearly, the shield has already crumbled, or I wouldn't be here in Libby licking my wounds. I may be concerned with maintaining as much of my reputation as I can, but I have a feeling Jackson doesn't care much about reputation or expect any kind of perfection.

"I was put on leave."

"Yes, you mentioned that."

There's an obvious bite to his voice suggesting he's upset about that on my behalf. It's weirdly complimentary and makes me feel a little better. Still, I have to swallow hard to clear my throat before I can continue.

"The official word is for health reasons. As I mentioned, my suspected heart attack was really high blood pressure coupled with an anxiety attack, which was embarrassing enough, but it wasn't all." I glance up and the equal mix of concern and curiosity I read in his eyes prompts me to go on. "It wasn't the main reason why I was sidelined."

This next part is hard, and I need some space to get through it without a meltdown. Turning my back on Jackson, I walk over to the sliding glass doors and fix my eyes on the view of the creek and the mountains beyond, as I try to find the right words.

"The last week of November last year, I shot and killed a sixteen-year-old in front of his parents."

Just saying the words out loud has the bile rise up from my stomach. The silence behind me is thick, but I push on.

"It was a domestic terrorism case. We were following up on a credible lead to a ranch property just outside Thompson Falls. A family of preppers, pretty isolated, minimal contact with the outside world. The information we received suggested they were possibly manufacturing bombs on the property. Because of the potential danger, we went in armed."

I shake my head, vividly remembering the sequence of events, the images flooding back faster than I can blink them away.

"They sent the kids out first. Five of them, the youngest couldn't have been more than three, just a toddler. It threw us off long enough for the oldest two kids to produce automatic weapons and open fire on us. Two of the children and the father were injured, but my bullet hit the oldest boy in the head and he died instantly."

I'll never forget the look of shock on his siblings' faces when they realized this wasn't some survival game their parents had trained them for, but real life, with real bullets, and real consequences. Even their mother seemed stunned this could be the outcome; one child dead and two more plus her husband gravely injured.

I hear soft footfalls behind me and quickly rush to finish my story.

"Anyway, we had helicopters with cameras overhead that captured the whole thing, so it was quickly deemed we did everything by the book and we received our absolution and congratulations on a job well done."

My last words sound bitter, even to my own ears. That's the part I've struggled with; yes, we foiled what turned out to have been an elaborate plan of coordinated attacks on a number of federal buildings in five different states. We found enough evidence to pick up an additional seven individuals who were all part of the conspiracy. We managed to save what could have potentially been in the hundreds or even thousands of lives lost.

I know all that, but a sixteen-year-old boy still lost his life at my hand.

"Did you talk to anyone?"

Jackson's voice is so close, it startles me. His strong hand settles on my shoulder, and when I glance up at the reflection in the window, I see him standing right behind me, his eyes aimed at the mountains as well.

Despite his physical proximity, by not looking at me, he's still giving me space, which I appreciate.

"My boss made me attend a few sessions. I didn't find them helpful. I guess I was numb. I tried to take a little time off, but I didn't last long, I did better back at work. Or at least I thought so. It wasn't until earlier this year I realized it was starting to have an effect on how I functioned. I felt a hesitancy every time I had to draw my weapon, my instincts weren't as sharp as before, and my confidence started slipping. Apparently, I didn't hide it well enough." I bark out a bitter laugh. "The anxiety attack was confirmation and my boss used the blood pressure issue as an excuse to sideline me until—and these were his words—I got my shit sorted out."

Jackson removes his hand and crosses it in front of me to reach my other shoulder, his forearm braced against my upper chest. It forces me to take a step back, right into his strong body.

"You lived for your job. No wonder you've looked so lost. I get it."

I've been able to hold my shit together until now, and I

don't even bother holding back the sob that gets the water-
works going.

Right now, in this moment, in this man's hold, I'm not
an agent, not a collection of skills or a sum of accomplish-
ments, but a flesh-and-blood human being.

"Let it out," he mumbles in my hair.

So I do.

I let it out, after months of desperately holding myself
together for fear of falling apart, I let myself purge.

# Eleven

*JACKSON*

"Sorry I unloaded on you."

I look up to meet her eyes. They're still a little red-rimmed from her epic crying bout. I was starting to get worried when the tears just kept coming and coming, as if she'd saved those all up for years.

Who knows, maybe she had?

"Don't be," I reassure her, turning back to the creek to watch my nymph bob on the water. "I appreciate you sharing with me."

I didn't think going out for dinner was a good idea after Stephanie's tears finally dried, so I decided to try and catch dinner. I'm hoping if I can pull a good-sized trout out of the creek, I could cook it on JD's charcoal grill on the deck. I noticed Stephanie must've done a grocery run recently because there is plenty of stuff in the fridge I can use to make us a decent meal.

I reel in my line and lift the rod over my shoulder before

I start casting it back out in smooth strokes.

"Is that a fish?" she asks when the nymph on the end of my line disappears as soon as it hits the water.

The slight tug on the line is confirmation, and I quickly jerk the tip of my rod up to set the hook.

"Feels like it."

The trout I reel in makes for a good distraction from the heavier subject of her meltdown. I get it, I've been there.

"That's probably enough for the both of us," she comments, picking up the landing net.

When I get the fish close to shore, she quickly dips the net in the water and scoops it up. Then she grabs a firm hold of the trout's jaw, lifts it up, and deftly frees the small hook from its mouth.

Another thing I can add to the list of things I like about Stephanie, she's not afraid to get her hands dirty.

"Mom died when I was young, so I grew up in a house ruled by testosterone," she explains when she catches my appreciative glance. "Fishing was a regular activity. Summer or winter," she adds with a grimace.

"Ice fishing?"

"Yes, Lake Michigan is good for perch and walleye. Sometimes lake trout."

She carries the fish to the deck and I follow with the fishing gear, dumping it by the back door.

"Got any experience cleaning them?" I ask.

She throws me a sassy look as she hands me the fish. "Even if I did, I wouldn't admit to it. The job's all yours, but I'll gladly help by chopping vegetables for a salad."

"Sounds fair."

Half an hour later, the trout is ready for the grill. Skin on, with the head and tail still attached, but the body cavity is stuffed with thinly sliced shallots, sliced lemon, a few twigs of fresh rosemary and thyme, and generous seasonings. I bound it with twine and drizzled the skin with olive oil. It sizzles when it hits the hot grill.

"That smells good already," Stephanie volunteers when she steps outside with a beer for me and a glass of ice tea for herself. "Where did you learn how to cook? Your mom?"

I try not to laugh. Ma's cooking skills are basic at best, which is why she happily leaves it to others.

"Lucy taught me. Bo's wife?" I clarify when she doesn't seem to recognize the name. "Lucy manages the horse rescue. She's worked for Ma for over twenty years. She's family and we all shared a house before I went off to join the Army and Ma moved in with Jonas. Lucy did most of the cooking and she's an amazing chef, better even than Ama—JD's mother—which is saying a lot."

I take a sip of my beer and check on the fish before closing the lid on the grill.

"Interesting," she muses. "So I grew up in a male-dominated environment, and you in a household of women."

"Hmm. I'm thinking it benefited us both. You're tough as nails and a force to be reckoned with, but still all woman. As for me, I picked up a few cooking skills and learned to put down the toilet seat, but I can guarantee you I'm all man."

She smiles at that as she sits down in one of the lounge chairs.

"I can see you're not lacking in confidence either," she observes teasingly, but I detect a wistful edge to her voice.

"I wouldn't say that," I admit, leaning a hip against the deck railing.

In the spirit of getting to know each other—she's been open with me, although I have yet to find out who this Ben is to her—it's only fair I give her the same courtesy.

"Don't get me wrong, I may have been a cocky bastard at one point, but all that self-assured bluster disappeared when I lost my leg. I wasn't in a good place for quite some time," I confess. "And even now, I'm still a work in progress."

"Of course; losing a leg is a life-altering experience."

"So is taking another person's life, however justified," I counter, shooting her a pointed look.

"I guess," she concedes, shrugging her shoulders.

It's quiet while I check on the fish and flip it over, but then Stephanie breaks the silence.

"You know, I consider myself a decent judge of character for the most part, but I think I may have missed the boat with you."

"How so?"

"You always struck me as a man of few words—a bit of a grouch, if I'm honest—but I was wrong."

That gets a chuckle from me.

"You're not wrong, I'm actually surprising myself, but I think the difference is you. I'm finding you're easy to talk to."

She's trying to hide her smile. "I'll take that as a compliment."

I close the lid on the grill and approach her, leaning over her chair. I hook a finger under her chin and tilt her face up.

"Good. You should."

Next, I close the distance and press a kiss to her mouth. Then another one as I watch her eyes flutter shut when I slip my tongue between her lips for a deeper taste.

Her soft sigh is oil to my fire, so I retreat before I take this kiss places I don't want to rush into.

"You are much too tempting," I confess, brushing the pad of my thumb over her plump bottom lip. "I didn't think I wanted to get involved, but you broke through my resolve."

The way the late afternoon sun catches her face makes her eyes appear lit from within as she looks up at me.

"I didn't do anything."

I gently shake my head.

"You exist, that's enough."

*Stephanie*

Dinner was delicious.

Jackson has serious cooking skills, and better yet, he enjoys using them. I'm not necessarily a slouch in the kitchen, but it's nice not to have to be the one responsible for putting dinner on the table.

Since he did the bulk of the cooking, I claimed the task of cleaning up, He left to run home to pick up his dog. I'm not sure what it means that he's bringing him back here, but he pointed out the dog needed some attention since he'd been cooped up since this morning. It appears Jackson wasn't ready to call it a night yet.

After I put the clean dishes away, I take care of the over-flowing trash bin in the kitchen. There's a large metal bin partway down the driveway where I was instructed to store garbage. It has one of those bear-proof locking mechanisms, and I was told it's emptied every few weeks.

I shove my feet in my Crocs, grab the trash bag and the can of bear spray Janey suggested is a better defense against wildlife than a gun whenever I wander outside in the dark, and head out the front door.

It's a beautiful night. Mild, I'd guess in the mid-sixties, which is surprising this early in spring. I didn't bother putting on a jacket and I'm quite comfortable. The sky is clear and dotted with so many stars. You don't see skies like this in the city, where light pollution washes out their glow.

I fill my lungs with fresh air, feeling the batteries I drained with my crying bout earlier slowly recharge. Now that the weather is better, I should do more of this; going out for walks, seeking out nature, instead of looking at it from inside four walls. Maybe I should take Janey up on her offer of taking me on a trail ride. I don't have a ton of experience, and it's been a while since I've been on a horse, but I'm pretty sure I can still remember where everything goes. As long as the horse is well-behaved, I should be okay.

Or maybe, if she's busy, Jackson could take me.

My feet crunch on the gravel as I let my mind conjure up images of the two of us on a blanket under the trees, a picnic basket within reach, and two horses patiently waiting in the shade. Distracted by the nice fantasy—one I'm happy to let play out in my mind as I make my way to the green bin—it takes me a moment to register the snap of a branch.

I stop and angle my head to the right from where I thought the sound came. There's a single light post by the garbage bin which makes it even more difficult to make out anything hidden in the dark shadows of the woods bordering the path. I should've grabbed a flashlight.

Dropping the garbage bag by my feet, I aim the bear spray at the trees, while reaching in my jeans pocket for my phone—which has a light—only to find it empty.

*Shit.* I left it plugged into the charger on the kitchen counter.

I'm startled by a sudden rustle, the sound of something substantially bigger than a bird or a squirrel moving through the trees. The next moment, a beam of light bounces off the tree trunks as a vehicle winds its way up the driveway, scaring off whatever animal was out there.

I quickly toss the trash bag in the bin, just as Jackson's pickup pulls up.

"Everything okay?" he asks when he rolls down his window.

His dog, Ash, climbs over him to stick his head out. He whines for attention, so I reach out to scratch his head.

"Just taking out the trash."

"Are you eager to get back inside, or can I interest you in a walk? This guy needs a chance to run for a bit."

"I'd love a walk. I was just thinking about that, it's a beautiful night out."

"Sure is. There's a nice trail along the creek on the other side. Let me just get rid of the truck."

I nod. "Meet you at the house." I probably should grab a sweater or something anyway, I can feel the temperature dropping.

Ash runs ahead as we set out on the trail, excitedly sniffing at random clumps of grass or tree trunks, proudly lifting his leg as he marks every spot.

"He just learned how to do that," Jackson fills me in. "For the longest time he squatted like a girl, but he finally figured out how to pee standing up."

I chuckle. "You sound like a proud dad."

"Guess I am."

He grins back and reaches for my hand, weaving his fingers through mine. It's done so casually, it takes me a moment to realize we're walking hand in hand, something I haven't done in many years.

High school, in fact, if I remember correctly. Walking to the bus stop with Brian Simeon in our sophomore year.

Public or even private displays of affection were nonexistent in my family. At least, not after my mother passed away.

The simple act of holding my hand in the dark of night, with no one to witness the gesture but the dog, somehow feels more significant. It also gives me a sense of safety, and any jitters of my earlier near-encounter remaining promptly disappear.

We walk without talking, giving my senses a chance to tune in to things I might otherwise have missed. Like the soft gurgle of the creek, the rustle of leaves at the slightest puff of wind, and the scent of damp earth and pine sap. I can feel the slight abrasion of the calluses on Jackson's hand, and the fresh air entering my lungs with every breath.

I guess this is what they mean when I hear some people talk about *being in the moment*. I never understood the meaning of that statement. My focus has always been ahead, calculating a next move, a farther step. Stillness of any kind has always made me restless, eager for a purpose or a direction.

But in this moment I am simply content; my mind is quiet and my feet move of their own accord.

I'm more relaxed than I have been in I don't know how long by the time we find our way back at the trailer.

"Is it too cold for you to sit outside?" Jackson asks. "I can make a fire."

"No, not too cold, It's beautiful out. Can I get you a drink? Beer, hot chocolate?"

I picked up some cocoa and mini marshmallows for rocky road brownies I was thinking of baking, but they'll work for hot chocolate as well.

"Sure, I'll have a hot chocolate."

He pulls me toward him for a peck on the lips before he

lets go of my hand and rounds the house to the back, while I go in through the front door.

Ten minutes later, I walk out onto the deck with two mugs in one hand and a blanket in the other. A fire is roaring in the pit at the edge of the deck, and Jackson is stretched out on one of the loungers, staring into the flames.

"Give me those." He reaches for the cups and sets them on the deck beside his chair. "Come sit with me," he then adds when I'm about to pull up the second lounger.

He pats the space between his legs and I barely even hesitate, sitting down between them and letting myself lean back when his arms circle around me. Then he takes the blanket and spreads it over us. Next he hands me my cup and I take a sip, feeling a slight sting of nostalgia when the rich flavor hits my taste buds.

"It's good," he confirms, drinking his own.

After we've set down our mugs, he pulls the blanket up under my chin and tucks his arms underneath.

"Comfortable?' he asks, his lips brushing the shell of my ear.

"Yes."

So comfortable, in fact, I could easily fall asleep like this.

But then one of his hands slides up my belly, lightly cupping my breast. The feeling of need spreads through my body like a warm liquid. Suddenly I want his hands and other parts all over me.

"Still okay?" he whispers by my ear.

I twist my head so I can look at him. "Very much so."

My eyes catch on his strong lips and I reach up, catching him behind the neck and pulling him down to me. The instant I kiss him, his hand claims my breast, and I moan softly into his mouth. When, moments later, his other hand slips into the front of my jeans and between my legs, I'm already wet.

Somehow, I'm not surprised to find out Jackson is selfless in his focus. My orgasm comes embarrassingly easy—probably from a prolonged period of no action—but any attempt I make to reciprocate is foiled.

"Just relax," he mumbles, his arms tightening around me.

By the time the fire has burned out, I'm half asleep, wrapped up in a warm cocoon under the blanket, and limp as a noodle. I don't even have the strength to protest when he helps me inside, walks me to my bedroom door, and presses a kiss to my forehead.

"Get some sleep."

The dog brushes past my legs and jumps on my bed, getting comfortable on my pillows.

"He's already settled in," I point out. "You could stay if you wanted."

He brushes a strand of hair off my forehead.

"Tempting. Unfortunately, I bumped into Jonas when I went to pick up Ash, and we've been asked to join a search for a missing couple of teenagers near Eureka. He wants to head out at daybreak."

He glances over my shoulder at the bed, where his dog is already asleep.

"But if you wouldn't mind looking after Ash for me?"

# Twelve

We found the teens holed up in an old hunting shack near Independence Peak.

Two starry-eyed kids trying to live out a Romeo and Juliet fantasy, almost getting themselves killed in the process.

From what I could piece together, the girl's parents weren't too keen on their fourteen-year-old daughter hooking up with a seventeen-year-old boy. The two had devised a plan to hike across the Canadian border to start a life together. Unfortunately, they got caught up in a rare May snowstorm in the mountains for which they weren't equipped.

The kids were lucky they found that shack, or the outcome could've been a lot worse than the trouble they met when they found their parents waiting for them at the hospital in Eureka. I'm sure they'll recover quickly from their adventures and the mild hypothermia they suffered, but I imagine other consequences will be longer lasting.

"Where have you been? Missed you around, kid."

Thomas is sitting in his regular spot on the porch when I walk past from the barn to my cabin.

My plan had been a shower and then to Stephanie's to pick up my dog...at least that's the excuse I'm sticking with. It wouldn't have anything to do with the fact I can't seem to get the woman from my mind, especially after hearing her soft sighs of pleasure while making her come on my fingers. But I can't walk past the old man after hearing the plea in his voice.

"Sorry, Gramps. Things have been busy; I know I haven't been around much."

What starts as a hoarse chuckle from him quickly turns into a rattling cough. Concern has me climb the porch steps, but when I get close to him, I see the sparkle of humor in his eyes.

"The FBI agent got your attention?" he manages after clearing his throat.

As I've heard from the other guys, there is no escaping Thomas when he's ready to dole out his romantic advice. Besides, he's right, I haven't been around much. Being the only two single guys left on the ranch, the two of us would often spend time chatting after dinner. Not long, since Thomas generally starts getting ready for bed by eight. Still, having become more of a spectator than a participant in life, even just those ten or twenty minutes of human interaction would be a big deal to him.

Resigned, I climb up the porch steps. There's no way to know how many more of these chats the old man has left in him.

"You could say that," I confess, taking a seat in the other wooden rocker.

"Pretty girl. Didn't know she was from around here."

"She's not, but she's staying at JD's trailer while she's on break."

"Break?"

I shouldn't be surprised the old man won't let that one slide.

"She's had a health scare she's recovering from, but she'll be fine."

That's about as much as I'm willing to give him.

"I bet she will, kid. I know you'll make sure of it."

I glance over to find Thomas's rheumy eyes looking at me sternly.

"Don't make more of it than it is," I caution him.

My words are easily dismissed with an impatient wave of his hand and a pointed, *"Harrumph."*

"Been waiting long enough, Jackson. Thought I'd never see the damn day, so don't go denying me the peace of mind my only grandson is finally settling down with a good woman. You're sweet on the filly, and that's all there's to it."

I bark out a laugh.

"If only things were that simple."

"They are," he insists. "You young'uns just like to complicate things when love is all that matters."

*Love.*

That's a big-ass word, and something I'm not sure I'm cut out for. At the very least, it's premature.

"Don't give me that look," he adds, narrowing his eyes. "Trust me when I say, there will come a time you'll regret wasting even one single day. I'd give anything to have just one more day with your grandma Mary. The love of my life, that woman, and I took way too long opening myself up to the possibility I might be the one for her too."

Even though I never knew his wife, Mary—who died long before I first met Thomas—I've become very familiar with her through his stories over the years. From what I understand, she was a force to be reckoned with, which isn't all that surprising, considering the two of them produced someone like Jonas.

Of course Thomas had been a catch in his own right back then, as he's told me before; he already owned his own ranch outside Amarillo, Texas.

I, on the other hand, work for my stepfather, live on his ranch rent-free, and have nothing more than my truck and my prosthesis to my name.

"It's not the same," I point out. "Not like I have much to offer."

"Why the hell not?"

As old and frail as he's getting, there is nothing wrong with Thomas's volume, which has my mother sticking her head out the front door.

"Is everything okay? Oh hey, honey. Didn't realize you were out here," she directs at me. "Ama left enough food in the slow cooker for everyone."

"I'll take a pass," I announce, taking the opportunity to get to my feet.

I need a shower and could use a long hard think about what the hell I'm doing, putting the moves on Stephanie. Because the old man is right about one thing; I am *sweet* on her, but that in itself is not enough.

She's here only temporarily and as soon as she finds her feet will be back to the career she lives and breathes for. This thing with me has been a distraction—a little break from reality, like a vacation fling—but it has no future. Unfortunately, I'm afraid it wouldn't stay a fling for me. Already I find myself more invested.

I should never have let down my guard.

"Come on, Ash. Let's go."

Jackson's dog has been sniffing furiously around the base of that tree and won't leave it alone. From the fresh scratches in the bark at least six feet off the ground and the clumps of fur sticking to the trunk, I'm guessing a bear was here recently.

I'm less worried about myself—I have my bear spray with me, and even slipped my gun in my pocket this time before heading back out on the trail—but I'm concerned about the rambunctious dog getting it in his head to face off with wildlife ten times his size. I wouldn't put it past him.

Dammit, I wish dogs came with leashes like they do in the city. Here, most dogs are trained to follow and listen without one, except Ash isn't listening much now.

"Ash, here!" I try again, this time my tone gets his attention.

I slap a hand on my thigh in encouragement. The dog takes one more longing look up in the tree, before finally turning toward me reluctantly.

I immediately turn on my heel and start walking back in the direction of the trailer. I need a bathroom and am not about to crouch down behind a tree. Not with bears around, thank you very much.

Also, I've seen what I'm pretty sure is poison oak or poison ivy, with the three leaves I was told to avoid. I'd rather not risk exposing my nether regions to that stuff. The memory of a particularly embarrassing episode at the summer camp my father sent me to when I was fourteen, and had the misfortune of innocently squatting in a patch of the stuff behind the girl's lodge because I was too afraid to walk to the outhouse, is burned in my mind.

Glancing over my shoulder, I'm relieved to see Ash is following. Pretty soon he's back out in front, sniffing blades of grass and low-hanging branches. He seems oblivious of the risks of squatting to do his business, and I'm glad we're out here where I don't have to pick up his poops.

The walk has helped to clear my head, which has been a little scrambled since Jackson left here last night. I had an amazing time with him and was on cloud nine as I was getting ready for bed, but the moment my head hit the pillow, doubts started creeping in, leaving me feeling vulnerable and a little raw, causing a minor panic attack. Emotions have been on a bit of a rollercoaster since then, making me feel unsettled.

I don't have my shit together yet, I have no idea what my future is going to look like, I don't have a clear path or a solid base, and I'm not sure how wise it is to start something new when I don't even know where I stand on my own.

My feelings are already involved, but I need to be cautious letting things move ahead between Jackson and me. It's so tempting to lean on him with all my weight, but he is a man who already has enough to carry on his shoulders. I need to find some solid footing of my own.

By the time I see glimpses of the trailer through the trees, the dog is trotting well ahead, like a horse smelling the stable. Then right in the bend, where the trail veers off to the house, Ash abruptly stops. He lifts up one of his front legs and perks his ears at something he sees up ahead. Next thing I know, he's off running, his sharp bark echoing through the trees.

I don't recognize the dark SUV parked next to my CR-

V. Ash is barking furiously, jumping up against the vehicle, and I can just make out a figure behind the wheel. Shifting the bear spray to my left hand, I shove the right one in my pocket where it curls securely around the grip of my weapon.

The passenger side window on the SUV slowly slides down as I approach.

"Can you get your damn dog away from my door? He's scratching up the rental."

*Fucking Ben Vallard.*

Not that it's a surprise he shows up in town—he told me as much—but how the hell did he find me? It's not like I left a forwarding address with the Kalispell office, and I definitely never volunteered the specifics of where I'm staying to Ben. That wasn't part of the plan. At least not mine.

"You wait there," I snap at him, pulling Ash away from the vehicle.

I feel Vallard's eyes on my back as I struggle to keep the dog under control while unlocking the front door. Hustling Ash inside, I slam the door shut behind us and hurry for the bathroom where I take care of my bursting bladder first.

"How did you find me?" I ask him a few minutes later when I open the door and find him standing right outside.

But when he makes a move to come in, I quickly step out and pull the door closed behind me. He lifts a sarcastic eyebrow in response.

"Local law enforcement was quite helpful. A Sheriff Hughes or something?"

"Ewing," I correct him.

I'm annoyed. Not at Junior Ewing, who I bumped into at the grocery store the other day, but at Ben, for being intrusive.

"If you wanted to talk to me, you could've just called."

"I could've, but I wanted to see you. It's been so long."

He casually leans a hip against the rental SUV's fender, tilting his head with that faint, cocky smirk on his lips.

The charm and the easy familiarity I once fell for—hook, line, and sinker—now just gives me an ick-feeling. There isn't a thing about Ben Vallard that is easy or casual; everything is carefully calculated to bring about a desired effect.

"Cut the bull, Ben. I stopped buying a long time ago. I told you all I know over the phone and the rest is up to you. You don't need to see me; you can take it from here."

"I could, but you would save me a lot of time showing me around, introducing me to Tracy."

"You're FBI, how much more introduction do you need?" I point out.

"I didn't know you had a dog?" he asks, abruptly changing the subject.

He's trying to keep me off-balance. I know his games.

"And why would you?" I fire back. "Aside from the fact we share an employer, you're nothing but a faded smudge on a distant past. Now, what is it you're hoping to gain by coming here?"

I plant a fist on my hip and glare him down.

"Aww, come on, don't be that way," he cajoles with a broad smirk, but when he realizes I'm not going to play, his face morphs into an impassive mask. "Fine. I need help on the ground here. Because there have been no reported sightings of Laine, my boss gave me only a couple of days to poke around. If I can't come up with confirmation the guy is in this area, he wants me in South Dakota to chase down new leads. You're familiar with the area."

I shake my head, conveying my response.

"I told you, I'm on leave. The only reason I agreed to get the information you wanted was because a policeman is dead—for that and more Laine belongs behind bars—and I was able to get it without the need for any credentials. But I'm otherwise useless to you, I currently don't have access to FBI resources. Hell, I don't even have my badge. Talk to Sheriff Ewing, maybe he can offer some assistance, I don't know, but don't look at me; I don't have any standing at the moment."

"Were you suspended?" he asks, his eyes narrowed on me. "Is that why you're hiding out in this little Podunk hole in Montana? I thought that shooting in Thompson Falls was ruled a good one."

I don't know what is more disturbing; the thought he may have been keeping tabs on me, or the fact he knows about the most pivotal moment in my career.

"No," I respond curtly, not wanting to get into the real reason, but I also don't want the story going around I was suspended from my job.

That kind of gossip has a tendency to get around, and the last thing I want is for it to reach my father's ears. Even after being retired for about fifteen years, he still has connections within the FBI, one of them standing in front of me now.

Ben Vallard was my father's last partner, and Dad was Ben's first. I've come to realize part of my attraction to Ben had been my father held him in high regard. Maybe I'd hoped hooking up with Ben would meet my dad's approval. Another pathetic attempt at gaining Dad's favor that blew up in my face.

Not that Dad ever found out about it, Ben had insisted on keeping things under wraps while they lasted, which wasn't long. Of course he'd never intended for our relationship to be anything long term and played me, something he wouldn't have wanted my father to know.

To be honest, I don't think it mattered, Dad probably would've found some reason to put the blame on me. Nothing I've done in my solid career for the FBI so far has been able to make him proud of me. I've long given up trying to impress him, and we barely even speak, but I still don't want word getting back to him I've been sidelined.

It would confirm what he's been trying to tell me all these years; I don't measure up. The last time he told me that to my face was at my brother's funeral years ago. He battled cancer and lost. Another dark mark on our family. I know it was grief talking that day, but it hadn't been the first time my father made it clear to me I wasn't worth the dirt on his shoes. That was the last time I actually saw him face-to-face.

"I'm recovering from a health issue that landed me in the hospital a while ago," I opt to share. "I'm on medical leave."

He draws his eyebrows together as he studies me. "What kind of health issue?"

I straighten my back and lift my chin a fraction higher.

"The kind that is none of your damn business. Now, like I said, I can't—"

I abruptly stop talking when I catch sight of Jackson's truck coming up the driveway.

*Oh fuck.*

I have a feeling I'm about to witness a pissing contest.

# Thirteen

*JACKSON*

It's not hard to guess who the guy is, standing in front of Stephanie's place.

Everything about him screams FBI; the SUV, the suit, the aviator sunglasses shoved back on his head. He gives off territorial asshole vibes right off the bat too, as he takes a step closer to Stephanie when I get out of my truck.

Well, that shit is not going to fly.

I wasn't even sure I was going to show tonight, but when I got back to my cabin to shower, I remembered I left Ash here.

Oh, who the hell am I kidding? I've been trying to talk myself out of starting something with Stephanie from the get-go, and yet I keep showing up. The brutal truth is; I'm a shadow of the man I was before, I have little to offer her, and she's so far out of my league, I shouldn't even be breathing the same air...but here I am. Again.

Except this time, I'm facing off with a guy I feel instinctively as a threat. He fucking looks at me like he's been there with Stephanie and aims to go there again. The message is so fucking thick in the air, I could sharpen my teeth on it.

I turn to my truck, pull the bag of dog food I brought from the back, and toss it over my shoulder. Then I walk straight up to Stephanie without looking at the asshole, hook my free hand behind her neck, and pull her in for a hard, claiming kiss.

"Hey, Hotshot," I greet her. "I picked the dog up some food."

Her mouth twitches. "I see that."

She knows exactly what I'm doing, but makes no attempt to stop me from making a blatant claim on her. I turn to look at the guy as I slide my arm around her shoulders and lean my head close to hers.

"So who's the suit? Friend of yours?"

I feel a great deal of satisfaction when she answers, "Hardly," and I watch the man's face turn to stone. Clearly, he doesn't like her answer, which means I likely read his vibes correctly.

"Ben Vallard is the colleague I told you about. The one I did the favor for."

"Right. You did mention that." I turn a fake smile on the guy, who looks like he tried to swallow a lemon whole. "So what brings you here?"

It takes a moment for him to respond.

"I'm here to follow up on a case I'm working on."

"Actually, Ben tracked me down because he wants my help," Stephanie interjects, throwing oil on the flames by correcting him.

"Does he know you're on a break?" I ask her, ignoring the agent across from us.

"Yes, I was just explaining to him about my medical

leave," she returns, leaving Vallard completely out of the conversation about him.

I can feel the anger radiating from the guy, he doesn't like being ignored. I love it and play along.

"Good, I don't want you to push yourself too hard too soon."

She puts a hand on my chest and smiles up at me. "I know."

The loud scrape of a throat draws my attention back to Vallard, who is glaring at Stephanie.

"If you hear anything useful, let me know. You have my number." He says the last with a quick glance in my direction. "And watch your back. You never know, if Laine is around, he might recognize you."

My grip on Stephanie's shoulders tightens.

"He'll have to get through me first," I deliver through gritted teeth.

All I get in response from the agent is a raised eyebrow before he gets behind the wheel of his SUV and backs away from the house.

"Well, that was about as fun as a root canal," Stephanie jokes, as the SUV disappears down the driveway in a cloud of dust.

I drop my arm from her shoulders and turn to her.

"You have history with him."

She nods. "A very brief and sordid history, yes. Thirteen years ago, when I was fresh out of the academy."

"Let me guess; he was the charming, experienced agent offering to take a new recruit under his wing. He promised you the moon, while screwing every other skirt who crossed his path."

"Skirt?" she fires back, catching me on the derogatory term.

"You know what I mean. Not a word I'd use to describe women, but you know he would. I know the type."

She turns her head and looks away.

"You're pretty close to the mark. Not my finest moment. Especially since he used to be my father's partner before Dad retired."

I'm starting to see why the topic may be difficult for her. It also confirms my suspicions about Vallard; the man wants back in there. But I meant what I said, anyone trying to get to Stephanie—including the agent—will fucking well have to get through me first.

"We all make stupid choices when we're young," I offer. "It's the only way to learn."

She reaches for the door and opens it, releasing Ash, who comes barreling toward me.

"Hey, buddy. Have you been behaving?"

"We just got back from a long walk," Stephanie volunteers. "He got hung up on some animal scent out there, but I was able to eventually get him to come."

"Yeah, recall can be a challenge, it's something we're still working on."

She leads the way inside; I pick up the bag of dog food and follow.

"You're probably hungry, aren't you?" I mutter at the dog, who is circling me.

"I hope you don't mind; I shared my breakfast of scrambled eggs and toast with him. He seemed so hungry," Stephanie confesses, an apologetic grimace on her face that makes me chuckle.

"I don't mind, but be warned, he's a mooch. I fed him last night before I brought him over, so he should've been fine." I drop the bag of dog food on the kitchen counter and look down at the half-full metal bowl of water on the floor at my feet. "I probably should've brought his bowls."

Stephanie brushes past me and pulls another mixing bowl from the cupboard, handing it to me.

"He can use that one."

Then she leans against the counter and I can feel her scrutiny as I scoop out some food for Ash and set it on the floor beside the water bowl. Ash doesn't hesitate and starts scarfing the food down.

"So is he staying?" she asks, sounding a little apprehensive.

"We both are," I return in a low voice. "If you'll have us."

The effect this woman has on me cannot be denied. Just thirty minutes ago, I was still trying to convince myself this whole thing between us simply couldn't happen, and here I am, begging to stay. The fact I found an ex of hers sniffing around may have had something to do with that bold request as well.

Her mouth drops open and I see her blink a few times before she clears her throat and responds, "Holy shit, you're not wasting any time."

I shrug. "Don't see the point of it. At least not anymore. I used to move slow, cautiously and methodically, so much so, the guys in my unit came up a tag they'd mock me with. But I've recently been made aware life is too short to waste time."

She smiles, which I take as a good sign. Then she asks, "What tag?"

I reach for her hand and bring it to my lips, pressing a kiss to her knuckles. I opened myself up to that question, but I have a hard time forcing the familiar nickname from my throat.

"High Velocity."

~

*Stephanie*

His voice is rough and I wasn't expecting the deep pain in his eyes.

I lift a hand to his face and stroke the rough stubble on his square jaw.

"What just happened?"

He lightly shakes his head and turns away, moving to the sliding doors where he stops to stare at the mountains. Unsure of what to do, I stay where I am in the kitchen, giving him a minute.

"They're all gone," he starts, his voice barely a whisper, but I'm so attuned to him, I hear every syllable. "One minute we're joking around—on our way back to base after a mission—the next I'm the only one left breathing."

The strength of my emotions at his confession over-whelms me, putting pressure on my chest as the deep ache I can feel from across the room settles there. There are no adequate words for me to share, so I stay quiet, letting him take the lead.

"The tag...it brings back memories I've tried to bury since that day. Too scared to even recall the good times, and there were plenty. It was a true brotherhood, you know? The guys and me, we liked to goof around. We could be cocky assholes. But when it came time to go on a mission, we were all business and worked together like a well-oiled machine. There's no hiding; you work, eat, and sleep together, twenty-four hours a day, seven days a week. These guys knew me better than I knew myself, and vice versa. I miss that. A lot."

My eyes are burning with tears for him when he turns to face me. Not only did this man lose his leg, he lost his brothers in one fell swoop. On top of the grief, I can't imagine the survivor guilt he must be feeling.

"I can see why," I offer softly.

He nods before continuing, "When Ma and Jonas first dragged my ass back to High Meadow, after sitting guard by my hospital bed, I was pissed. But I think in some way it gave me back that sense of belonging, which is probably why I haven't made any effort to move to a place of my own."

"Makes sense." I take a few steps closer.

"I told you I was a work in progress."

It's my time to nod. "As am I. In fact, last night after you left, I was trying to convince myself I come with too much baggage to start something serious with you. Too many open questions, too little direction. I'm standing on quick-sand and desperately need to feel solid ground beneath my feet. Regain my confidence. But now..."

I let the words drift to where he's standing still as a statue, his intensity palpable.

"But now?" he repeats.

I bridge the distance and lay my hands on his chest, looking up at him.

"Now I think perhaps I was wrong. I can't bring back your brothers, but I can listen and help you hold on to their memories. Just as you can't absolve me of all my problems, but already you make me feel heard and seen and cared for more than anyone else ever has. Maybe we can help each other recover some of what we've lost."

His arms clamp around me, almost lifting me off my feet as his mouth slams down on mine in a fierce, almost brutal kiss. I welcome any bruises the pressure of his mouth or the imprints of his fingers may leave behind. I feel oddly safe as I let myself get swept away in a passionate storm I have no way of escaping.

Half stumbling over the low coffee table, we somehow end up in front of the couch, where Jackson's hands urgently strip down my jeans and panties. Then he releases my mouth, sits down, and pulls a condom from his pocket, before shoving his jeans halfway down over his ass. Then he carefully rolls the condom down his beautiful cock while his eyes devour me the entire time.

"I need you to ride me."

I don't need any more of an invitation and climb astride on his lap. Immediately, his mouth finds mine as his hand guides his cock to my opening. I groan deep in my throat as I feel him brush the blunt head along my slit, gathering up the wet collecting there.

The stretch burns as I take him inside, but the over-whelming fullness of him feels so good. I feel his hands clamp down on my ass cheeks, guiding my movements.

Our mouths are fused as we pant and grunt down each other's throats on this wild ride to completion. I feel Jackson buck under me as he reaches his release shortly after I orgasm.

I'm not sure how long we sit on the couch, clinging on to each other as we try to catch our breath.

"I'm sorry."

I sit up and look down in Jackson's face. "Sorry? For what?"

"That's not how I'd planned our first time."

"Really? Because hard and fast is the perfect opening act, in my opinion," I suggest, flashing him a smile, which he returns.

"Opening act?"

"Don't tell me you're a one-trick pony?"

"Hell no."

I climb off him and reach for his hand, but instead of letting me pull him up, he pulls me back down on his lap, this time sideways.

"Before you take me to your bedroom...I'm nervous."

"Why? Your leg?" I guess.

"The few times I've... Anytime I... I haven't been completely naked," he stammers. "Not since losing my leg."

It breaks my heart, but I force myself to keep it light-hearted.

"Well, I'm glad I'm your first, and just so you know, I haven't had a man in my bed in about twelve years, so I'm a little nervous too."

He looks shocked at that. "No sex in twelve years? How the hell—"

"I didn't say that. There's been sex, but not in my bed."

That puts a smile on his face and he shifts me off his lap, before getting up himself, and pulling up his jeans but leaving them open.

"Show me the way."

# Fourteen

*Jackson*

Her hair smells like fresh air with a hint of something citrusy.

I woke up moments ago with her body wrapped around me, her head on my shoulder, and Ash whining at the door.

I don't want to leave the bed though. I could let Ash do his own thing outside, which I would do at the ranch, but there's no guarantee he won't take off if I don't keep an eye on him. I just don't feel like putting on my prosthetic just yet.

It had been much easier than I thought it would be, taking the thing off in her presence. She didn't shy away from it, which I was afraid of at first. I thought maybe she'd just avoid looking altogether, which would've been awkward. But she looked and she asked questions, and didn't freak out when I revealed the gnarly scars.

She also didn't treat me with kid gloves in bed. In fact, she was an eager participant in trying to find creative positions for us to try, for a good portion of the night, which is why it's not my stump that is raw this time. Not that it stops my dick from going hard at the feel of her soft skin against mine.

I take in a deep breath and stroke my hand down the curve of her back.

"Are you sniffing me?" she mumbles, her lips moving against my neck.

"Maybe. You smell good."

She abruptly lifts her head, looking at me through slightly swollen eyes.

"There's something off with your olfactory senses then. I smell like sex."

My mouth spreads in a wide grin.

"Sex smells good on you."

She shakes her head. "You're insatiable. You can't possibly—"

"Oh, but I can," I interrupt her, grabbing her hand and guiding it to the hard evidence under the sheet.

Instantly her eyelids go half-mast and she licks her lips as she curls her fingers around my shaft, only making things worse. But then Ash spoils what could've been some early morning delight by scratching at the door and whining even louder.

"I should let him out before he pees on your couch."

Stephanie bends down, pressing her spectacular tits against my chest as she drops a kiss on my lips.

"I'll take care of it. I need to pee anyway."

I reluctantly let go of her as she climbs out of bed, but can't take my eyes off her as she moves toward the door, bold and buck naked. I'll be damned if that confidence isn't as much of a turn-on as the generous curve of her ass is. The woman has a killer body underneath that tight exterior, and she knows how to use it.

For a few moments I lie back, my hands folded behind my head, taking stock of my body. I feel good, relaxed. If my teammates saw the smile I can feel myself wearing, they'd know right off the bat where—and how—I spent the night. They're getting to know me pretty well too.

I hear the sliding door open and force myself to get out of bed and into the shower. Maybe I can cook us breakfast, since we appear to have missed dinner last night. At least I did. I'm starving.

When I walk into the kitchen ten minutes later, freshly showered and wearing yesterday's clothes, I find Stephanie by the sliding door staring outside. Ash is standing beside her doing the same thing, except he's growling softly. Stephanie hears me approach, snaps her head around, and if Ash's growls didn't alert me, one look at her face would've told me something is wrong.

"What is it?"

My eyes drift outside and I see the bear right away. The animal is close to the deck, digging through what looks like a garbage bag.

*Shit.*

"Looks like he got into your garbage. Gotta make sure you lock that latch."

"I did. I do. I don't even think that's my trash bag. He wasn't out there when I took Ash out, but he was when I got back. I was barely able to grab Ash and get inside. This is a little too close for comfort," she adds with a little shiver. "At least that first bear was across the creek. I knew there were bears, I just didn't know they all seem to hang out here."

I walk up to her and pull her in my arms.

"I don't think they do, usually. I mean, you'll see the odd one, but for the most part they try to avoid human interaction as much as they can."

As if to illustrate my point, the bear grabs a corner of the bag and starts dragging it toward the shelter of the trees.

"Well, all I can say is, I'll be carrying that bear spray and my gun whenever I so much as stick my head outside from here on in," she mutters as she steps out of my hold. "I'll put on some coffee but then I need a shower."

"Go shower. I'll get some breakfast going."

My offer is met with a sweet smile and a brief brush of her lips. Then she disappears to the bedroom.

I glance out the sliding door to where the bear disappeared into the woods one last time, before I turn my attention to the coffeepot.

It's not uncommon for bears' territories to cross or overlap, so the fact a second bear shows up this close to the trailer within a relatively short time span could be purely coincidental. But it's definitely piqued my attention. It's possible some idiot is dumping their trash somewhere nearby, which wouldn't be the first time, but other than being illegal, it can also create a hazard. I'll be keeping my eyes out.

Whether it was the bear, finding Stephanie's ex on her doorstep last night, or the fact a violent criminal she once put behind bars is out and possibly close by, my protective instincts have been shifted into high gear. I'll be sticking close for sure, with or without an invitation.

Fifteen or so minutes later, when Stephanie walks in, her damp hair loose down her shoulders, I have cheesy scrambled eggs on avocado toast and coffee ready.

"I could get used to this," she comments, taking a bite from her toast.

I shoot her a grin across the small table and jump at the opening.

"I'm sure we can come to some arrangement. I was already planning on bringing a bag when I come back tonight."

She pulls one eyebrow up high.

"Tonight?"

Shrugging, I point at Ash, who has made himself very comfortable on her couch.

"My dog's more comfortable here."

I grin when she starts laughing.

"Shame on you; using your dog as bait," she accuses me, but her eyes are sparkling with amusement.

"Hey, if it works..."

*Stephanie*

Janey is waiting for me in the doorway with question marks all over her face.

"What's Ash doing with you??"

Jackson had just left this morning when she called to invite me over for lunch at her place. I jumped at the chance. Not only would it get me out of the house, but I'd love to get her perspective on what's happening with Jackson. Don't get me wrong, I enjoyed the hell out of last night and waking up with him this morning, but I still worry this might be moving too fast.

I've been so focused on my career; I haven't actually dated in a really long time and don't know what is normal.

I'm hoping Janey—who's known Jackson longer than I have—may be able to give me some insight.

Bringing the dog was an afterthought. Call me silly, but I didn't feel right leaving him at home alone when that bear might still be out there. Plus, I know he's buddies with Ginger.

"I didn't think you'd mind."

"I don't, but that doesn't explain how he ended up with you," she says, bending down to give Jackson's dog some attention, before gesturing me inside.

Her house has undergone something of a transformation since I was first here last year. It had still been pretty outdated then—Janey having only recently moved in—but now boasts beautiful wide-plank hardwood floors, a comfortable open concept living space with as crowning jewel the fantastic new kitchen. Beyond that, out the sliding glass wall at the back, it opens up onto a large outdoor living space, where she is leading me right now.

"You don't mind sitting outside, do you? It's a nice day and we can let the dogs play."

"Not at all."

When we're settled into the comfortable outdoor furniture with a glass of iced tea, she pins me with a look.

"Lunch has another ten minutes in the oven. So...the dog?"

I take a deep breath and blow it out.

"Has been staying with me for a few days," I explain.

"Interesting. Just the dog, or the owner as well?" she probes with a sly grin.

My instinct is to clam up. I've never had a lot of girlfriends, don't have a girl posse. In fact, technically, Janey is the only real friend I have, and I'm not used to sharing stuff. Talking about personal things feels a little unnatural, but I came here hoping to get her take on things, so I force myself to open up.

"Last night, both. Jackson came over a few times and a couple of days ago he brought Ash and left him with me. Then last night Jackson stayed over as well." I take a deep breath and blow it out. "And it sounds like he's coming back tonight."

"Wow. Good for you," she responds with a wide grin. "Jackson's a good man. I love this for both of you."

"You don't think it's too fast?"

She waves a dismissive hand at me. "Pfff, it's not like you just met him. You've known him for a while."

"Barely. Besides, I thought he was a bit of a grumpy ass."

"I'm guessing you know better now."

I nod. She's right, I do. He's kind and thoughtful, is a hell of a kisser, and—as I discovered last night— is a force in the bedroom.

"It was no different with me and JD. I thought he was a bit of an ass at first too, but then I got to know him and I was pretty much swept off my feet. These guys are all cut from the same cloth; once they set their eyes on you, they don't mess around. They're not wasting time."

"So I've discovered," I admit, but Janey must hear something in my voice, because she tilts her head to the side.

"But you're not sure..."

"I'm sure I like him, but I feel like I'm stuck in a bit of a bubble. Everything is perfect inside, but when I try to look out, everything is blurry. Everything is shifting, and I'm not sure of anything anymore."

"I get that. I do. It feels like a seismic shift is taking place in your life and you don't quite know how to balance your-self and where to find steady ground."

That's exactly how I feel, and I'm so relieved to know she understands. "Yes, that's it."

She leans forward and pats my knee.

"Right, so then what you do is grab on to something steady and solid until you regain your footing."

She sits back again and picks up her glass, taking a sip, while I quietly consider her words.

"Jackson is a good man," she softly repeats. "Not perfect, but genuine, and I know he will do right by you. Don't be afraid to lean a little while you sort out the rest of your life."

Inside, the timer for the oven goes off, and Janey gets to her feet.

"Can I help?"

"Sure, you can toss the salad and top up our drinks."

When we sit down at the outdoor table with the delicious-smelling oven dish with quesadillas and a big bowl of salad between us a few minutes later, I send Janey a smile.

"This looks amazing, and thank you for the pep talk."

She grins back. "Let's hope it tastes that way. Eat up. And, um, I may need a pep talk myself."

"You?"

She dishes out the quesadillas and gestures for me to serve myself salad. I brush off Ash, who smells the food and shoves his head in my lap.

"Yeah. I meant when I said I know what it feels like when the earth shifts."

I already had a bite heading for my mouth when I promptly put down the fork.

"Why? What do you mean?"

She looks at me and her eyes get glossy as she bites her lip.

"I'm almost forty years old, I'm newly married, my

clinic is thriving, my house is the way I want it, and life is good…"

When she pauses, I prompt her, "But?"

"I saw my doctor yesterday."

My imagination spits out every possible diagnosis that could follow a statement like that while I hold my breath, waiting for her to drop what I'm sure will be a bomb.

But then she says, "I'm pregnant."

# Fifteen

JACKSON

I reek to high heaven.

Foaling season has started and we have more pregnant mares than we have birthing stalls in the barn, so we've been splitting the field adjacent to the barn into smaller sections —like a staging area—and have moved some of the mares in there. The ones that look to be close to delivering are moved inside the barn.

Doc Richards drops in every so often to monitor how things are going but, unless there are complications, we manage the births ourselves. For the most part that means simply observing as nature takes its course, but occasionally some intervention is required.

Like with the small bay mare, who didn't look anywhere near to delivering when I last checked, and ended up dropping her foal in the field. I didn't even notice the small bundle in the grass at first. The mare was on the other side of the makeshift pen and appeared spooked. The foal was still mostly covered in the sack and I had to tear a hole to free its nostrils, but I don't know how long it had been lying there. The little thing was limp.

In the birthing stalls we have a few tools at hand, like oxygen, so I scooped up the foal and hoofed it to the barn. We were able to perk up the little one, but when we brought the mare into the barn, she wouldn't have anything to do with her foal. Fortunately, two stalls down from her, another mare had lost hers earlier this morning and with a bit of coaxing, she allowed the little guy to nurse on her.

My current condition is the result of rolling around in birth guck and horse shit all afternoon, but I'm otherwise feeling good. Nothing like the sight of newborn foals, stumbling around on legs too long for their bodies, to put a smile on your face.

It's already after seven by the time I head for my cabin, I hadn't realized how late it had gotten. When I left Stephanie's place this morning, I promised I'd bring some bear meat to grill for dinner. I pull out my phone and give her a quick call as I walk past the porch of the main house. Thomas lifts a hand in greeting as I pass.

She answers my call with a soft, "Hey."

"Hey yourself. I'm just calling to let you know I'm running late, I'm sorry. I should've warned you sooner, but things have been hectic here."

"Oh, no worries. We can do this another night."

Dinner, maybe, but I fully intend on seeing her tonight.

"If you haven't already, grab yourself something to eat, and I'll be over, right after I wash this goop off me."

"Goop?"

"You don't wanna know. Foaling season started and we've had four mares deliver today."

"I'm so jealous, I love foals, those awkward, gangly legs," she shares.

I push open the door to my cabin and am greeted with silence. No dog to greet me because I left him with Stephanie.

"Okay, change of plans," I suddenly announce. "How about you pack an overnight bag, grab the dog, and head over this way? I can scrounge us up some food and show you the new additions."

I'm surprised how fast she jumps on it. I thought maybe she'd need a little coaxing, but her resounding, "Yes," comes before I've even finished my last sentence.

After ending the call, I quickly tidy up the dirty socks I left on the floor by the couch and clear away the handful of dishes I've left in the sink. Then I hop in the shower.

When Stephanie arrives half an hour later, I'm clean and have a small pan of stew staying warm on the stove. Ama had left a large pot simmering at the main house for the stragglers. Dinner is generally a fluid concept at the ranch, and not a rigid time slot.

"Smells good," she announces after I kiss her right inside the front door.

"Ama's stew, not mine," I clarify. "It comes with a chunk of fresh sourdough bread she baked this morning."

Her stomach rumbles in response.

"That sounds so good. I'm starving."

No surprise, dinner is a little late. I'm pretty damn hungry myself. I dish us each out a good portion of stew and set the half loaf of bread on a board in the middle of my small table.

"Come sit. Beer?"

Stephanie shakes her head as she takes a seat. "It doesn't play nice with my medication. I'll stick to water."

"I also have orange juice, and a bottle of some green tea stuff I don't drink, or I can make you regular tea."

I can't remember who left that bottle here. It may have been Ma; she went through a phase where she tried to fix me with all kinds of stuff that was supposed to be good for me. I think the green tea may have been a remnant of that time. I'm surprised it survived in my fridge; I ended up tossing most everything else she brought me.

"I'll take the green tea."

We don't talk much, but I can't keep my eyes off Stephanie as she scarfs down the bowl of stew I put in front of her. Every so often I catch her eye and she throws me a smile. I like that she doesn't pick at her food and doesn't apologize for enjoying it.

"More bread?" I ask her, when she drops her spoon in her empty bowl and sits back.

"Sadly, I'm going to have to pass, I'm already stuffed."

I get to my feet and hold out my hand. "Then come with me, we'll walk it off. I'll clean up later."

I hold on to her hand as we walk out the door, Ash darting ahead of us to do his business. It's a nice night, fairly warm, even though the sun has dropped behind the mountains and dusk is setting in.

"Are you taking me to see the babies?"

I grin at her eager expression. "Yeah, before it gets too dark. There's one left in the barn we're keeping an eye on, and the other two mares and their foals are in the field behind the barn."

"Out for a stroll?"

I hear Thomas's voice come from the shadows on the porch. He usually goes back out there for an after-dinner drink before he heads up to bed. I stop as we pass in front.

"You remember Stephanie, Grandpa? Stephanie, this is Thomas Harvey."

"Yes, we met last year," she responds. "Good to see you again, Mr. Harvey"

"Pleasure's all mine, but call me Thomas. If you're hoping to see those foals, you best hurry. It'll be dark soon."

"We'll stop for a chat on the way back, if you're still up," I promise him.

He raises his hand in response.

We check out the two foals in the field first, and for the next ten minutes Stephanie is totally taken with them. Both mares are gentle and allow us to approach their little ones.

"I can't believe how soft their noses are. Boggles the mind these are going to be big honking animals one day."

"Won't be that long. Horses grow up fast," I point out. "Why don't we head inside to see the third one."

"Didn't you mention four mares delivered?" she asks.

"We lost one foal."

"That's so sad. That poor mother."

"Actually, we had a first-time mare who rejected her little colt, so we put him with the mare who lost her own foal. That's why we're keeping those two inside, to make sure they're bonding well."

It's clear they're doing fine when we lean over the stall door. The little guy's short tail is wagging as he's nursing and the mare is calmly munching on some hay. They look like they're fine.

I notice the porch light of the main house is on by the time we head back, and I see Jonas has joined his father. Those two often sneak out there at night for a cigar, I can smell the smoke from here.

But when we get closer, I notice only Jonas has a cigar in his mouth.

Thomas looks like he's sleeping.

～

*Stephanie*


*Oh shit.*

I could tell something was off the moment I caught sight of those two on the porch.

In my line of work, the truth is in the details, so it pays to be observant. That's not something you can simply turn off. It's ingrained, almost like a second instinct.

Which is why I immediately notice Jonas is holding his father's hand in his, while smoking a cigar with the other one. The second thing that stands out is the slackness of the old man's face. There is no muscle tone whatsoever left, and he is slightly lilting to the side.

I recognize death. I've seen too much of it and studied it too closely to miss the obvious signs.

Jonas's unfocused eyes tell the story when we approach.

I can feel the exact moment Jackson realizes; his steps falter and his hand twitches in mine.

"Dad?"

Jonas nods as he slowly turns his eyes to Jackson.

"His favorite spot in this whole damn place was this porch. Killed him to leave his ranch in Texas but he came to love it here, from this spot, watching the ranch life he couldn't participate in anymore. He didn't want to miss out on anything or anyone."

Alex, Jackson's mom, steps out on the porch and smiles at us, but then she notices her husband, and her smile is replaced with a look of concern.

"What's wrong?"

"Pops..." The single word from Jonas is enough to clue her in.

"Oh, no...Thomas."

I watch her approach the old man and bend over, putting a hand against his wrinkly cheek and pressing a kiss to his forehead. Then she turns to her husband, who wordlessly reaches for her. She responds by crawling onto his lap and I watch as tears slowly start rolling down her face. I didn't know Thomas well, but my eyes are burning too.

Jackson still hasn't said anything and is holding on to my hand as if it's a lifeline.

"Jackson," his mom calls out. "Honey, call the family. Tell them to come."

I am out of place, this is too personal, too intimate.

"I should go," I whisper.

His hold tightens as his hand almost crushes my fingers.

"Don't...Please," he adds as an afterthought. I hear the emotion thick in his voice. "Stay."

Alex is apparently of the same mind when she turns to me.

"If you wouldn't mind putting on a big pot of coffee, while Jackson makes the calls."

I nod, "Okay," and move with Jackson as he leads me up the porch steps and inside the house.

Thank God the coffee machine is pretty standard and I find a tin of coffee in the cupboard overhead. While Jackson is sitting at the large island, making phone calls, I start setting out mugs, and find sugar and creamer. Next, I dive into the massive fridge, find the makings for sandwiches and setting it all on the counter.

"What are you doing?" Jackson asks, walking up behind me.

"People are going to come and will want coffee, maybe a drink, so there should be food too."

I've blocked out a lot of what happened after my mother died, but I distinctly remember that part. I recall being angry, at first, that people could even think about food or drink at a time like that, but I was twelve, and didn't know people found comfort in sharing memories over a drink or a meal.

I turn in his arms when they slip around me, and lift my hands to his face.

"I'm so sorry."

He opens his mouth to respond but closes it again, nodding instead, as I lift up on my toes and press a light kiss on his lips. For a moment, he closes his eyes and drops his forehead to mine, but then he straightens up.

"Okay, let's get to work."

Half an hour later, I carry a tray with coffee and sandwiches out to the porch where, to my surprise, a crowd has already formed. It looks like almost everyone associated with the ranch or the High Mountain Trackers has come.

It puts a lump in my throat to see how Thomas is being honored. He is still slumped over in the rocking chair, but now propped up by a few pillows and his lap covered in a blanket Ama is straightening, his community gathered around him. Alex and Jonas are still as they were, but others are sitting on steps, leaning against posts, and most of the men appear to be smoking cigars. Conversation is muted and no one seems too surprised to see me here.

Janey, who is sitting on the porch steps beside a petite blond woman I don't recognize, smiles at me.

"Want me to make you some tea?" I ask her, realizing she probably passed on coffee because of her pregnancy.

"I'm okay. Stephanie, have you met Lucy yet? Bo's wife? She runs Hart's Rescue."

"No, I haven't. Hi."

"You're the FBI agent."

Her tone is a bit abrupt, but perhaps I interrupted something.

"Yes, at least for now; I'm technically on leave."

"So you're just visiting," she concludes with a bit of a snark.

"Lucy..." Janey gently cautions.

I'm not getting friendly vibes from this woman and I'm not sure why, until I catch her dart a concerned glance over my head in Jackson's direction. That's when I make the connection. This is the woman who taught him to cook. His mother's friend. She's worried about him, which is why I decide to give her honesty.

"For the moment. Right now, my future is in flux but I'm starting to get a clearer picture."

She nods, but then her eyes narrow and her voice lowers to a near whisper.

"This is going to be hard on him. He loved Thomas and he's had enough loss in his life. Don't know how much more he can handle, so if you—"

"Lucy?" I hear Jackson coming up behind me. The next moment his hand drops on my shoulder. "I see you two have met."

"Yes, we have," the petite woman is quick to answer, darting him a warm smile.

It's clear she cares about him deeply and is concerned for his well-being, which I can understand. But Jackson is a grown man, and I'm not so sure he'd appreciate her meddling, which is why I change the subject back to refreshments and turn to Janey.

"Sure I can't get you something else?"

"You know what? Maybe I'll have some tea after all," she returns, giving me the escape I was looking for. "I'll come in with you."

As Janey gets to her feet, I notice Lucy scrutinizing her closely.

"Wait a minute... Tea? Since when do you drink tea?" My friend looks like a deer caught in headlights as Lucy's face morphs into one of shock. "Are you pregnant?"

"Pregnant?" The echo comes from Ama, who walks over, drawing everyone's attention to our little group.

I feel guilty when Janey shoots me a pleading look, but her mother-in-law is already locked in on her.

"Janey?" she prompts.

"I'm so sorry," I mumble under my breath, recognizing my innocent question may have caused this situation.

Jackson must've heard me and gives my shoulder a squeeze, as JD enters the picture, stepping up beside his wife and pulling her close to his side. He's the one who answers his mother.

"We just found out. We were gonna wait for a better time, Ma."

"Actually," Jonas pipes up, setting his wife on his feet before getting up himself. "This is a perfect time. I'm gonna grab a bottle of the good bourbon and a box of Cubans I've been saving for a special occasion. I'm sure Pops would be tickled he gets to be part of a celebration of new life."

Ama already has her arms around Janey and her son, smiling big through her tears.

It's coming up on midnight when everyone is standing in front of the house, like some kind of honor guard, watching as the funeral home van disappears down the driveway, carrying Thomas inside.

"Come on," Jackson whispers in my hair. "Time to turn in."

There are goodbyes and hugs, as everyone disperses to their respective homes.

This was both the weirdest and most heartwarming experience I've ever been part of. These past few hours have given me a deeper sense of family than I've had with my own.

"How are you doing?" I ask Jackson later, when I crawl into bed with him.

"I'm okay," he claims, but I have a feeling reality is only just setting in for him.

"Is there anything I can do for you?"

He turns his head on his pillow and his brown eyes look black, glowing like polished onyx in the dark.

"Just hold me."

## *Sixteen*

*JACKSON*

On my way back to my cabin, I stop at the bottom of the porch steps and look at the empty chair.

Despite the impromptu celebration of life on this porch a couple of nights ago, morale on the ranch is low.

The absence of Thomas is affecting everyone. Each time I glance over or pass by and spot his empty rocking chair, my heart grows heavier. A few dark thoughts have started swirling again, and this morning I had to force myself to get out of bed.

Stephanie stayed with me that first night, but I didn't stop her when she left the next morning after I told her things would probably be a bit hectic on the ranch until the funeral. I did ask her to take Ash, and although I feel better knowing she at least has the dog for company, I'm struggling with guilt because I haven't been in touch with her since.

I'm raw and I'm weak. I'd needed her to hold me

together that night after Thomas died, needed her to keep me grounded. I let her go home because the temptation would have been too great to keep leaning, when I should be the one supporting her. She's dealing with enough on her own, she shouldn't have to deal with my dark moods.

"You're an idiot."

I look up to see Ama standing in the front doorway. Her dark eyes are angry.

"Me? What did I do?"

"Do you know the old man spent his last days waiting for you to get your shit together? Do you think it was a coincidence the night you bring her to the ranch is the night he let go? He was hanging on from sheer will to see for himself." She shakes her head and gestures with her right hand like she's swatting at a fly. "And what is the first thing you do? You blow the woman off."

Her words shake me—the thought I meant that much to Thomas deepens the ache in my chest—but that doesn't stop me from reacting defensively.

"I didn't blow her off."

Ama raises a sarcastic eyebrow. "No? Then how come she's called the house several times over the past few days to find out how you're holding up because you won't answer her damn calls yourself?"

Now that guilt I was already feeling sharpens even further. I wish I could punch something to block out the intensity of emotions tearing at me.

"She's better—"

"Don't you dare finish that sentence, young man," Ama interrupts with a bark. "You'd be spitting in the face of everyone who loves you, and you should damn well know there are many of us. And don't insult Thomas's memory, because other than his son, there wasn't a single person here he loved more than you."

With that she turns on her heel and heads back inside, slamming the door behind her.

I feel like I've just been flattened by an eighteen-wheeler and I'm down, my insides spilling out.

"Ma's right, you know." JD's hand clamps on my shoulder as he steps up beside me. "The old man couldn't have loved you more if you were his own blood. He'd be pissed to see you blow this thing with Stephanie."

He gives my shoulder a squeeze before heading toward his truck, where he stops to shoot me one last look.

"Not to mention your girlfriend has the skills to seriously hurt you if you don't get your head outta your ass."

I watch as he gets behind the wheel, backs out of his spot, and turns down the driveway, heading home to his pregnant wife.

*Fuck.*

Tomorrow is Thomas's funeral. A simple graveside affair, right here where he wanted to be buried on top of the hill behind the barn. He'd wanted a spot from where he could oversee the ranch.

Jonas asked JD, Dan, and I to dig the grave, which we did this afternoon. I'm covered in the dirt and soil that will be covering him tomorrow morning, and I really fucking want Stephanie by my side when we lower him into his last resting place. I need her there.

I take time to shower and change, but twenty minutes later, I'm in my truck. I could've called or sent a message, but Stephanie deserves a face-to-face explanation. I just hope I haven't already done too much damage.

As a peace offering, I pick up a couple of brisket sandwiches at Foxy's on the way. I'm sure I can put away both if it turns out she's already eaten, but I don't want to show up empty-handed, and there isn't anything else between the ranch and her trailer.

When I take the turn that brings the trailer into view, I immediately notice the dark SUV parked out front.

Fucking Vallard.

~

*Stephanie*

"What do you mean, she's gone?"

I ignored his first three attempts and know I shouldn't have answered this call, but curiosity got the better of me. Or maybe I just wanted to hear a human voice.

It's been crickets here the past few days. I've tried to connect with Jackson a few times, but for some reason he seems to be avoiding me. Now, I know they probably have their hands full with arrangements for Thomas's funeral and all that entails, but maybe a one-line text wouldn't have been too much to ask. Just a simple "hey, now is not a good time," would've sufficed. It would at least have stopped me from going full stalker mode and calling the main house to check up on him.

Yeah, I sank that low. I've never chased a man in my life and, to be honest, it doesn't feel good on this side. But I'm worried, I wonder how he is coping, and I can't help thinking his silence holds a more ominous message than a simple, "I'm busy."

All that to say, it was messing with my head and in an unguarded moment I took Vallard's call instead of ignoring it, like I'd done the other times. He didn't waste any time hooking me back in by announcing he can't locate Tracy Elliston.

"I've been sitting on her place for days. According to the salon where she works, she took time off to look after her ailing mother in Helena, except some research revealed her mother died of cancer five years ago. I need your help. I'm coming over."

"No, I don't—" I start, but I'm talking to dead air. The bastard hung up on me.

Barely five minutes later there's a sharp knock. I grab Ash by the collar and hold on to him while I open the door.

"How'd you get here so fast?"

I'm at least a ten-minute drive from Libby.

He shrugs and smirks. "I was having dinner at that little dive down the road. I was giving you one last chance to answer my damn call, or I would've shown up on your doorstep unannounced."

Ben lets Ash sniff his hands and I let go of his collar.

"Not sure what you want from me." I state, a little less than gracious as Ben closes the door behind him.

"My gut says Laine is in this area but If I don't produce some proof of that in the next few days, my boss will send me to South Dakota. I need to talk to Tracy Elliston, but I have a suspicion she's hiding somewhere and my time is running out."

"If you're right, and Laine came here, who's to say the two of them aren't in Canada by now?"

He shakes his head stubbornly.

"No. I don't buy it. Laine is still here somewhere; I can feel it."

I'm pretty sure it wouldn't do any good to try and point out his gut feeling could well be indigestion, so I don't bother. Besides, he may be right. Tracy never mentioned his name to me, but the details she gave me about the man in her life leave me no doubt he's at least been in the area.

"For argument's sake, let's suppose you're right. I still don't understand what you want from me?"

"You have a connection with her, use it to see if you can flush her out. Try to call and see if she'll answer when she sees your number. I haven't had much luck."

"Have you tried tracking her cell phone?"

"That wouldn't necessarily tell us anything, she could've had her calls forwarded to a burner phone, and right now I don't have time to wait for warrants to follow that trail. I need something concrete."

"What about her car?"

"I've asked the sheriff's department to keep an eye out, but I doubt she'd leave it out in the open if she's trying to stay hidden."

He spreads his hands and with a sad puppy look on his face, pleads his case.

"See if you can get hold of her. Go into the salon and say you're a friend looking for her. You were there before, weren't you? I have a feeling the owner knows more than she's letting on. If she recognizes you, she might be more inclined to tell you what she knows."

There are other ways for him to track down Tracy Elliston through the salon—a phone tap for instance—but it would require a warrant and would take time. He's right about that. We have a lot of resources available to us in our line of work, but there are rules and steps we have to follow. It's not the instant access they like to portray in movies.

I won't put myself out there, but Ben is right, it might be easier for me to get information on where Tracy is.

This whole thing is puzzling; she was already gone by the time Vallard went looking for her. How would she have already known the FBI had arrived in town? Is it possible something else happened to send her into hiding? Did I somehow inadvertently trigger her? Maybe I didn't quite pull off my cover as well as I thought. I guess it would all depend on when exactly she went missing.

"Do we know when she took off?" I ask Ben. "Did her boss at the salon mention what day she left?"

He opens his mouth to answer, when Ash suddenly starts barking enthusiastically as he rushes to the front door. My heartbeat kicks up a notch, and I already know who is here before I answer the sharp knock.

Part of me is pissed he's been avoiding me, but I do understand it. I'd probably be doing the same in his shoes, I suspect we're alike in preferring to hide out and lick our wounds in private when we're hurt. My suspicion is confirmed when I open the door.

Jackson doesn't look well. His eyes are dark and sunken, his color is much too pale, and I detect a small tremble in his hand as he reaches for his dog first. I'm not sure what he's looking for when he straightens up and searches my face, but I can feel the intensity of his scrutiny. Then I realize he would've seen Ben's vehicle parked outside.

Before he has a chance to misinterpret what is going on, I step into him, bracket his face with my hands, and press a kiss to his lips. When I step back, he grabs on to my hip with a hand and pulls me in for another brief kiss. As he lifts his head, I can see the emotions swirling in his eyes, before he straightens up and aims a glare over my shoulder.

"Vallard, right?"

I turn to catch Ben's scowl at Jackson's intrusion.

"That's right. I'm sorry, who are you again?" he returns with an edge.

Petty play, since I'm positive Ben not only remembers

Jackson's name, he probably looked into his background as well. This is just a transparent attempt to undermine Jackson's presence here.

"Don't be an idiot," I accuse him sternly. "I believe you and I about finished up our work business anyway. I'll see what I can find out on Tracy Elliston and be in touch."

I reach for Jackson's hand to pull him inside and away from the open front door. Then I raise an eyebrow at Ben, conveying a clear message.

His face is hard when he passes me and stalks out the door.

"He rope you into helping him again?"

I push the door shut and turn to face Jackson.

"Tracy disappeared. She's the woman I was looking into for him earlier. Something spooked her and she took off. Vallard thinks I may be able to help find her."

His jaw is tight when he responds with, "I see."

Wonderful. He shows up on my doorstep after avoiding me for days, and he's the one pissed off. I curb the urge to blast him and wait for it to pass. I remind myself he's hurting, probably not quite himself, and to boot finds Ben Vallard sniffing around again.

I take a deep breath and opt to stay calm instead.

"I'm only going to ask a few questions as Tracy's friend. Nothing dangerous, simply gathering information and passing it on."

The tension drains from his face as he takes a seat on the couch and leans forward, resting his forearms on his knees.

"Can I get you anything to drink?" I ask, moving into the kitchen to grab the kettle. "I'm making some tea."

"Sure," is his lackluster response.

"Bad day?" I ask while I get a couple of mugs from the cupboard and deposit a tea bag in each.

"Bad week." I turn to look at him and find his eyes on me, guilt written on his face. "I'm sorry, I'm not very good at sharing."

I shoot him a grin.

"I noticed. Guess that's something we both have to work on."

# Seventeen

*Jackson*

She's understanding, but it would almost be easier if she was straight-up pissed at me.

I would've deserved that more than the gracious way she welcomed me.

I take the steaming mug from her hand as she sits down beside me. She seems comfortable with the silence as she carefully sips her hot tea and stares out at the creek. It takes me way too long to think of the right words to say.

"I spent the afternoon digging a hole on top of a hill at High Meadow. An eight by three foot hole, about six feet deep. Sometime tomorrow I'll be putting the dirt back, except Thomas will be in that hole."

In my peripheral vision I see Stephanie put her tea down and I feel her eyes on me, but I keep mine fixed on the view.

"I barely remember my father's funeral. I only have vague memories of uniforms, a lot of pomp and circumstance, and a ton of strangers wanting to shake my hand. But I do recall being angry. So damn angry. It was my coping mechanism at thirteen years old."

I snort at myself, thinking of the shit I put my mother through. Not only back then, but as recently as a few years ago when, once again, rage was my go-to response to pain.

"I was still in the hospital and missed the funerals for my fallen brothers, but I was angry then too. I guess at the unfairness of it all. But this time, with Thomas, I can't bring myself to be mad. He lived a long, good life, he loved fiercely, and he died on his terms."

My eyes burn when I turn to look at Stephanie.

"It's easier when I'm angry. Somehow, it hurts less."

The next moment her arms are around me and I bury my face in her neck. All the rioting emotions that have been ripping at my insides these past few days erupt. I toughed through the death of my father, those of my best friends, and yet I lose my shit over an old man who left this life glad at the prospect of seeing the love of his life again in the hereafter.

I'm not sure how long we sit like this, arms around each other, my hot tears leaving a wet spot on Stephanie's shirt. When I lift my head, I notice hers have left tracks down her face.

I probably should be embarrassed for the meltdown, but I'm not. Not even when she lifts her hand to my face and wipes the wetness from under my eyes.

"Thomas may have triggered them, but something tells me these tears held a lifetime of repressed emotions," she whispers, pressing her lips to mine.

"Probably," I concede in a hoarse voice.

"They say purging is good for the soul."

I bark out a dry laugh and joke, "That may well be, but it's hell on the reputation."

She smiles. "Your reputation is safe with me." Then she tilts her head to the side. "How do you feel?"

I shrug. "Exhausted, a bit empty, but lighter."

Stephanie slaps both hands on her knees before getting to her feet.

"You probably haven't had dinner yet. Let me put something together."

"I came prepared. Picked up a couple of brisket sandwiches at Foxy's but forgot all about them in the truck when I saw Vallard's vehicle out there. Let me go grab them."

The outside air feels good on my face, and I take a few deep breaths in as I walk to my truck.

Only to find all four of my tires flat.

*What the fuck?*

I bend down to inspect one of my front tires and notice a deep slash in the rubber. The other three received the same treatment.

Un-*fucking*-believable.

Pissed off, I snatch the bag with sandwiches from the passenger seat and stalk back inside.

"Your buddy Vallard slashed my damn tires," I snap, walking in.

Stephanie looks surprised. "What?"

She darts passed me outside, where I find her crouched beside my truck.

"Stay back," she orders.

I observe as she pulls her phone from her pocket and starts taking pictures of the tires and the dirt around my truck.

"What are you doing?"

"Shoe prints." She points to the ground. "These smaller

ones are mine. I believe those belong to you; see how your right shoe leaves a flatter imprint than your left? That's because your weight distribution is different on the prosthetic side. But these..."

She indicates a full print next to a partial one right beside the rear passenger side wheel.

"Someone crouched down here. I'd say a men's size twelve. See the deep treads? Looks like a hiking boot to me."

She's right; the shape and pattern of ridges and grooves suggests the prints were made by hiking boots.

"Vallard was wearing dress shoes," she volunteers. "Plus, this isn't his style."

I visualize the smug bastard standing in Stephanie's living room in his suit and tie, wearing brown leather lace-up shoes.

"Maybe he changed and came back," I suggest, though it sounds lame even to my ears.

It would be so much easier to blame it on that jealous piece of shit. The alternative is much more ominous. Who would go to the effort of slicing all four of my damn tires? Why?

"Do you want to call triple A?" Stephanie asks.

"Nah. Sully's wife, Pippa, owns an auto shop just up the road. I can get it towed tomorrow after the funeral."

I watch her walk toward me, her blond hair glowing gold in the setting sun and her features cast in shadows.

"That is," I add when she stops in front of me. "If you don't mind me staying the night."

Her brown eyes blink up at me, a soft smile on her lips. "I don't."

"And if you could maybe give me a ride to the ranch tomorrow?"

She lays her hand on the middle of my chest.

"I can."

"And if you'd come with me to the funeral?" I ask.

"You bet," she returns before steering me back inside.

*Stephanie*

I'm at the sink, staring out of the window as I quickly wash the last of the dishes.

The trailer has a small dishwasher, but I prefer washing by hand. It's therapeutic in that it's mindless and allows my thoughts to flow freely. Historically, those thoughts would be associated with one or another case I was working, often leading me into new and unexplored directions. I've even solved cases with my hands in warm water.

But not tonight. Tonight, my mind is preoccupied with Jackson, who is sitting on the couch, watching the end of a newscast on the small TV. After eating the lukewarm brisket sandwiches he brought over, we took Ash for a walk, and settled in for an episode of *Landman*, which we discovered we both enjoyed.

I glance over my shoulder at Jackson, who catches me looking.

If I wasn't half in love with the guy already, I would be now.

I grew up in a household and worked in an environment where real men weren't supposed to show any emotion, which was considered a show of weakness. Heck, even as a girl and woman I was judged, which is how I developed a hard shell and learned to swallow any emotions, not allowing them any daylight. There might have even been a time I subscribed to that way of thinking, but not anymore.

I've come to believe—and today even more so—stoic endurance is not a sign of strength, but of cowardice. Hiding your feelings behind a straight mask is not a show of resilience, but rather one of fear. We need courage to express honest emotions, and gain strength when we pick ourselves up after.

The last thing I do is prep the coffee machine so all I have to do tomorrow morning is flip the switch, before I walk over to the couch.

"Come to bed?"

I hold out my hand, which Jackson grabs in his as he stands up and follows me into the bedroom.

"Be right back," I tell him, slipping into the bathroom.

When I come out, he's sitting on the edge of the bed wearing a gray pair of boxer briefs, releasing his prosthesis from his leg. One look at his face tells me he likes what he sees. Deciding to walk out buck-ass naked is new for me. Seduction is not really my thing, nor is it really the objective, but I wanted to reward the trust he showed me tonight with my own vulnerability.

Sure, he's seen me naked, in parts, but tonight I'm offering myself up to his scrutiny. I'm far from perfect; my breasts are too small, my thighs too thick, and I have swimmer's shoulders. He can probably see the stubble on my legs from where he's sitting, because I haven't shaved in a week.

Yet, with the way his eyes stroke my body from the top of my head to my toes, he makes me feel beautiful. Desirable. When he motions me over, creating a V between his leg and his stump for me to fit, I don't hesitate.

My arms instinctively wrap around his head and shoulders when he presses his face into my soft belly and his hands reach behind me to grab hold of my ass.

"*Fuck*, you feel so good, Hotshot. Perfect."

He gives my belly button a leisurely lick before tilting his head back, his dark eyes sparkling as his fingertips slide down my butt crease.

"Taste amazing too," he mumbles as he dips his fingers between my folds, finding me already wet. "I want more. I want you to climb on my face."

As he lies back on the bed, he pulls me with him, and I let him arrange me until I'm kneeling on the bed, poised over his head. I'm vacillating between self-consciousness and lust as I look down in his eyes. Then, as he locks me in his focus, he pulls me down on his hot mouth.

I close my eyes, drop my head back, and let myself be swept off by a tsunami of sensations, as his talented lips, tongue, and fingers make my body sing. He's all that keeps me grounded when I come so hard, it feels like I scatter with the force.

He eases out from under my collapsed body and kisses his way up my back, until I can feel his lips pressing against the shell of my ear.

"Stay just like this," he whispers.

I'm still on my knees, my body slumped forward—ass up and face pressed into a pillow—when I feel his hands on my hips a moment later. Then I feel a light pressure as he brushes the blunt head of his cock along my crease, before sliding inside me in a slow but firm stroke.

Still a little swollen and sensitized from the earlier onslaught of his mouth, Jackson is gentle as he makes love to me. This time when I feel my orgasm crest, it's a rolling wave instead of a wild tsunami.

The last thing I remember is Jackson rolling us to our

sides, his body curved around me from behind. I feel warm and safe, and fall asleep almost instantly.

~

"Wake up! Stephanie!"

Something acrid fills my lungs as I try to force my eyes open. I'm already being pulled from the bed and am disoriented as my mind tries to grasp what is going on.

"Fire," Jackson's voice sounds close to my ear.

Just like that, I'm wide awake, and now I can hear it, even if I can't see a hand in front of my eyes.

"We have to go out the window."

"Ash," I rasp, before launching into a coughing fit.

"He's here. You first, then I'll lift him out."

Jackson sounds hoarse himself as I instinctively follow the flow of cold air to the window. I grab the ledge and with his help, hoist myself outside, landing hard. That's when I notice I'm still naked, but I don't have time to worry about it, because already Jackson is lifting the dog through the window.

I can smell singed hair when I cradle the surprisingly calm animal in my arms, and when I crouch down with him, my brain finally registers our predicament. Everything out here is cast in a red glow as flames shoot up from the roof. The trailer looks to be almost entirely engulfed.

"Jackson!" I yell for him when he doesn't immediately follow the dog out.

Next thing I know, what looks like a wadded up bedsheet is lowered out the window, immediately followed by Jackson's prosthesis. Then comes the man himself, head first, as he launches himself out of the burning house.

Still hanging on to the dog, I scramble to get him to

186

safety as an ominous groaning sound heralds nothing good. Jackson is right behind me on one leg, dragging the sheet behind him. Moments later there is a loud reverberation as the roof of the trailer collapses, sending sparks and burning debris flying.

I'm knocked to the ground as Jackson throws himself on me and the dog, covering our bodies with his own.

# Eighteen

*JACKSON*

Stephanie looks pale in the harsh light of the ambulance.

She also looks pissed, mainly at me since I insisted she get checked out before me.

After I made sure she and Ash were safe outside, I was able to grab a few random things I wrapped in a bedsheet. Some clothes, stuff off the bedside table which included Stephanie's phone, and a couple of things I'd manage to snag from the top of the dresser. Not enough, not nearly enough, but it was all I could get before the heat got too much. I was lucky, I almost tripped over my prosthesis hopping back to the window and was able to rescue it too, but unfortunately the heat already got to parts of it and it's going to need some repairs.

After the roof collapsed, I knew any efforts to go back in another way to try and salvage anything else would be moot.

Stephanie ended up calling 911, but I knew they'd be at least ten minutes if not more. While waiting for emergency services to get here, we got dressed in the few things I was able to grab off the floor. We're both barefoot and dressed haphazardly at best, but at least the important parts are covered.

"Minor smoke inhalation. Rest, avoid irritants, and if your throat feels raw, you can take some cough medication," the EMT tells her before adding, "If anything changes, get checked out in the emergency room."

The woman turns to me. "Now, let me see what you've got going on."

As it turns out, I get off with a few second degree burns, which are treated on the spot at my insistence. For smoke inhalation I receive the same instructions Stephanie got.

I climb out of the ambulance just as Jonas pulls up, the pale face of my mother visible through the windshield as she leans forward in the passenger seat.

"Jackson!"

The moment the SUV stops, she's out and running for me. I'm not too stable on one leg, but manage to brace myself against the side of the ambulance when she hits me full force, her arms banding around me.

"Jesus, kid. Scared the living crap out of your mother," Jonas mutters when he walks up, carrying my spare prosthesis.

From the slight waver in his voice, it sounds like Ma wasn't the only one affected.

"Shit, Alex," he grumbles. "Let the man put his leg on before you take him to the ground."

Ma reluctantly lets go as I'm handed my leg, and Jonas tucks my mother under his arm.

"How is Stephanie?" she asks.

I look around to see where she went. She went with the sheriff's deputy to answer some questions when I was being looked at in the ambulance. That was fifteen or so minutes ago.

"Junior!" I yell out when I catch sight of the sheriff, who must've just gotten here as well. "Have you seen Stephanie? She was with Dale earlier."

"She's not with him now. Dale is back there." He cocks his thumb over his shoulder at the water truck, where I can see the deputy talking with some of the fire crew.

Stephanie is nowhere in sight, and suddenly the same sense of panic I felt when I first woke up, disoriented as smoke filled the room, making it difficult to see where I was, is back.

"I'll go see where she went," Jonas offers, reaching out to give my shoulder a squeeze before he takes off.

"She's not wearing any shoes," I mumble as my eyes scan the clusters of first responders and the surrounding area.

"I brought you some clothes. I wasn't sure..." Ma pauses. "I grabbed some things that might fit Stephanie too, just in case. Jonas will find her. And JD will be here soon too, we called him on the way over."

She's rambling, and I can hear the barely contained emotion in her voice, as I struggle to strap on my spare pros-thetic. It's not fitting properly without the liner, which is probably still in my closet somewhere at the cabin, but this will have to do for now.

"I didn't think about footwear. Should I call JD back and ask him to bring some boots or something?"

"Ma, it's fine," I reassure her. "I need to go find Stephanie."

I watch as Jonas approaches a group of firefighters and see one of them point toward the creek. Wobbling a little on the ill-fitting limb but going as fast as I can, I set off in that direction.

It's surprising, with all the commotion around the trailer, how quiet and peaceful it is back here. The moon is out, reflecting its silver light off the water, and any noise from the scene I left behind fades into the background.

But I don't see Stephanie.

At least, not immediately.

A sharp bark draws my attention to a rocky outcropping jutting into the water to my right, where the creek makes a sharp bend. I see her then, sitting with her feet dangling in the water, Ash standing guard by her side.

It's tough going on the uneven ground on one bare foot and one unstable prosthetic, but I make it over to the rock. As Ash comes up to greet me, I notice Stephanie is still staring out at the water. I sink down beside her.

"I burned down JD's trailer," she mumbles without looking at me.

"Why do you say that?"

"I left the candle burning in the kitchen."

The candle she talks about is a small tea light on the kitchen counter she lit before we sat down to watch TV.

"No, you didn't. I looked over when we went to bed and it had burned out."

It's not until I drape an arm around her shoulders and pull her close, that she turns her face up to me. Tear streaks cut through the soot on her face and her eyes shimmer with unshed ones.

"I don't know what happened—I'm sure we'll know more once the fire inspector gets here—but it wasn't a burning candle."

She nods and I brush some hair out of her eyes before grabbing the edge of the shirt I was wearing today, and wipe some of the wet dirt off her face.

"I can't believe everything is gone. JD's trailer, everything I brought with me, my laptop…" She chokes out a half laugh, half sob. "Even my Honda. Did you see?"

I did see. It must've been when the roof caved in the burning debris fell onto her SUV, because there wasn't much left of it either. My truck, which was parked back a bit, received a little heat damage, but other than that—and of course, the four slashed tires—it seems to have survived.

"It's stuff. You can get other stuff. I'm sure JD is insured, plus, he took his most important belongings with him when he moved in with Janey. He'll be fine."

She shakes her head and turns back to the water.

"It's not *all* just stuff. Some of it was irreplaceable."

"Like what?" I gently probe her.

"My mom's hairbrush," she whispers. "After all these years, I can still smell her shampoo. Or maybe that's just my imagination, but it was the only tangible thing I had left of her."

*Stephanie*

"Come with me."

I'm abruptly pulled to my feet and almost dragged back toward the emergency vehicles.

"What are we doing?"

But I don't get an answer as Jackson pulls me along, aiming for the south side of the trailer. The one side still standing, albeit minus a roof. The side of the bedroom were we narrowly escaped through the window.

"There," he says triumphantly.

He's pointing at what looks like a pile of dirty laundry,

but is in fact the sheet he tossed out the bedroom window with some clothes wrapped inside. When he picks up a corner and shakes it out, several items come tumbling out. A bottle of moisturizer, a half-squeezed tube of toothpaste, the charger for my phone, a pair of my panties, and...my mother's brush.

"I couldn't see, I just grabbed what was there. But I remember something felt like a hairbrush," he explains.

I throw myself in his arms, and start crying all over again.

I know it's silly, it's just a brush, but to me that piece of plastic is worth more than my clothes, my laptop, and my Honda combined.

"You found her," I hear Alex's voice from behind Jackson. "Good. Let's get you guys back to the ranch to get cleaned up. The sheriff says he'll meet us back there later."

Twenty minutes later, I'm in a shower the size of my apartment in Kalispell, and Jackson is shampooing my hair. I try not to think and enjoy the sensation, but inevitably my thoughts go back to the fire.

If I didn't leave that candle burning, then what could've been the cause? The investigator in me immediately wants to connect it to Jackson's slashed tires, which is something I should've looked into right away. But I gave Jackson's mental state priority last night, and pushed everything else to the background. I'm wondering if that was a mistake.

"I can hear the wheels in your head churning," Jackson observes when we dry off in the large fluffy towels Alex left out for us. "Wanna talk it out with me?"

It's what I would do with my fellow agents. We'd meet up, hash out details of the case, and toss around ideas. More often than not, we'd walk away with at least a plan of attack.

"The damage to your truck and the fire...I'm having trouble trying to believe that was coincidence."

"Agreed," he concurs. "Although, I fail to see the motive for either. Slashing my tires was small potatoes—I was actually wondering if Vallard had a petty streak—but the fire is a different level."

"You think it was set?"

He shakes his head, sending water droplets flying. "Not a doubt in my mind."

A sharp rap sounds on the door.

"Get your asses dressed," Jonas barks from the other side of the door. "The sheriff is here; he wants to talk to both of you."

That kicks us in high gear, and I throw on the sweats Alex left out for me, before helping Jackson pull the stubborn sleeve over the still-damp skin of his stump. I twist my wet hair up in a messy bun with a clip I find on the vanity, and follow Jackson downstairs.

It's not even five in the morning, yet when we walk into the large kitchen, the place is already bustling with activity.

It's a ranch, I'm sure they get an early start, but that doesn't explain why Ama is already in the kitchen, working on what smells like a full breakfast, complete with bacon. Or why JD and Janey are both here on a stool at the large island. I awkwardly wave at James, Sully, and Fletch, who are sitting at the dining table, and smile back at Dan, who is pouring coffee from a large thermos into a row of mugs on the sideboard.

Janey gets to her feet and comes over to greet me with a big hug.

"So glad you're okay," she whispers in my ear as she holds me in a viselike grip.

"Where is Ewing?" Jackson asks behind me.

"Waiting in Jonas's office," Ama is the one to answer. "But grab a coffee first."

I see she is wearing a dress, something I haven't seen before. She's usually in jeans. When she turns her back I notice she cut her hair. She had a long braid down to her behind before, but the hair she has tied back in a ponytail now barely reaches her shoulder blades.

"Your hair..."

She glances at me over her shoulder with a sad smile. "It grows back."

Then it hits me, it's Thomas's funeral this morning. She's dressed up and cut her hair to honor him. That's why people are assembling so early.

I turn and face Jackson. "You should stay and have coffee with your brothers. I'll handle the sheriff."

"Good luck with that," Janey mutters under her voice as the guys collectively chuckle.

All Jackson does is shoot me an intense look I can't quite decipher, grabs my hand, and starts marching down the hallway to the office, dragging me along. We're going to need to have a word about that later.

"The fire was set," Ewing confirms moments later what we already suspected. "Fire inspector found some large blister charring around the dryer and the roof vents. Not sure what was used yet, but he suggests some kind of liquid accelerant was sprayed into the vents and set alight."

"Someone has it in for you," Jonas directs at me.

"Or me," Jackson suggests. "My tires were slashed earlier in the evening."

"I noticed that. I was going to ask you about it," Ewing states. "Tell me what happened. From the beginning."

Over the next twenty minutes, Jackson and I fill the sheriff in, telling him everything we know. I even shoot him the snapshots I took of the damage to Jackson's truck, since those were taken prior to the fire. By now those footprints I photographed are probably covered by many others.

"Regardless of who the target was," I observe. "Whoever set the fire did a piss-poor job of it."

"Hmm," Ewing hums his consent.

But Jackson brings up another possibility.

"Unless someone is toying with us," he suggests. "Distracting us."

# *Nineteen*

*STEPHANIE*

"Let the boys take care of him."

Alex drapes an arm around Ama's shoulders and steers her down the hill, leading the way back to the ranch house. Janey hooks her arm through mine and we follow behind, with Pippa, her sister Nella, and Sloane herding the kids, while Jillian and Lucy bring up the rear, moving along any stragglers.

Part of me revolts at the gender-based division, but at the same time it feels right for Thomas to be looked after by "his boys." If anything, it's a show of respect to the end of a more traditional generation. Times may have changed, and we may have evolved beyond the gender bounds, but this farewell is not about us, it's about Thomas, and the last respects paid to him.

The ceremony was a simple one with little fanfare, and just a few brief graveside blessings by a Baptist minister, who left right before us. Thomas wasn't a churchgoer anymore, but he was apparently raised Baptist and met his wife at a church event seventy years ago.

I got a little teary-eyed as Jonas recounted his parents' love story at the graveside, but couldn't hold back the sob when he stated his pops was back where he belonged, in his mother's arms.

The man was loved, no doubt about that. I can only hope when my time comes, I'll have earned even just a fraction of the love and respect he was shown today. But I doubt my family would show me any—they haven't cared enough to in life—and I only have a scant handful of people I can call friends. If I went today, I know Jackson would mourn me, Janey would, and maybe a few others would be sad, but there wouldn't be many who'd even notice me gone.

If I'm honest with myself, I have to admit I haven't made enough of an impression on people's lives. Sure, I've helped take bad guys off the street, but most of what I do is anonymous to those whose lives it would have impacted. I live and breathe my work, a lot of which is working under the radar, and I've been hiding there. I'm good at what I do, but I'm not so sure anymore it's what I want to spend my life doing.

"You're quiet," Janey observes, giving my arm a squeeze. "Are you all right?"

I nod and dart her a quick smile. "Yeah, just contemplating life and future, that's all."

She barks out a laugh as we climb up the porch steps.

"Is that all?" she teases before continuing on a more serious note, "Funerals have a tendency to encourage soul-searching, don't they?"

"I'd already been doing the soul-searching, but I'm starting to draw some conclusions."

"Oh?" She raises her eyebrows as she shoots me a look.

"I think I'm going to quit my job."

The thought never fully formed until the words are already spilling from my mouth, but the relief I feel is instant. I know in my heart it's the right thing to do. It feels like severing the ties on a toxic relationship, which is in essence what I'm doing.

I joined the Bureau to prove myself worthy to my family —to my father—but I think it's safe to say that'll never happen. Sad that it took me almost a decade and a half to realize that. Then I made a major mistake when I stumbled into a relationship with Vallard, a fellow agent, and have spent the years since trying to prove myself better than that lapse in judgment.

I've been spinning my wheels trying to be the person I think others want me to be, and I'm realizing I'll never get there. Nor should I have to.

For most of my adult life my work has defined me, I thought that's who I was. But if I've learned anything since coming here, it's that the person behind that badge holds value by merit of who she is, not what she does. Jackson has shown me that, so have Janey and JD, and all the others who have welcomed and included me because of who I am, not what I do.

"You're quitting your job?" Alex, who walked into the house ahead of us, turns around and asks.

I can feel a number of surprised eyes on me and suddenly feel put on the spot, even though I put myself there. I blurted it out without considering the consequences. Or the fact I probably should've talked to Jackson before anyone else. It's a pretty big life decision that impacts my future, and I think we've reached a point in our relationship where those things should be discussed.

Still, the cat is out of the bag now.

"Yeah…I think so."

"That's a big step," Alex points out with a serious expression on her face. As Jackson's mother, I can see why she might be concerned. "What will come next?"

I guess that's the million-dollar question, one I haven't had a chance to seriously ponder.

"With her background and experience? She could do anything," a voice I recognize as Sloane's pipes up on my behalf. "The sheriff's department is constantly stretched thin, and we still have a defunct police department that could use someone with the appropriate know-how to try to breathe new life into it. She'd be an asset to any law enforcement agency or even a private organization like the High Mountain Trackers."

"Well, I'm not sure—" I start, a little embarrassed but secretly pleased at the vote of confidence.

But Ama cuts me off.

"I'd like to see a woman on the team to take those boys down a peg," she states, as she moves through the large kitchen like a force of nature.

"Yes," Alex agrees with a grin. She's setting out a tray of sandwiches, removing the plastic film covering it, while Pippa works on the coffee and Ama moves a large pot of something from the back of the stove to the front burner. "Too much testosterone between the lot. Time some of those boys slowed down anyway."

"You ride, right?" Lucy wants to know.

"Well…umm."

"Sure she does," Janey answers for me, leaning over and adding under her breath. "You can come and practice on Sterling."

Sterling is Janey's mare, a pretty pinto.

I feel a little uneasy, because somehow, somewhere, this

conversation has taken on a life of its own. Other than prompting the discussion with my surprise announcement, it went in a direction I had little input in.

"Glad that's settled then," Ama declares, clapping her hands together.

Then Jonas's deep voice rumbles behind me.

"Glad what's settled?"

*Jackson*

The straight shot of bourbon Jonas poured for us at the old man's graveside is still burning its way down my esophagus as we shovel the dirt back in the hole we dug yesterday.

The old man's oversized Stetson Jonas placed on the coffin before we lowered him into the ground is already almost covered, as we take turns with the shovels.

I'm sweating buckets in the midday sun, but my heart is much lighter and my head a lot clearer today, despite our overnight adventure. Needless to say, there wasn't a lot of sleeping after Ewing confirmed arson. There hadn't been a lot of answers we were able to provide—other than to share the single smoke alarm never went off—but both Ben Vallard and Mitchel Laine's names came up. Ewing indicated he'd be contacting Vallard and he'd be in touch if there was anything to report.

I don't think being sidelined made Stephanie very happy, but she didn't push it. At least not then, and not this morning when she stood next to me, her fingers entwined with mine as we said goodbye to Thomas. Though I have a feeling she's not the type to stay complacent for long, and she's definitely not one to cower and hide when someone puts a target on her back. I just hope she doesn't go off on her own without telling me.

Dan takes the ATV with the shovels back to the barn, while the rest of us walk back down to the ranch house. My spare limb doesn't fit as comfortably as the damaged one does, so my limp is far more pronounced.

"Take my truck this afternoon," Jonas offers as he falls into step beside me. "I assume you're gonna want to get to the prosthetics clinic as soon as possible. And Stephanie may want to make a stop at her place to pick up a few things. That is, if she plans to stick around longer."

"She'll stick around," I assure him. "For now."

She and I talked about it this morning. I asked her what she wanted to do, and she said she wasn't ready to leave Libby. So I told her she could stay with me in the cabin. It's not ideal, being right next door to the ranch house, but at least the ranch is safe. The extensive security system ensures no one comes around here without being noticed.

I glance over at the man beside me and catch him studying me.

"What are you gonna do when she leaves? Goes back to her job?"

Good question. She made it clear she's not ready yet, but that doesn't mean she'll never be. I'm not so sure about long-distance relationships, especially when neither of us have very predictable schedules. If she decides to go back, I'm not sure what kind of future we'd have. Do I feel good about that? Not particularly, but that's a decision she's going to have to make.

I give him the only answer I have. "We'll cross that bridge when we get to it."

He enters the house before me and as he steps into the kitchen I hear him ask, "Glad what's settled?"

"Stephanie," Ama, who is stirring a large pot on the stove, explains. "She's quitting her job and moving to Libby."

Stephanie looks mildly panicked as her eyes find mine. "I never...all I said was that I was thinking about leaving the Bureau. I..."

"And the discussion took off without her," Janey jumps in with a big grin. "We got carried away. She never actually said she would move to Libby."

JD chooses that moment to poke his head around the door.

"Sorry to interrupt but, Stephanie, do you have a minute?"

Stephanie's eyes dart to me before she nods at him and follows him out into the hallway. I'm not far behind and join them out on the porch.

"I put a call in with the insurance company this morning and they'll be sending a claims adjuster out, hopefully sometime this week," JD starts as I step up beside Stephanie, draping my arm over her shoulders. "I'm going to need to hand over a complete inventory of items lost or damaged, so if I could bother you to put together a list of your things? Since you were a guest in my house, I'm gonna include them on my claim. If you happen to have any receipts or proof of purchase that would probably be helpful."

"I can do that," she answers, nodding. "Again, I'm so sorry for—"

JD raises a hand to stop her. "You're not responsible."

"Still," she persists. "If it wasn't for me..."

"Look, the only reason I hadn't sold the trailer or gotten

rid of it some other way yet, is because I was procrastinating. Now I can scratch it off my honey-do list. I didn't lose anything I had emotional attachments to and the only thing of significance to me is the land, and that's still there. Plus," he adds. "I'll get the insurance money back."

"Are you sure about that? Ewing confirmed it was arson," I point out.

"Oh, we'll get it. Eventually," he modifies. "I'm sure the insurance company will want to investigate, which is why I figure we'd include as much documentation as we can, it'll save time later."

"I'll do whatever I can," Stephanie volunteers. "Any paperwork I have would be at my apartment in Kalispell though. I was going to check my own insurance information as well. I was hoping—"

"We can go this afternoon," I offer. "I have to take my prosthesis in to the clinic for repairs anyway. We'll take Jonas's vehicle and we can stop at your place to pick up what you need."

"Lunch!"

Ama's voice easily carries through the house and out to the porch.

JD grins and shakes his head, muttering under his breath, "Better go in before she blows a gasket."

# Twenty

JACKSON

"What's going on?"

Stephanie is sitting up when I try to sneak into the bedroom.

Dammit, I was hoping she could sleep a bit longer, since we didn't get much the other night. I was up early and ended up on the couch out in the living room, watching some news on TV, when Jonas's message came in. Unfortunately, I had to get in here for my clothes.

"We got called out on a rescue." I sit down on the mattress beside her. "I'm not sure when I'll be back and I may not have cell reception, but if you need me for anything, check in with Ama. We've got two-way radios and a satellite phone in the office in the ranch house you can try."

"I'll be fine. I've got a few things I need to take care of in town, and I want to pick up some groceries."

When I open my mouth to remind her she's welcome to

anything from my fridge or from the kitchen in the big house, she places her fingers against my lips.

"I know what you're gonna say, but I'll feel better if I have my own stuff."

I bite my lip and nod. We had an argument yesterday afternoon in Kalispell when she insisted I stop at a car rental place because she needed wheels. I told her she could use one of the ranch trucks if she needed to get around, but she was adamant and followed me home in the little SUV she was able to get.

The entire visit to Kalispell had been a little tense. Every time I tried to bring up her decision to quit her job, she evaded the subject. Other than, "I'm considering my options," she didn't give me much feedback, which made me uncomfortable. On edge. Which is what had me up at three thirty and unable to sleep this morning.

"Fine."

As soon as the clipped word leaves my lips, I regret it. It's petty and I'm cranky. Ticked because I want her to let me in all the way, I want to look after her and she won't let me, and I'm frustrated because I have to go out on this call and I don't want to leave her alone.

"Look, I've been taking care of myself for a long time. My life has been shaken up these past few months, and we've just had a shitty few days, and it makes me feel a little better knowing I'm still able to. Even if it's just going to the bank or the grocery store on my own. It has nothing to do with you."

I take a deep breath and let that settle in. If I'm being completely honest with myself, I want her to need me. It would make *me* feel better, but I hadn't really considered how it would make her feel.

"Fair enough. Understood," I concede, which earns me a sweet kiss on the lips.

But I can't help myself from asking, "Are you going to call Vallard back?"

The agent was blowing up her phone all yesterday afternoon, but she let his calls go to voicemail. Part of me wonders if that was because I was with her. She knows I'm not a fan of her getting more involved in this case, and I'm even more convinced that's not a good idea since the fire. But I can't lose sight of the fact Stephanie is a trained and experienced FBI agent, leave of absence put aside. Hell, in all truth, she's better equipped than I am to deal with scum like Mitchel Laine and even sleazeballs like Vallard.

"I should probably check in with him. He'll be wondering where I am."

I bite my lip and nod, limiting myself to, "Just be careful."

Jonas and Sully are loading up the back of the truck when I get to the barn.

"Are you okay to ride?" is the first thing my stepfather asks.

He probably wants Sully to man base camp.

I rap my knuckles on the socket of my artificial limb. "Got a new gel sleeve for this one and it fits like a glove. I'm good."

I had to leave my good prosthesis there, but with this new sleeve, the old one fits better than it ever has. Even though a marathon may be out of the question with this limb, it should be fine for riding.

"Good. Go give Dan a hand loading the horses, and as soon as JD and Wolff get here, we'll grab some coffee and have a quick brief before we roll out."

When those guys arrive a few minutes later, we have the

horse trailer loaded up, and all the equipment—including the brand-new, high-end drone Jonas apparently bought—is in the back of the truck. We congregate in the big kitchen, where Ma has coffee going and is slapping together some egg and Canadian bacon sandwiches.

"Where is Ama?"

The woman is normally here by six, ruling the kitchen. My mother does her best, but she's no Ama in the kitchen, evidenced by the slightly charred toast and crispy eggs.

"She needed a break," Ma answers curtly.

"Yesterday was hard on her," JD explains. "Dad's taking her home for a visit for a couple of days."

From what JD has shared with me over the years, home is the Flathead Reservation where he grew up. They still have family living there.

I know Ama had a very strong bond with Thomas. They bickered all the time, but she cared for him deeply. She looked after him like a daughter would for her father, when the rest of us went about our daily business, so I'm not surprised his loss cuts her to the core.

"Okay, here's what we have," Jonas starts. "Two guys tried to climb up to Snowshoe Peak and fell forty feet down a rock wall last night. One of them is in pretty bad shape, the other guy managed to stabilize him, thanks to some first-aid training. They were in a dead zone though, so the one guy was forced to leave his friend to find a signal. He was barely coherent by the time he got through to dispatch. All we have is a ping on a map and a starting point at Leigh Lake trailhead. We need to find both, and extract them. Jillian is on standby to bring in the dogs if we can't get a visual on those guys."

My mother hands him a travel mug and a breakfast

sandwich wrapped in paper. He gives her a resounding kiss on the lips before turning back to us.

"Guys, help yourselves and let's roll out."

Ma sees us off from the porch with a "Be careful out there," when we get into the trucks.

Just as we pull away from the ranch and pass the cabins, I catch sight of Stephanie stepping outside, a coffee mug in her hand. She smiles and blows me a kiss when she sees me in the passenger seat.

I don't realize I'm grinning until I glimpse my reflection in the side mirror.

*Fuck*, I look happy.

*Stephanie*

It feels a little weird to be out in athletic wear when I have no intention of hitting a gym, but, other than work suits, that was all I had left in my closet back at my apartment.

All the casual clothes I had—and there weren't too many to begin with—got lost in the fire. So yoga pants and a zippered hoodie it is until I can find myself some more serviceable clothes, which is on my list of things to tackle today.

There's a discount store called *Stytches Bent West* that is supposed to carry some discount and consignment stuff Janey recommended. She says they sometimes have unique things, not that I'd know something unique if it slapped me in the face, but I'll have a look.

Jackson's mom, Alex, suggested the *Blessed in the 406*

boutique which is supposed to carry more mainstream jeans and tops.

But first I'm stopping in at the salon to see if I can get some more information on Tracy's whereabouts.

"Can I help you?" the young girl behind the counter greets me.

"Hi, yes. I was wondering if Tracy is in today? I don't have an appointment, but I had a house fire a couple of days ago and I can't get the smell of smoke out of my hair. I've washed it three times already. I was hoping Tracy might have some suggestions?"

"Oh no. That place by Foxy's Bar? My boyfriend is a firefighter and told me the folks staying there narrowly escaped. Was that you?"

Both the hairdresser and her client, sitting in the chair closest to the front desk, are gawking at me right now.

"I heard about that," the woman with half her head in foils contributes, inserting herself into the conversation. "Heard it was a total loss. I'm so sorry that happened to you."

"Thank you," I mutter, for lack of anything better to say.

"Smoke alarm woke you up?" the customer probes.

"Something like that," I respond.

The smoke alarm didn't wake us, but I'm not about to share that information. I'm still trying to figure out how it was possible for the alarm not to sound when I personally saw JD put a fresh battery in the day I moved into the trailer.

I told Ewing as much in Jonas's office. He asked me who all had been in the trailer since I got there, which is how Ben Vallard's name came up. Except, I had eyes on Vallard at all times while he was inside, I would've seen him tamper with the smoke alarm.

Ewing indicated the smoke detector would be checked out by the forensic lab, to see if it had been interfered with or whether it could've been a simple malfunction. It happens.

He'd also wanted to know about the trailer's security. Other than the door locks, there hadn't been much. I guess there hadn't been any need with just JD living there. Plus, it's not the kind of place that would've promised a profitable haul for a random burglar passing by. All of that to say, it is possible someone snuck in at some point and tinkered with the smoke alarm.

In any event, all that is speculation until we know for sure the detector was purposely disabled, and I'm not going to open up a public discussion on the subject.

"So, do you think Tracy could help?" I return the conversation to my original request.

"I'm sorry, Tracy is out of town, visiting family," the receptionist shares.

"Really? That's so odd, Tracy never mentioned anything about that."

A statuesque redhead—I'd guess her to be mid-to-late forties—wearing a pair of orange platform Crocs comes walking up to the desk. I guess she was working at one of the chairs closer to the back, judging from a pair of scissors still in her hand.

"You were looking for Tracy?"

I turn to her with a smile. "Yes, she's a friend, and I tried to call her but my calls keep going to voicemail, so I decided to try and catch her here. I have a bit of a hair emergency I was hoping she could help with, but I'm told she's out of town? That seems so weird, I was in here not that long ago and met her for lunch after, and she never mentioned anything about going away. Odd."

The redhead nods. "I remember seeing you. I'm Donna Farley. I'm Tracy's boss, and also a friend. Why don't you step into the back with me? Let's see what we can do about your hair problem."

I follow her to the back and through a set of beaded curtains to a private section of the salon, where she ushers me into an office, closing the door behind us.

"Have a seat."

She slides behind the desk and I take the visitor's chair in front. It seems odd she'd take me into an office to look at my hair, but I suspect that's not the reason I'm here.

"Is something wrong?" I ask, playing up the role of concerned friend. "Did something happen to Tracy?"

"You're new to town. Tracy mentioned you."

It's not an answer to my question, but it is telling nonetheless.

"She did? Yeah, I haven't been here that long yet. I'm still getting my bearings, so it was nice to make a new friend. Is Tracy okay?"

The woman leans forward, studying me through narrowed eyes, and I do my best to look as non-official as possible. It seems to work, because she finally sits back, leaning her head against the chair.

"How much did she tell you?"

I'd like to think I know what she's referring to but I need to tread carefully.

"About what? Um...we talked about new beginnings. She'd picked up on some problems I had with an ex. We discussed men, both past and present. Mostly my past and her present. I told her about the abusive relationship I left, and she mentioned finally meeting her longtime, online boyfriend for the first time recently. I know he was an ex-con. Did something happen?"

Donna presses the heels of her hands against her forehead.

"I don't know. She called me a week ago, told me she had to leave, and if anyone asked to tell them she was out of town indefinitely, looking after her sick mother."

That's the story Vallard was given, but I'm not supposed to know about it, so I force a look of confusion on my face.

"But...I could've sworn she mentioned her mother was dead," I volunteer.

"She is," Donna confirms. "Has been for years. When I asked Tracy if she was in trouble, she said she didn't have time to talk but would get back to me as soon as she could." The woman's worried eyes meet mine. "I don't think she was alone."

"The boyfriend?" I suggest.

"I'm sure of it," Donna states, her face now filled with anger. "I told her the guy was a bad idea, but she wouldn't listen. Now the FBI is coming around asking questions."

"FBI?" I echo, feigning ignorance.

She nods. "Walked in the other day, asking her whereabouts. I gave the agent the story Tracy wanted me to tell, but I'm afraid I haven't seen the last of him. What if I'm in trouble now for lying to them? Tracy may be gullible but she's a good person, who hasn't had many breaks in life. I'm trying to protect her, but the longer I don't hear from her, the more I worry I may be making a mistake lying for her."

When I walk out of the salon forty-five minutes later with a freshly washed and coiffed head of hair, I still don't know where Tracy could be, but I'm more convinced than ever she didn't exactly go voluntarily.

Poor Donna. The woman seems truly conflicted, and I

feel bad I'm deceiving her. She thinks I'm a battered woman and feels safe talking to me about our supposed mutual friend. She never would've confided in me if she knew I was an FBI agent.

At least, I am for now. I'd been tempted to stop in at the office yesterday afternoon when we were in Kalispell, but Jackson suggested I take a bit more time to really think it through before handing in my resignation. That annoyed me at first, but then I realized there really wasn't any hurry, and it would probably be a good idea to put some plans in place for my next steps before I burn my bridges behind me.

To be honest, I'd been pretty combative with him on several subjects yesterday, and for the most part he was undeserving, but stress and emotions and uncertainty had me lash out at him. The poor guy had an arguably worse week than mine, but he still managed to be a lot more patient and understanding with me than I was with him.

Something I'll have to make up for when he comes back.

# Twenty-One

STEPHANIE

"Super cute."

Janey nods her approval at the embroidered cowboy boots I picked up on a whim.

She'd called while I was out shopping and asked if I wanted to come over for dinner at her place. I ended up going straight there after shopping.

I'd hauled all my bags inside and am busy stuffing some of my groceries in her fridge to stay cool, while she ransacks the other bags.

"Consignment. I picked them up for forty-five bucks. I thought that was a pretty good deal."

Shopping was always a necessary evil to me and I generally avoid it like the plague, but I have to admit, I had fun digging through those two small stores this afternoon. Maybe it's because it feels like part of this new life I'm creating. I've never really given myself a chance to think about what it is I want. I was always more concerned about what was expected.

It's a new experience for me, and I'm determined not to feel guilty about having fun doing it. Even though I just dropped a quick five hundred dollars in less than two hours, and I haven't even replaced my laptop and e-reader yet.

"I love this."

Janey dug through the bag of mainly plain jeans and shirts I picked up, and spied the pretty floral peasant blouse I found. I'm not usually one for frilly clothes, but I thought it might be nice to wear for a dinner date, or something.

"Did you find it at *Stytches*?" Janey wants to know.

"No, the other one."

"*Blessed in the 406?* You're kidding." She holds the blouse in front of herself. "It's nice and flowy. Might cover up a baby bump, at least for the summer months."

"About that," I redirect. "How are you feeling?"

She drops the top back in the shopping bag and leans back in her chair, placing both of her hands on her belly.

"Fine, I guess. Nothing a cup of ginger tea and a handful of saltine crackers can't fix."

"Morning sickness?"

"Yeah. Although it isn't just in the morning. That's a big misnomer." Suddenly she breaks out a big smile. "But I saw my doctor this morning for my first official visit. He asked me for the first day of my last period, which took me a bit to remember. Turns out it was the end of February, but things have been so busy since the snow melted, I didn't really pay attention. He's sending me for an ultrasound to confirm, but it looks like this baby is due somewhere around the beginning of December."

I break out a grin of my own. "An early Christmas present."

She snorts. "Yeah, one that requires a little work to unpack."

My phone starts to buzz in my pocket. Ben Vallard's number appears on the screen. He's been trying to get a hold of me and I tried calling him after my visit to the salon earlier but was bumped to voicemail.

"I'm sorry," I tell Janey, holding up my phone. "I've gotta take this."

"Of course."

I slip out the door onto the front porch before I answer.

"Hey."

"Sorry, I was tied up when you called earlier. What have you got?"

He gets down to business right away, which I appreciate. I have no desire to engage in social chitchat with him. In fact, I would love if we could get this case resolved and I could get this man out of my hair for good. I have a new life to explore and don't particularly want to drag old baggage along while I'm doing it.

"Nothing concrete, but I had a chance to talk to Donna Farley, Tracy's boss. I played the role of Tracy's new and concerned friend and the woman opened up a little. She admitted Tracy asked her to lie about her whereabouts, but she doesn't know where she actually is and is worried about her. From what she told me, I got the sense wherever Tracy went, it wasn't exactly voluntary. Donna suspects the new boyfriend had a hand in her disappearance and my gut tells me she's right."

I hear Vallard mutter a curse on the other side.

"Goddammit, that doesn't really help me much," he grumbles. "Have you tried just calling her?"

"Goes straight to voicemail," I inform him. "Which could mean the phone is off, or she doesn't have service where she is, or calls have been forwarded directly to her mailbox. Either way, she's not answering my calls either. Your best bet is to ping her phone."

"I know it is, but I'm in hot water with my boss already. I was supposed to be back yesterday and have been avoiding his calls. I'm not gonna get any help there. I'm on my own."

"Are you sure you're on the right track?" I ask him. "Because it sounds like you may be blowing up your career over this."

I'm one to talk, I'm ready to turn my back on the FBI myself, but that is for personal reasons. Ben is risking his livelihood over a lead on a case that isn't even technically his. There is no concrete evidence to support his theory Mitchel Laine was responsible for all those robberies across several states. Or even that it's Laine who took off with Tracy, forcefully or otherwise.

"I'm right about Laine. No doubt about it," he states strongly. "He's responsible, he's here, and he has Tracy. And yes, I'm willing to stake my career on it."

At the moment I don't really have a career to stake anything on anymore, but my gut tells me he's right about Mitchel Laine as well.

"All right then, got any favors you can call in? Any friends in the Bureau willing to bend a rule or two for you?"

It wouldn't be the first time and unlikely to be the last. Favors are called in all the time.

"I'm not sure I have a lot of goodwill going my way at the moment," he admits. "And if it gets back to my boss I went behind his back, I'd be on my ass on the street faster than I can blink."

Fair enough.

I could let it go at that, but the smell of smoke still clinging to the inside of my nose is a reminder I already may be too invested in this case, even though perhaps not by choice. I'm going to have to let my gut do the talking again because I have no evidence either way, but I don't believe Vallard was responsible for slicing Jackson's tires or setting the fire last night.

He's just not the kind of guy to get his hands dirty, and besides, what motive could he have?

"Let me see what I can do," I offer. "I'll call you back."

Then I end the call. It sounds like he's determined to see his investigation through, with or without the backing of the Bureau, so the only way to get him out of my hair is to help him get the evidence he needs. I happen to be on good terms with my colleagues and might be able to get someone to slip me some info.

I pull up a familiar number and hit dial.

"Agent Wilcox."

I smile at the sound of his voice. We've worked together for the past five or so years, and have had each other's backs. I realize I miss him.

"Hey, Shane, it's Stephanie."

"No shit. What the fuck happened to you? One minute you're in the hospital, the next moment you're gone."

He sounds pissed, and has a right to; I haven't exactly stayed in touch.

"Long story, but it's gonna have to wait. I need your help with something."

Despite being angry with me, Shane doesn't hesitate.

"What do you need?"

～

*Jackson*

· · ·

Sully spotted the first guy around two this afternoon.

He'd taken a seat against a boulder at the edge of a small clearing, and had been visible when the drone flew over.

Unfortunately, it took us almost four hours to get to him, only to find he had succumbed to his injuries right where he sat down. The only thing visible on the outside was an open head wound, and massive bruising along his lower ribs. The general consensus was he must've sustained internal injuries and bled out over the course of some time.

Poor guy.

Of course, that made finding his buddy even more urgent, but also more of a challenge, since dead men can't give directions. The best we can do is try to retrace this guy's tracks, but with the light fading fast, that is becoming virtually impossible.

Sully is still flying the new drone, which is outfitted with a thermal imaging camera, but a lot of things give off a heat signature after a mostly warm, sunny day. It can distinguish small temperature differences, which helps filter out whether you're looking at a person or a rock. It's effective when you are searching a small area, but pretty tedious and slow when you have the entire side of a mountain to explore.

The satellite radios Dan and Wolff are carrying on their hips crackle alive with Jonas's voice.

*"Give me an update, guys."*

Wolff answers, "We've got the first guy wrapped up and ready to transport down. It's no use stumbling around blindly. We're almost out of light. Want us to head back?"

*"No. Not with little visibility and on tired horses. Camp down where you are. If there is any chance this other guy is still breathing, I want you out there and looking at first light instead of having to haul back up the mountain."*

Knowing we'd have to haul out one, perhaps two extra people, we brought Hannah, our pack mule. She hauled up some of our supplies, like food and water for us and the animals. We each carry our own sleeping bags and small survival shelters, designed to keep you somewhat protected from the elements.

It takes us ten minutes to set up camp, and JD already has a fire going to heat water for the MREs, while the rest of us get the horses secured and settled in with some water and food. Then Dan and I haul a few fallen logs around the fire to serve as benches while we wait for dinner to rehydrate in the foil bags.

I like nights like these. The environment is much different, but the camaraderie around the fire reminds me of the many nights in the field with my special ops team. It was always either the lull before the storm, or the relief after completing another successful assignment that set the tone. Tonight, it's a little of both.

When I finish my beef stew in a pouch, I slide my ass down to the ground, lean my back against the log, tilt my head back, and listen to the muted conversation between my teammates. Every so often the moon peeks through the clouds, bathing the mountainside in a faint, blue-silver light that catches on the rocks and treetops. If it was a completely clear night, we'd be able to see the skies filled with millions of stars, but even only the occasional glimpse is worth the view.

It would be a perfect night, if not for the body of a forty-one-year-old father of two lying twenty feet from me, wrapped in a plastic body bag.

"You're quiet tonight," Dan observes, sitting down on the ground beside me and mimicking my pose. "Are you sore?"

"Nah," I deny, even though my body sings a different tune.

"You're a fucking liar."

I grin at the brotherly accusation. I guess it shows a level of acceptance when your teammate bluntly calls you out. It feels weirdly good. Like I'm part of something again. I've felt a bit like the team's stepchild until now. In part because my recovery limited my abilities, but I also kept myself apart, feeling I didn't quite measure up or belong.

That's changing though; right now, out here under the stars, I feel equal. In more ways than one. It's not only because I rode side by side with these men all day without needing, or being given, any special consideration. Tonight, I also feel a connection because, for the first time, I know there is someone at home waiting for me too.

It's a fucking great feeling.

"Put your damn weight behind it!"

I brace myself on my good leg, dig my fake heel into the dirt, and lean back into the rope I have wrapped around my waist. Sweat is pouring down my face as Wolff and I haul the immobilized body of the second climber up from the canyon below.

We set out at first light this morning, and with Sully already flying the drone overhead, it took us only a little over an hour to locate the guy. No one expected to find him alive, but he was. Alive and talking. Not very coherently, mind you, but given his condition after the fall, coupled with two nights of exposure to the elements, that wasn't a surprise. Aside from his physical injuries, I can only imagine what this experience will do to his psyche, especially once he discovers the friend who went to get help for him is dead.

Experiences like this mess with your mind.

I should know.

A hoarse cry comes from the inflatable full-body cast we wrapped the man in as we manage to haul him over the last rock lip onto level ground. Wolff is already moving to his side, while I bend forward, trying to suck air back into my lungs. A few moments later, I feel a clap on my back to find JD standing beside me. He must've climbed up beside the injured man to try and keep him steady as we muscled him out of the canyon.

Dan and JD have the most experience climbing and rappelling, so they went down to stabilize him the best they could for transportation. This was only the beginning though. We still have to get him down the mountain to proper medical care.

While Dan makes his way back up to us, and Wolff tends to the climber, JD and I put together the rescue litter so we can mount it behind Hannah, who already has the dead guy strapped to her back. It'll be slow going down since we have to find a route with as few obstacles as possible so the injured guy doesn't get banged around any more than is necessary. It already won't be a fun ride for him, considering he'll be staring at his dead friend's body all the way.

"Let's move the dead guy," I suggest. "I'll take him on Banner."

My horse, Banner, is one of the steadiest horses on the ranch. A canon could go off and he wouldn't flinch. Besides that, he's sturdy and can handle the extra weight.

"Why? Hannah can handle both," JD points out, looking confused.

"I know." I turn to where Wolff is talking to the guy in a

calm voice. "But he'd have to look at that body bag for God knows how long."

Understanding washes over his face as he nods. "Gotcha."

The sun is high in the sky, baking us as we finally lumber into base camp five and a half hours later. The fire department's EMS team is waiting with an ambulance they managed to get up to the trailhead. We had to stop several times to check on our patient, and a communal sigh of relief goes up when we're finally able to hand him off to the paramedics. It's one thing to find him alive, it's another making sure he stays that way while extracting him.

That leaves his dead friend, whose body I had strapped to the saddle in front of me the whole way down. Not an experience I care to repeat, but better me staring at his body bag than his friend, who was devastated enough as it was to find out he didn't make it.

I'll remember his name, like those of many who went before him.

Enzo Baffa; he died a hero.

# Twenty-Two

STEPHANIE

"They found them."

I look up to see Alex walking down the path toward me.

I've been sitting out here for a while, nursing my coffee, which is stone cold by now, and watching the sun rise to its highest point in the sky over the ranch. It's warm, and it is a beautiful day to be out and enjoy the view, but my patience is wearing thin.

Wilcox promised me last night he would try and look into the location for Tracy's phone if he could find a quiet moment to do it unobserved, but I haven't heard from him yet. I'm not used to waiting.

I plaster on a smile for Jackson's mother, even though it takes me a moment to clue in to what she's talking about.

"The two hikers. They found them," she clarifies.

"Of course." I shake my head. "Sorry, my mind was else-where. That's great news."

"Jonas says it'll be a while yet before they can get them down the mountain, but he thinks the crew should be home in a couple of hours."

"Good. That's good. That is...are they okay? The hikers, I mean?"

I can already tell from her wince at my question, the news may not all be good.

"He asked me to dispatch an ambulance so it'll be waiting at the trailhead. He didn't ask for two ambulances."

I have no trouble understanding the implication of a single ambulance. One injured, which leaves me to deduce the other is no longer in need of medical care. Immediately, my thoughts go to Jackson, and I worry about his mental state, but I'm not sure if that's a subject I should discuss with his mother, so I refrain from asking how he's doing.

She may have worries of her own though, because she sits down on the small porch beside me and lets her gaze drift out to the view.

"It can be tough on the guys," she begins. "It's great when they can rescue and bring people back alive, but unfortunately, all too often, they find death instead—sometimes very ugly—and in some cases they carry that burden with them. Questioning themselves if they've done all they could. Were they fast enough? If they'd gone north instead of east, could they have been in time?"

She sighs, wringing the hands in her lap.

"For some of them, it can trigger memories they'd rather not revisit. I know Jonas still wakes up in the middle of the night from nightmares from time to time. These men rarely talk, some are so closed off they never do, and others just get angry. All we can do is be there for them to grab hold of when they need us."

She looks at me with a plea in her eyes, and I know it's not Jonas who's on her mind, but Jackson. I cover her clasped hands in her lap with one of mine.

"He talks to me. I'm sure not about everything, but some of it," I assure her. "Maybe it's because I've shared some of my own struggles and experiences with him. But regardless, I think he knows I'm here for him."

Alex shakes her head, clearly struggling not to cry as she grabs on to my hand.

"Only one thing worse than seeing your man in pain, it's seeing your child in agony and knowing there is nothing you can do for him. I am so glad—so grateful—he has found a strong, compassionate woman to lean on when he needs to."

Oh dear. I feel my own eyes burning and my nose starts to sting. What do you say to that? You can't say thank you to a compliment as profound, a trust as deep as she's offering me.

So I say nothing and hold on to her hand as I let a tear of my own roll down my cheek.

For someone who used to pride herself on her tough exterior, I sure am turning into a bit of a powder puff.

I don't get a chance to indulge in the discovery of my softer side for long because my phone—which I'd propped up on the porch railing—starts ringing. Shane Wilcox's name pops up on the screen. The call I was waiting for.

"I'm so sorry, I have to take this," I apologize, snagging the phone as I get to my feet. "I'll be right back."

"I'll leave you to it." Alex stands up as well.

"No, please...this'll only take a minute."

I quickly slip inside as I answer the call.

"What have you got for me?"

"Hello to you too," Shane responds sarcastically.

"Sorry," I mumble.

"You're forgiven. It took me a while, I guess you were waiting by the phone."

"Something like that."

"That phone number, I didn't exactly get a pinpoint reading on it—which is always a problem in rural settings and in particular the mountains—but I'm sending you the information. What I *can* tell you is that the phone didn't travel too far."

"What do you mean?"

"I've gotta go, but check the map I just sent you."

The line goes dead.

I immediately check my emails and open the one from Shane.

Well, I'll be damned. I can see what he means that it's not a precise location, the circle on the map is at least a couple of miles in diameter. But it's covering an area I'm familiar with, just north of Troy, and bisecting the circle I can clearly make out Waterfront Road, where Tracy Elliston lives.

Annoyed, I immediately dial Ben Vallard, who answers on the third ring. I don't give him a chance to say anything.

"This was a waste of a good favor," I launch in on him, while texting him the image Shane sent me. "Her cell phone is still at the trailer."

"No, it's not."

His quick and confident response throws me for a minute.

"How would you know that? Ben...were you in her trailer?"

It might be different if she was reported as a missing person, but she isn't, and for him to gain access to her trailer without cause could get him into big trouble.

"It doesn't matter. Her phone is not there," he insists.

"Look at the screenshot I sent you."

Some rustling can be heard on the other end, followed by a muffled curse.

"Are you still sure?" I prompt him.

"Yes. It's not in her trailer," he confirms.

All kinds of different scenarios play through my mind. She could have dropped it, but it's hard to believe she wouldn't have discovered that quickly and returned. Unless, of course, she dropped it but wasn't able to return. Because someone was restraining her, or worse, she was injured or dead.

I shake my head to stop my mind from running away from me. I need to stick to the facts and her phone may be a source of information, if I can get my hands on it.

"We have to look for it."

"It'll have to wait until I get back this afternoon. I'm in Eureka, running down a lead."

I don't want to wait around. Tracy's been missing for days already, if she was in any way hurt, we may well be too late already, but I'm not about to take that chance.

"Fine," I tell Ben, already shoving my feet into a pair of runners.

I'll deal with the fallout later.

I'd almost forgotten about Alex, who gets to her feet when she sees the keys dangling from my hand as I step outside.

"Is everything okay?"

I realize I'm being pretty rude, running out on Alex when I'm the one who invited her to stay in the first place. She deserves an explanation.

"I'm so sorry. I have to run out to Troy. I have to check on someone. She may be in trouble."

She puts a hand on my forearm.

"Alone?"

I plaster a reassuring smile on my face.

"I'm an FBI agent, I'll be fine."

"Are you armed?"

Unfortunately, the fire destroyed my Glock. I guess I could lie, but this is Jackson's mother.

"I've been well-trained in hand-to-hand combat. I can hold my own," I attempt to placate her.

Her face sets in a stubborn expression I vaguely remember my mom wearing from time to time.

"I'm sure you can, but I'd feel a whole lot better if you were armed. Come with me, you can have your pick from what's in the gun safe in the office."

I'm not going to say no to that. I'm quite confident in my abilities to at least make it difficult for someone to over-power me, if it came to that, but it's nice to have the security of a weapon when you don't know what you're walking into.

I follow her to the ranch house, where she unlocks the large safe for me. I select a Smith & Wesson, compact and light enough to slip inside my waistband so I can keep my hands free. To my surprise, Alex reaches for a second compact weapon, expertly slipping in a clip before shoving it in the pocket of her jean jacket.

"What are you doing?"

She jerks up her chin and stares me down.

"I'm your backup. I'm coming."

I start shaking my head. "I don't think that's a good—"

A hand in my face cuts me off.

"I'm a mother; my son would disown me if I let anything happen to the woman he loves."

I glance at her with my mouth open.

*Love?* Whoa. That word hasn't come up, it's way too soon for feelings that big.

Isn't it?

He'd be moving pretty fast, but that shouldn't surprise me.

Not from a man who earned the nickname, High Velocity.

*Yikes.*

~

*Jackson*

I can't wait to take this damn fake leg off and hop in the shower.

I'm grimy, sweaty, and I probably reek to high heaven, and despite the new sleeve, my stump feels like rare hamburger at the moment.

Thirty-six hours is a long time to be wrapped in silicone without air circulation, especially inside my old prosthesis. Sitting in the saddle for a day and a half, the edge of the socket rubbed the inside of my thigh raw. I'd be surprised if I didn't break the skin.

But, all complaining aside, we did manage to get one hiker out before the animals could get at him, and were able to keep his friend alive long enough to get him down the mountain and in the hands of medical professionals. Obviously, it would've been nice to rescue them both, but one is better than none.

"You're limping," Jonas observes when I round the back of the trailer to help unload the horses.

We're back at the barn, and I'm eager to get the horses looked after so I can call it a day.

"I'm fine." I rap my knuckles on the rigid socket. "This old thing was made for walking, not riding."

Unlike my newer model, which was designed for a variety of physical activities.

"How long before they fix the other one?"

"I'm hoping a week or so. They'll call me when it's done."

Jonas nods as he unlatches the trailer gate and I help him lower it. Then he turns to me.

"Go home, have a shower, you're bleeding."

He points at my jeans where I notice a stain forming on the inner part of my thigh. *Wonderful.*

As I turn to head to my cabin, I pull my phone from my pocket. I'd left it powered off, since there was no signal up there anyway, but I want to check if Stephanie left me a message. I noticed her rental gone when we drove up.

> Running a few errands. Hope to be back before you get there.

That was sent at a little before two, it's coming up on four now. I send her a quick message back as I walk up to the front door.

> Just got back. Hopping in the shower.
> See you soon.

Inside I strip down, remove my limb, and check the damage. It's not bad, just rubbed raw and oozing. I take the sleeve into the shower to give it a good rinse. I think I'll make do with crutches tonight, give my leg a rest. I don't plan on going out anyway, other than perhaps the main house to grab some grub. I'm sure Ma has something cooking, Jonas said he gave her a heads-up we'd be home soon.

I stuff my dirty clothes straight in the washer before taking a nice leisurely shower. I'd half expected Stephanie to come in at some point, but when I come out of the bathroom fifteen minutes later, she still hasn't returned. I check my phone again, but she hasn't responded to my last message. I immediately dial her number, but after several rings, I get bumped to her mailbox. I don't bother leaving a message.

I try not to get worried as I get dressed, but I find myself fitting my prosthesis back on after all. I'll just head over to the ranch and check in with Ma, maybe she talked to Stephanie and knows where she may have gone.

Jonas is by himself in the kitchen, his phone to his ear and thunder in his eyes when they lock on me.

"Fucking pick up, Alex," he growls before slamming his fist down on the counter.

"What's going on?"

"Nothing good," he grumbles, brushing past me and marching to his office.

I follow to find him standing beside the gun safe, pointing at two empty spaces.

"I noticed them missing when I went to put my rifle away. Now why the hell would your mother take two handguns from the safe? Hell, the only reason she knows how to use them is because I made her practice.”

He throws his arms up in frustration. “Her wheels are here, where the hell could she’ve gone off to?”

“Stephanie is gone too, but so is her rental,” I volunteer, a tight ball forming in the pit of my stomach. “She left me a message saying she was running errands. Ma may have gone with her.”

“Yeah? And what fucking errands require them to be armed?”

The phone he’s still holding in his hand pings with an incoming message.

“It’s your Ma.”

I look over his shoulder to read along.

> Can’t talk now. Stephanie may be in trouble.

“What the fuck is going on?” Jonas bursts out.

“Where are they?” I bark, and his thumbs immediately type out a single word.

> Where?

My heart is pounding in my ears as we wait for a response. When it finally comes, it turns my blood cold.

North of the river in Troy. Old trailer. There were shots, I'm hiding.

"Tell her to stay put," I snap at Jonas, snatching a rifle and a handgun from the safe. "I think I know where they are."

# Twenty-Three

STEPHANIE

"I need you to stay here."

Instead of driving all the way up to the trailer, I pull off to the side of the driveway a few hundred feet away. I'd rather walk the rest of the way in and keep my eyes open, but I don't want Alex to leave the safety of the car.

"How am I supposed to back you up if I stay in the car?" she objects.

"We can exchange phone numbers, and you can keep an eye on me from here." We swap phones and enter our numbers. "And if anything happens, I want you to get out of here," I add as I take my phone back, and leave the keys in the ignition for her.

The last thing I want is to put Jonas's wife and Jackson's mother in any danger.

She doesn't look too pleased with me, but I ignore her as I slip my cell in my pocket and the borrowed gun in the back of my waistband, and get out of the vehicle.

Something is not sitting right with me.

The whole drive over here my mind has been going a mile a minute, trying to come up with some kind of theory that would explain everything that has happened. But some of the pieces simply won't fit.

Then, as I pulled into the driveway and saw the trailer in the distance, something hit me. If Tracy's phone is pinging around here somewhere, it doesn't bode too well for her because it would indicate she's either hurt, dead, or taken against her will. But if that's the case, then where is her car? Why isn't that gray Pontiac Vibe still parked in front of her trailer?

Unless she, or someone else, moved that vehicle to support the story about her leaving for Helena. Still, if that were the case, why would she toss her phone out somewhere around here? If she was afraid someone would use it to track her, wouldn't she try to destroy it? Take the sim card, toss it in the lake. Anything but leave it lying around near her trailer. It wouldn't fit with the story she'd be trying to create.

No, wherever Tracy is, I don't think she went voluntarily. Everything I've learned so far would support that. Which means I need to watch my back, because I have no clue what the endgame is here. I don't know how it ties in with the fire or even the tires on Jackson's truck, but my gut tells me those things are connected, and it feels like I'm in the middle of it.

Except I have no idea how I got there.

Without losing track of my surroundings, I scan the ground for a phone or anything else that might give me a clue of what happened to Tracy. Ten minutes of that and I realize I'm looking for a needle in a haystack. I pull my cell phone from my pocket to study the image Wilcox sent me.

The red-shaded circle covers a larger area than just this

property. It includes the surrounding land and a scant handful of homes—mostly trailers like this one—spread out through the woods. Unless I stumble over it, I'm never going to be able to find the phone by myself.

On a gamble, I hit redial on Tracy's phone number, hoping perhaps I can hear it. It rings once and then the call is dropped. When I check my phone, I see I only have one bar. Dammit. With so many mountains around, it's always a bit of a crapshoot whether you get decent reception or not. I guess no shortcuts for me.

I keep searching, checking the number of bars on my phone every so often as I slowly make my way around the house. I'm afraid if I dial the number too often, I'll drain the battery on her cell and then I won't be able to get a bead on it at all, so I try to pace myself.

At the back of the property, I stumble onto what looks like a game trail; a narrow path through the fairly dense underbrush. What draws my attention though is the sight of shoe prints in the still damp earth between the ferns. The ridged edges and distinct pattern hold my attention. Opening the photo library on my phone, I locate the image I took by Jackson's truck, right beside one of its deflated tires.

The shoe print—boot print is probably more accurate —looks identical, up to and including the small imperfections, likely made by gravel stuck between the treads.

I stick out my women's size eight foot, hovering it over the print, confirming the boot that left the imprint is about a twelve. Too big for Tracy, I'm sure. I would've noticed if she had men's size twelve feet. Besides, she doesn't seem the type to wear hiking boots. I snap a few quick pictures.

These prints haven't been here that long. Someone has been here within the past day or two at most.

Glancing back, I can't see the driveway from here, which

means Alex can't see me either. I don't want her to worry, so I try to call her, but this time I don't even get a ring before the call is dropped. Often times text can still get through since it requires less signal strength for transmission, so I quickly shoot off a message.

> Checking out a path behind trailer. Won't be long.

I don't wait for a response and slip the phone back in my pocket. Reaching around the small of my back, I check to make sure I can easily reach the gun I tucked back there. Then I set out on the path, following the direction of the prints and making sure I don't step on them.

I pass the rear of a few houses, but I'm still spotting a print here and there, continuing on the trail. When I reach the back of another property—this one looks more like a junkyard than a home—I no longer see any prints ahead. Checking out the place, I notice several old vehicles, an old motorhome, rusted bedsprings, a couple of big drums, stacks of old tires, and even an ancient tractor scattered around the property. There are even some raised garden beds, at one time probably used to grow vegetables or something, but they are wildly overgrown with weeds. The trailer home itself doesn't look much better than the sorry state of the yard. The only exception is the green tarp covering some vehicle right behind the building.

The folds in the clean plastic still look crisp and new, and my interest is piqued, but so is my sixth sense. It feels like I have eyes on me, and I furtively glance around me, my hand finding the butt of my gun at the small of my back. The fact I don't see anyone doesn't necessarily mean anything, there are plenty of opportunities to hide in this junk-riddled yard or the trees beyond.

I stand still for a minute or two, simply listening for any movement, but I don't hear much beyond the expected muted sounds of nature. Nothing moves.

Standing still won't find me Tracy though, so—staying alert—I slowly approach the covered vehicle.

Part of me already knows what I'll find underneath. Call it intuition or a gut feeling, but when I lift the edge of the tarp and reveal the distinct red logo against gray paint, I'm not surprised.

Instinctively I sniff the air for the scent of decomposition. It wouldn't be the first time we find a vehicle, only to discover the victim inside. I don't smell it though, and I have a sharp nose. The scent is distinctive enough not to be confused with the smell of damp or rotting vegetation, which there is plenty of. No guarantees until I get a good look, but that's going to have to wait until Vallard gets here.

He didn't seem in too much of a hurry when I spoke to him earlier, but I bet he'll put his foot on the gas when he hears I found her car. I drop the tarp and produce my phone, hoping for a pocket of decent cell reception. The two bars staring back at me are encouraging.

But before I have a chance to dial, a shot rings out. I drop the phone and duck down, but it's not until I try to reach behind me for the gun, I notice my right arm won't work. When I look down, I see blood dripping down my hand.

Then the pain sets in.

I fight to keep a clear mind, and slip my left hand behind my back. It's a bit awkward since the gun is angled the wrong way, but I manage to get my hand on the butt and pull it free. I guess those target shooting sessions my father subjected me to, where he made me shoot both right- and left-handed, are coming in handy now.

I try to peek around the vehicle to see if I can pinpoint the shooter, when another sharp gun crack forces me back down. Whoever is shooting at me is doing so from the far side of the trailer. Ignoring my injured arm, which feels like it weighs a ton and burns like it's on fire, I slide down on my stomach, inching my way under the vehicle. Praying I don't run into a snake, I crawl and claw my way to the back of the car, where I have a better view peeking out from under the bumper.

Someone used an old drum under the downspout on the back corner of the trailer to collect rainwater, probably to water those garden beds, but I'm guessing that was a good while ago. The rusted drum, full to the brim and spilling over, provides decent protection for someone trying to stay out of sight.

Ignoring the sweat and dirt stinging my eyes, I try to steady my left hand wrapped around the gun and line up my sight. It would be an awkward shot if I was taking it with my right hand, but even more so with my left and under these conditions. Still, the barrel is a large enough target.

I fire off two shots in quick succession. The first one is too high, clipping the top rim of the barrel, so I immediately adjust my sight and fire again. There is no reaction. No responding shot, no sounds of someone scrambling to get out of range. Odd, I would've bet the bullets aimed at me came from that direction.

With adrenaline fueling me, I scoot forward a little and push up the edge of the tarp to look for vantage points. Not a lot of alternative cover on that side of the trailer. Unless he was lying flat on the shallow roof of the trailer.

*Shit.*

If he was up on the roof, that would suggest he had time to prepare, which can only mean one thing; he was watching. I bet if I hadn't been looking at the ground to look for tracks, I'd probably have seen game cameras or something like that mounted along the trail.

I scan the roofline, which only has a very slight pitch, but see nothing. No movement. If he was up there, he isn't now.

Or she.

Somehow, I automatically assumed the shooter is a man, and in the back of my mind decided it's got to be Mitchel Laine, but who's to say it isn't Tracy Elliston taking potshots at me?

I don't have time to waste trying to figure out who has their finger on the trigger. I could stay put and wait for Vallard to show up but, as much as I dislike the man, I can't have him walk in on an ambush. Not to mention, Alex is out there waiting for me in the car. I can't risk her safety.

Taking a moment, I try to have a quick look at my shoulder. The entire right side of my torso is on fire, but all I can see is a relatively small entry wound almost on top of my shoulder, supporting my guess I was shot from above. At least the bleeding doesn't seem too bad, it's not gushing.

Rather than waste time trying to patch myself up, I decide to forge ahead. With the gun firmly clenched in my left hand, I wiggle my way out from under the car, keeping a sharp eye out for movement around me at all times. A brief and random thought flashes through my mind, wondering how my blood pressure is faring at the moment. Probably not too good. But on a brighter note, I'm not having a panic attack.

Clearing my head with a shake, I force myself to focus as I inch my way closer to the corner. Crouching down, I now use the rain barrel to shield me from view from the side of the house. The ground at my feet is saturated, making a squishy sound as I shift a little to find a more comfortable position. Then I slowly lift my head to clear the edge of the barrel in my vision.

Nothing, other than a few stacked flowerpots and a partial bag of potting soil that look like they've been here a while. At some point someone cared about this place, but now it reeks of neglect.

"Drop the gun in the barrel."

Every hair on my body stands on end at the sound of a gravelly man's voice right behind me. But it's the pressure of a barrel at the back of my neck that has the fingers on my left hand open up. A couple of droplets splash up when the gun hits the water with a plunk.

"Cell phone too."

My heart is heavy when I send that down to the bottom of the barrel as well.

If I had the use of both arms, I'd use this moment to attempt a tried and tested maneuver to disarm him, but it would be suicide to try with one arm. I will have to wait for another opportunity. If he wanted me dead, he could have easily killed me. The fact I'm still breathing means he still has use for me, and therefore there is time for me to plan.

The only time I ever heard Mitchel Laine speak, prior to today, was to ask for his lawyer. He never spoke during the numerous interviews or even during his trial, staying mum through the whole ordeal. That doesn't mean I didn't recognize his voice instantly.

"Where is Tracy?" I ask.

But instead of answering, he grabs hold of my ponytail, and with his gun still pressed in my neck, starts marching me to the front of the trailer. There, he forces me through the front door, kicking it shut behind us. But before I have a chance to take stock of my surroundings, he lets go of my hair and with a violent shove in my back, sends me sprawling face-first to the floor.

I'm given no time to recover when a dirty hiking boot is planted in my neck, keeping me pinned to the dirty linoleum.

"Get the zip ties," he barks.

My eyes track the sound of shuffling and find Tracy bruised, naked, and on all fours, scrambling for a ratty backpack sitting on the floor by a threadbare couch. I watch as she digs through the contents and comes up with a pair of black zip ties. It's not until she turns around I see the full extent of her injuries. She's almost unrecognizable. That bastard used her as a punching bag. Her eyes are almost swollen shut, blood is crusted under her obviously broken nose, and a deep slice on her cheekbone probably should've had stitches.

When her barely visible eyes catch on me, her lips form an apology.

"I'm so sorry," she whispers on a sob as she crawls toward me.

# Twenty-Four

*JACKSON*

"That's the rental."

I point at Stephanie's vehicle, tucked up against the trees on the side of the driveway. It looks to be empty.

We left Jonas's truck parked on the opposite side of the road, right by a river access trail. Let them think we've gone fishing. My mother's last message mentioned a trailer and Troy in the same sentence. Only one place I could think of where Stephanie might be going; Tracy's place. She probably spoke with Vallard, I'm just not clear on what the hell Ma is doing with her.

Junior Ewing will be pissed we didn't wait for the sheriff's deputy to get here, but neither Jonas nor I are about to sit on our hands until he arrives. We called him as we were leaving the ranch, but he said he had his hands full with an explosion at the Country Inn in downtown Libby he'd just been called out to, but he promised to send one of his deputies.

We passed the Country Inn on our way to Troy and could see it was a chaotic scene. Smoke billowed from the rear of the property, and it looked like the entire fire department had rolled out and was trying to stop the fire from spreading throughout the hotel. I'm guessing people got hurt, because we spotted at least two ambulances in the parking lot as we drove by, as well as a number of sheriff's cruisers.

It was clear emergency services would have their hands full for a while, so I'm not holding my breath for that deputy he promised. Besides, other than flash a badge, there's nothing some snot-nosed community college graduate can do that Jonas or I can't do better.

"Where the fuck is she?"

Jonas scans the trees for a sign of my mother, who is nowhere to be seen. She did say she was hiding, but I know my mother, I doubt she stayed put like Jonas told her to do.

"She still not answering her messages?"

Jonas checks his phone again, clearly annoyed. "No, and let's just hope it's because she was smart enough to turn off the ringer, and not for any other reason. Let's check the trailer."

We've been quiet in our movements so far, speaking in low voices and attempting not to announce our approach, but we're about to step out into the open. I move the rifle I brought to my left hand and pull the handgun from my waistband with my right. I have no idea what we're walking into, only that at some point there was shooting. I'm not taking any chances.

The trailer looks empty, but it's clear there's been activity recently.

"It rained overnight," Jonas observes, pointing at what

looks to be a muddy footprint on the front step. "Which would mean that was left sometime this morning."

Makes sense, otherwise the rain would've washed it away.

"Small print. Woman?" I suggest.

"Probably." He tries the front door, which is locked.

"Looks like whoever it was tried to peek in the window here. The grass is trampled."

Jonas leads the way around to the back of the house where he points to a narrow trail that seems to run along the back of the neighboring properties. It's really no more than a game trail, but Jonas crouches down and appears to examine the ground.

"I count at least three different prints." He indicates several overlapping tracks.

One looks to be the same small boot print as from the front step. It's smooth, with little ridging, and is superimposed on two others. Those look to have been made by something a little heavier, with deep treads like a hiking or a combat boot. All prints are aimed in the same direction though.

I follow Jonas, keeping a sharp eye on our surroundings and making sure our flanks and rear are clear, while he keeps his attention ahead on the trail. We never served together, but seem to instinctively fall into our respective roles.

I almost run into him when he suddenly slows down.

"*There*," he mouths, pointing toward what looks to be a junkyard, at an old Chrysler LeBaron which is rusting underneath an old, knotty tree.

Squinting my eyes, I try to make out what he's looking at. A slight movement catches my eye and now I see my mother, most of her hidden from view from this angle. I give Jonas a thumbs-up in acknowledgment. Ma is crouched by the taillight on the driver's side, hidden in the shadows of the large tree. She appears to be shielding herself from view from the rundown mobile home on the property.

Then I hear a muffled voice, coming from the direction of the trailer. A man's voice.

Jonas hears it too and turns to me, a finger to his lips. Then he gestures for me to take cover while he approaches Ma. I don't argue, it's hard to move in complete silence with a prosthetic leg, and the last thing we want to do is startle my mother into giving herself away. Whoever is inside that trailer could be watching right now.

For an old guy, Jonas is still pretty limber, making himself as small as possible and using his surroundings as cover, as he moves toward the Chrysler. At the same time, I find cover behind an old RV and tuck the gun back in my waistband before lifting my rifle to my shoulder. Pressing my eye against the scope, which has a 15x magnification range, I find the trailer in my sight, keeping an eye out for any movement.

A piercing scream has the hair on my neck stand on end, and it takes every ounce of my control not to depress the finger I have lightly curled around the trigger.

With a quick sideways glance, I catch Jonas closing in on Ma, who is getting up out of her crouch. I watch him band his arms around her from behind, covering her mouth with a hand as he pulls her back. Then he begins retracing his steps, holding her close to him.

Time slows down to a crawl, and I fight with everything in me not to go charging the trailer I'm, once again, closely watching for movement. If Stephanie is in there, I won't be helping her by announcing our approach, and possibly turn her into a human shield. Unless it's Tracy in that trailer, and that scream belonged to her.

There's really no way to tell, which is why we need some more clarity I hope my mother will be able to provide.

"Fall back," Jonas mumbles as he passes, pulling Ma to shelter.

With one last look at the trailer home, I lower my rifle and join them, ducking behind the ramshackle motorhome. Ma does not look happy, and neither does Jonas, who is trying to stare her down. You'd think by now he'd know that's a battle you can't win with her.

"What the hell were you thinking?" Jonas growls, cracking first as expected. "Sneaking around the woods by yourself, fueled by more balls than brains."

I'm not sure that's the way to approach Ma, but it's too late to intervene, she's already building up steam.

"Watch your mouth or you'll find out what I can do with *your* balls," she spits. "And for the record, I wasn't by myself, I was with Stephanie—"

"Who is a goddamn FBI agent," he interrupts. "For fuck's sake, Alex."

"She's the mother of my future grandbabies, you moron, and she was in trouble."

Jesus, this is not helpful, so when Jonas opens his mouth to respond, I hold up my hands to cut them off. The comment about grandbabies I tuck away for later consideration.

"Enough," I hiss, focusing my attention on my mother. "In as few words as possible, what the fuck happened?"

Ma nods sharply and takes a deep breath, while Jonas audibly grinds his teeth together.

"Stephanie was looking for a phone and told me to wait in the car, which I did. Then she disappeared behind the house and messaged me she found a trail she was checking out. The only reason I left the car then was so I could keep an eye on her."

"Christ," Jonas groans, dropping his head in his hands.

"From a distance," Ma hisses, before she turns back to me. "Anyway, I didn't have any cell reception or I would've called. Especially after that guy showed up when I was checking around the trailer."

"What guy?" I interrupt.

"I don't know, I heard something, turned around and some guy was checking out Stephanie's car. I've never seen him. He had the door open and poked his head inside. I couldn't really see what he was doing, but when the first shot rang out, he backed out of the car with a gun in his hand, so I ducked down and hid under the trailer."

"He shot the gun?" Jonas prompts.

"No, the shots were a distance away."

"So more than one?" I try to clarify.

"A single shot first, I hid, and the guy came up the drive, moved right by the trailer and around the back. That's when there were two more shots, in quick succession, and he started running in the direction of the sound. Three in total, I think. Or maybe four."

"And you thought it was a good idea to follow?" Jonas snaps.

"Stephanie is out there, people were shooting, and now this strange guy waving a gun is heading in her direction. Hell yes, I thought it was a good idea to stack the odds in her favor."

I motion for them to keep it down; the volume of this hushed conversation is starting to creep up.

Suddenly, I hear a woman's voice yell, "Please, no!" followed by the sharp crack of a gunshot.

An ice-cold fist closes around my heart.

Surely the universe couldn't be this cruel.

~

*Stephanie*
    *Earlier*


This place is a pigsty.

Aside from the empty food wrappers and containers, the crumpled up beer cans everywhere, and the stench of rotting garbage and body odor, every surface seems to be covered in a thick layer of grime and dirt. I don't think this place has seen a mop or a sponge in decades.

If I could wipe my face, I would, but the best I can do is rub the cheek that was pressed into the dirt on the floor on my shoulder. My hands are tied tightly behind my back with zip ties, so those are basically useless. My ankles are bound with more zip ties, but at least I'm still able to kick out. That is, if that coward would come close enough. Instead, he's sitting on a stool at a Formica kitchen table at a safe distance, sipping a damn beer.

Mitchel Laine. Damn, time hasn't been kind to him.

He can't be more than forty-five but looks at least a decade older, with a rapidly receding hairline and a face even a mother would have a hard time loving.

Yet Tracy fell for him. He must have a way with words, because I don't see the attraction. Of course he had five years of virtual anonymity to groom her before meeting her in person.

*Tracy.*

My eyes find the woman, hunched down in a corner of the kitchen. Poor thing, she can't have had any idea what she was getting herself into. When I get her out of here, I'm sure this experience will leave deep scars long after her body has healed.

Because I *will* get her out of here, if it's the last thing I do. Unfortunately, my right arm is useless and there's no way I'll be able to get out of these zip ties with one hand. Also, my gun is at the bottom of the rain barrel, and Laine's weapon on the kitchen table is right in front of him. Not that I'd trust myself to shoot anything at this point, it's tricky enough left-handed, but I'm also starting to feel a little lightheaded. Maybe it's blood loss, or maybe I'm going into shock. Either way, I may need a little assistance.

For now, all I can try and do is keep Laine talking until help arrives. I know Vallard will eventually find his way here—he may be a shit person, but he's a good investigator—or maybe Alex will call in the troops when I don't return.

I remember Laine had a massive ego and a penchant to rant when I collared him all those years ago. Maybe if I provoke a little, I can get him to talk.

"So what's the plan, Mitchel?" I challenge him.

There has to be a reason he didn't simply put another bullet in me and finish the job.

His beady eyes focus on me, but instead of answering, he takes another swig of his beer.

"Don't tell me you don't have one? You had years inside with nothing better to do."

A muscle in his jaw ticks at my taunt, but still no word. I try a different tack.

"Bet you weren't expecting to find me here, were you?"

He unexpectedly barks out a hoarse laugh at that.

"Stupid bitch. Why do you think I'm here?" He turns his head and jerks it in Tracy's direction. "For that bitch? Please. A means to an end, lady."

Tracy's whole body jerks as if he kicked her.

"What end, Mitchel? That's what I'd like to know."

The grin he sends me is bone-chilling.

"Don't play me for an idiot. You know exactly why I'm here; the money."

I'm confused, and the moment I take to process what he's saying doesn't make it any clearer.

"What money?"

"The money you bastards stole from me."

He slams down the empty can and snatches up his weapon, aiming it at me as he gets up on his feet. Tracy whimpers in her corner.

"I don't know what you're talking about."

"Don't give me that, you're in this up to your eyeballs and you know it. It was all a setup to get me to take the fall while you guys took off with my money."

Agitated, he starts pacing, waving his gun around, and I breathe a little easier now it's no longer pointed at my head. In the meantime, I'm desperately trying to make sense of what he's saying.

"We fucking grew up together," he rambles, shaking his head. "Got through high school together, shared pot and girls, and ran into trouble as a team."

I have no idea who he's talking about, but it isn't me. For one thing, I'd have known about any connections between us when I arrested him all those years ago. From what I recall, he grew up in or around Detroit, and Traverse City has always been home to me. Not to mention, he's a fair bit older than I am. Our paths wouldn't have crossed.

But I don't interrupt. Let him rant; as long as he's talking, I'm not only learning, I'm buying time.

"Hell, we broke into cars in the hospital parking lot

together," he continues. "We were tight, even after landing on opposite sides of the fence."

*Opposite sides of the fence?*

"Who are you talking about?" I can't help asking.

He swings the gun around and steps close, pressing the barrel against my forehead. Tracy screams.

"Shut up, you dumb cunt," he barks at her before turning back to me. "And you, don't play dumb with me. You know exactly who. Where is the money, bitch?"

"I swear, I don't know anything about any money."

My eyes find Tracy, who is watching us with tears streaming down her face and her fist shoved in her mouth.

"She doesn't."

I snap my head around at the sound of Ben Vallard's voice, coming from the doorway, and am immediately flooded with relief. *Thank God.*

"Like hell she doesn't," Laine snaps, apparently not at all surprised by Vallard's sudden appearance. The gun in his hand doesn't even waver an inch and is still firmly pressed against my head. "She wasn't just your partner; she was in your goddamn bed. Keeping it all in the family, isn't that what you said? I knew you'd fucking follow me, and you followed me straight here, didn't you?"

*Wait.* Keeping what all in the family?

I watch as Ben's eyes turn to slits and the corner of his mouth pulls up a fraction.

"You're making it so easy," he taunts. "What were you thinking, vandalizing trucks and setting fires? That was you, wasn't it? What were you trying to accomplish?"

"Drawing you out, you moron," Laine reacts. "And it ultimately worked, didn't it? Here you are, and I have a gun to your girlfriend's head, ready to blow it off unless you give me back what you stole from me."

"You're a little behind the times, my friend. She's not my girlfriend, and frankly, you'd be doing me a service. The fewer witnesses left, the better."

My heart lodges in my throat.

"Please, no!" Tracy yells.

The last thing I hear is the loud reverberation of a gunshot and I find myself once more with my face pressed against the dirty linoleum, before everything goes dark.

*Twenty-Five*



It takes every ounce of what little strength I have left to shift the dead weight on top of me.

At this point, I barely even feel my arm anymore, that whole side of my body is going numb, and I'm not sure if that's a good or a bad thing. At least I'm able to breathe again.

He shot him.

Ben Vallard shot Laine, who had a gun pressed against my head. He didn't care.

I'm able to raise my left hand to check for damage, but find my forehead intact.

Lucky.

My eyes find Vallard crossing the room toward Tracy, who is softly crying in the corner. Laine's heavy body still has me pinned and I'm paralyzed as I watch Ben stop a few feet away from her, raise his gun, and shoot her in the head, execution style. I stare in disbelief and swallow a sob as her body hits the ground with a dull thud. A pool of blood slowly spreads under her head like a halo.

The poor woman never had a chance.

"What? No!"

Vallard swings around and seems surprised when he sees me struggling to get out from under the weight pinning me down. Shock and fear and rage fuel me enough to heave Laine's body off me.

"I thought for sure old Mitchel here would take you out with him. That man hated you with everything inside him," Ben calmly informs me.

He looks at me with a faint smile on his face, his arms crossed, holding the gun like some poor imitation of the classic James Bond pose. It's almost like he's mocking me. The thought I ever invited this man's hands on my body turns my stomach.

"He held you responsible, you know?" he continues, before chuckling. "I thought it was quite funny, considering the old man and I were the ones who made sure his ass ended up in jail. He was a loose cannon. He was only supposed to hit banks out of state or at least in outlying jurisdictions, and just the ones we cased for him, but he decided to pick a target on his own. It was too close to home, that was his first mistake, and then he beat that old bird to a pulp. That was the end of the run for old Mitchel."

He barks out a laugh and turns his head, letting his gaze drift out the large picture window, like he's reminiscing or something.

"Even as a kid he was too gullible. It was so easy to get him to do shit and eat the consequences. He got the bad rap and I got off scot-free. I remember my parents telling me not to hang out with him because he was a bad influence. If only they'd known the bad influence was me."

My brain is still scrambling to make sense of what is happening and what he's telling me, when a soft moan draws my attention to Mitchel Laine's body. Is he still alive?

"I told him to keep his mouth shut, no matter what, and he'd be out in no time. I'd make sure of it. Heck, he even bought it when I told him I'd keep his cut safe for him."

He likes to listen to himself talk, *that* I knew about him. One of the telltale signs of a narcissist, along with his inflated sense of self, his arrogance, his callousness, and his manipulative behavior. That's not news to me. But it never occurred to me until now that most of those traits also fit the profile of a psychopath, and that comes as a shock.

I stay quiet and let him orate, absorbing the information he gives me, while I start plotting a way out of this situation with another part of my brain.

Because of one thing I'm sure, Ben Vallard has no intention of letting me go. If I'm to walk out of here, I'll have to make that happen myself.

With his back partly turned to me, I let Ben boast how he let Mitchel Laine believe I was involved in their arrangement, while I inch my way toward the prone man's body. I'm sure I saw his chest move, but helping him isn't the only reason I'm trying to get close; it's the butt of the gun I see poking out from under his shoulder. He must've landed on it when I rolled him off.

"...bastard took off the moment they let him out early. I was too late to welcome him to the outside world with a bullet between the eyes. No one would've been the wiser, but he made me chase him clear across the damn country..."

I can just touch the edge of the gun with my middle finger and try to slide it free, but it's stuck, wedged between the floor and Laine's shoulder. I need to get closer.

"...and when I figured out he was headed your way, I

couldn't believe my luck. I knew all I had to do was wave you in front of him to draw him out of hiding. He always believed you were in on it. I knew he'd want revenge. All I had to do was stick close to you and wait for him to make his move."

When he suddenly turns to face me, I move as well, pushing myself up and leaning forward over Mitchel's upper body. I can feel Vallard's eyes on my back, and I hope like hell, from this angle, he won't be able to see the gun I'm trying to shield.

~

*Jackson*

For a moment we're frozen, the sound of the second shot still reverberating in the air.

I'm the first one to move, but a strong hand grabs my arm and holds me back.

"Stop, breathe, and fucking think before you get yourself or someone else killed," Jonas growls in my ear.

With fear and adrenaline surging through my veins, I need my stepfather's clipped order to remind me of the basics. You don't barge into volatile situations without intel, and right now—other than Stephanie is in that trailer and guns are being fired—I don't have any. I don't know how many people are in that trailer, who is armed, who is hurt. Aside from Stephanie, I don't know fucking friend or foe. For all I know, she's already dead, but I won't know until I get more intel.

I force down the fear and the panic, and suck in a deep breath through my nose.

"I need an eye on the inside."

Jonas nods at me. "Good. Yes, but not much opportunity back here."

He's right, there are only two windows; a small, frosted bathroom window, and I'm guessing the other is to a bedroom and has closed blinds. From the front is the better bet.

"I'll go around. I'll stay out of sight. See if I can find a vantage point, use the scope on my rifle."

"No," Ma interrupts, shaking her head furiously. "I can't—"

Jonas turns to her and cups her face in his hands. She grabs on to his wrists.

"Yes. He knows what he's doing. I wouldn't let him go if I didn't trust one-hundred-percent he's got this."

She doesn't say anything, but drops her head down as Jonas continues to talk to her in a low voice.

"This is what I need from you. I need you to retrace your steps back to the other trailer and wait for the deputy to show up. Then I want you to get him to radio his boss and pass it to you, so you can fill Junior in on the situation here. And for God's sake, do not let that deputy come blundering into this scene because that won't end well for anyone. Fucking tackle him if you must."

If the situation wasn't so dire, I might've laughed at his last words, because if anything could get Ma on board, it was that comment.

But if I don't get moving there may not be much left to laugh about at all.

"I'll be back," I promise with a nod at my mother, before rounding the back of the motorhome and ducking into the cover of the trees.

Since I can't move silently anymore, it's safest to get

some distance, circle around, and approach from the front. With some luck I'll be able to find a tree with adequate handholds I can climb. One that offers me enough of a view inside the trailer so I can get a bead on this clusterfuck.

It's weird, finding myself slipping back into a zone I used to be so familiar with. One where your senses are attuned only to those things you need to see, feel, or hear, and the world around you becomes like a funnel, aimed directly at the objective of your assignment. In the zone, time doesn't exist, and the only reminder it passes is the sound of your own heartbeat.

It's an old, tall pine tree. A Ponderosa pine, in fact: Montana's state tree. What draws my attention at first is the thick cover of the branches and the way the top appears to lean slightly toward the large window and the partially open door I spotted at the front of the trailer home. But it's the shoulder-high stump of a second tree right beside it that has me look a little closer. The top of that tree must've broken off at some point, leaving jagged splinters sticking up. It looks like maybe it was struck by lightning, a scorch mark where the trunk is split down to the soil.

It's perfect. I'd never be able to get up to the shelter of the tall pine's branches without that stump to serve as a ladder of sorts, and from there, I should be able to pull myself up.

I sling the rifle over my shoulder and make my way over. With my back leaning against the stump, I quickly remove my prosthesis, and lay it down at the base, before tucking my loose pant leg in my waistband. It's ungainly and will only get in my way. I'll do better with one leg and two arms; it'll give me more flexibility.

I probably have some serious splinters in my hands, but I make it up into the tree with relative ease. I settle in on a branch that is thick enough to hold my weight, close enough to allow me a clear view inside the window, yet still provides sufficient cover so it'll be hard to spot me.

Lining up my sight, I get my first glance inside the trailer. It's not perfect, there is some reflection on the window that slightly distorts my view, but I'm able to make out one figure standing over what looks like the naked body of a woman.

Bile lurches up from my stomach, but I force it down and will myself to focus.

Movement draws my eye to the far side of the room, where I spot another body—this one looks to be a man— and the slighter figure of a woman with her back to me, leaning over him. As I watch, her head snaps around at the standing man.

*Stephanie.*

It plays out like a slow-motion movie, the way she turns her body, revealing a weapon in her left hand. Then I catch a glimpse of the man's face. Fucking Ben Vallard, and he's raising a gun of his own.

Years of training and experience have forged a direct connection between my eyes and my trigger finger.

No thought is necessary, only instinct.

*Stephanie*

"What are you doing?"

"He's still alive."

I'm surprised how weak my voice sounds. Maybe it's because my mind is working overtime to sort through all the pieces of information he's giving me and trying to sort them in some kind of order that makes sense.

"With a hole in his head?" He snorts. "If he is now, he won't be for long. Leave him."

"You were never in Eureka, were you?" I toss out at him.

"Ding-ding-ding, give the girl a prize. You're finally clueing in to that? No, I wasn't. And if you're banking on help to arrive, that's not coming any time soon either, I made sure of it. They'll have their hands full with the explosion I set off at my hotel."

*Jesus*, this man is diabolical.

"By the time they get here, no one will be left alive. The story that will go down is that I got here a fraction of a second too late, Laine already finished you off and I had no choice but to defend myself when he turned the gun on me."

The gun he's talking about is now firmly clenched in my left hand in front of me, but I need to stop my hand from shaking, because I'll only get one chance.

"The evidence won't support you. How do you explain your bullet in Tracy's head?"

When he barks out a harsh laugh, I whip my head around. The man I see is no one I recognize.

"Evidence can be manipulated. It's not that hard. I learned that from the best." A grin spreads on his face as he leans forward a few inches before adding, "Your father taught me."

He's toying with me. He knows how I've always tried to live up to my dad's expectations. This is what psychopaths do, they use little bits of information they've been given to play games with their victims.

But I'll be damned if I become his next one.

He seems startled for a brief moment when I swing

around, my fingers steady around the butt of Laine's gun and my finger ready on the trigger. The moment I have him lined up in my sights I depress.

I'm not prepared for the hollow sound of an empty magazine, and my lungs deflate.

Slowly, the man I once shared a bed with raises his weapon.

In a single moment, all that could have been, the life I could've led, the man I could've loved, the family I could've had, flashes with painful clarity in my mind.

Then I close my eyes and wait for the end.

# Twenty-Six

*Jackson*

My training dictates I keep my eyes fixed on my target through the scope, until I'm one-hundred-percent sure I've completed my objective and the threat is eliminated.

But I saw the man's head explode as the impact of my high velocity round felled him like a tree, so I doubt he'll be getting up ever again, and I didn't see anyone else moving inside.

*Screw training.*

I scramble down from the branch I was perched on, nearly falling the twenty feet or so I'm up off the ground, but I make it down in one piece. I would've made an easy target, but since no one took potshots at me, I assume the threat was eliminated with Vallard.

Growling in frustration, I realize I'm going to have to strap on my limb if I want to get to Stephanie fast. I was so focused on Vallard, I lost track of where she was. I keep my eye on the trailer, hoping to catch a glimpse of her but instead I see Jonas barreling around the corner, a gun in his hand and yelling at Ma—who is hot on his tail—to stay the hell back.

Needless to say, she's not listening. The moment she spots me she comes running for me, and I barely have the socket fitted over my sleeve when she almost tackles me.

"Oh my God, I was so scared. Are you okay? And Stephanie?"

Up ahead, Jonas is already ducking into the front door of the trailer, leading with his gun. His training shows too. I untangle myself from my mother's arms and hurry after him.

"Stay back until we know it's secure, Ma," I call back over my shoulder.

When I step through the door, the first thing I see is Jonas, kicking away the gun lying inches from Vallard's prone body. But my focus is to his right, where I saw Stephanie through my scope. She's not sitting up now, but is slumped over, the upper half of her body draped over who I presume is Mitchel Laine.

Fear for what I might find does not stop me from rushing to her side and brushing away the hair covering her face. Her eyes are closed, but when I press my shaking fingers against her carotid artery, I find a pulse and a sob of relief escapes me. But there's so much blood, it's hard to know where it's all coming from.

When I carefully roll her off the body and on her back, I sense more than see Jonas crouch down on the other side of Laine's body, but I'm focused on Stephanie.

"What've you got?" he asks.

"Shoulder wound. Can't find anything else, but she's lost a lot of blood."

"Out of my way," Ma snaps, appearing out of nowhere.

"Move," she urges, unceremoniously shoving me aside as she crouches down beside Stephanie.

She immediately starts ripping at Stephanie's shirt, exposing a nasty looking wound in her shoulder.

"Help me roll her," she orders.

When we have her on her side, Ma quickly examines her back, before motioning for me to roll her back.

"No exit wound. The bullet's still in there. We need to get her to the hospital ASAP." She tugs at my shirt. "Take this off, I need it to apply pressure to the wound."

"This one is alive too," Jonas informs us. "Although barely, he's got a fucking hole in his head the size of a golf ball."

"It's going to take too long to get an ambulance here," I point out, as I pull my shirt off over my head. I'm not concerned about that piece of shit, he can croak, but I'm worried about Stephanie. "The volunteer ambulance service in Troy was shut down last year. We're gonna have to drive them out."

I hand my shirt to Ma as Jonas gets to his feet.

"I'll go for the truck; we can fit both of them in the back. Call Ewing, get him to organize Life Flight into Kalispell. With the explosion in Libby, the hospital will already be overwhelmed. They fly Koalas and should be able to take two patients at once. Tell them to land at the Troy airfield, we'll meet them there."

"What explosion in Libby?" Ma asks, but her husband is already running out the door, and I'm busy trying to get the sheriff on the line.

Less than five minutes later, I'm in the back seat with Stephanie, and Jonas is loading Mitchel Laine into the cargo space with the help of the deputy who followed my stepfather's Yukon here. The guy tried to make noise about us leaving the scene, but Jonas took care of that in a hurry. He's now agreed to stay put and guard the crime scene until Junior Ewing—who is on his way—gets here.

Since one of the dead bodies is that of an FBI agent, I'm sure the feds will be crawling all over this place in no time. I have no doubt they'll want to talk to me, since I'm the one who took that man down, but I don't give a flying fuck, they're going to have to wait until I can get Stephanie looked after.

Ma crawls in the back with Laine and Jonas gets behind the wheel. He doesn't mess around; three minutes later we pull onto the small airfield.

I had my fingers resting on her pulse the entire time.

*Stephanie*

The first time I opened my eyes, there was a man in a helmet, hanging over me and the noise was overwhelming. I don't remember anything after that.

This time when I open my eyes, I see the friendly smile of a woman in surgical scrubs.

"Hello there. You're at Logan Medical in Kalispell. You may feel a little groggy, but that is normal since you just came out of surgery. There is a call button clipped to your gown if you need anything, and a doctor will be in shortly to talk to you."

She's gone so quickly; I doubt she heard my whispered reaction. "Surgery?"

I had surgery? How did I end up in Kalispell?

I try to lift my right hand to find this call button she mentioned, but it won't move. Then I notice my heavily bandaged arm and shoulder. My head starts to pound when I try to remember what happened, so I close my eyes.

I must've dozed off again, because this time when I wake up, my entire right side is throbbing with excruciating pain. I quickly close my eyes as a moan escapes me, and I try to find the call button I remember the nurse telling me about.

"Here." The button is pushed in my hand, as I blink open my eyes and find Jackson's face hovering over mine. "Welcome back, Hotshot. I think it's probably time for some pain meds."

I try to nod but it shoots a sharp pain to my shoulder, which already feels like it's on fire. My thumb finds the call button and I hold it down until a nurse rushes in a few moments later. She administers something through my IV, and it thankfully doesn't take too long before the pain becomes more manageable.

"Is that much pain normal?"

She smiles at me. "With this type of surgery, I'm afraid so, but when the doctor gets here, she'll probably put you on a pump. That way you don't have to wait for us for your next dose, you can manage the timing yourself."

The surgeon, a woman I'd guess to be in her mid-to-late fifties with gray hair curling out from under her surgical cap, smiles sweetly as she approaches my bed. She looks more like a cookie-baking grandma than she does someone who cuts open people for a living. As soon as the thought enters my brain, I'm embarrassed to realize I'm stereotyping and how shortsighted it is.

She sits down on the edge of my bed and introduces herself as Dr. Littleton, oblivious to the fact I just mentally placed her in a flour-dusted apron instead of the surgical scrubs she's wearing.

"You were brought in late yesterday afternoon with a gunshot wound to the shoulder. You'd lost a great deal of blood and were in shock, which we dealt with first. As soon as we safely could, we took you up to surgery to find the bullet ended up lodged in your right scapula. Shoulder blade," she clarifies.

I'm still trying to come to terms with the fact I apparently lost a substantial chunk of time somewhere, when her next words draw my focus back.

"We were able to recover the bullet, but it had done extensive damage. You had a break in your shoulder blade that required plates and screws to stabilize. There was also damage to your soft tissue, muscle and such, all of which will heal over time. But the most serious damage was done to your brachial plexus." She uses her hand to illustrate as she explains. "It's a collection of nerves that runs down from the neck and shoulders into the arms and hands, controlling movement and sensation. Sometimes nerves can regenerate but your case required surgical repair, which involved an entire team. Now, we were lucky we happened to have a neurosurgeon available to step in, because the sooner these repairs can be done, the better your chances of recovery. We were able to harvest a nerve from the back of your right leg and graft it into place in your shoulder. The harvested nerve was a sensory nerve, which means there will be a section of your skin on the back of your leg that no longer has sensation. However, in its new place, it should be able to return some, if not most, of the function of your right arm."

"Wait," I interrupt, my heart rate going a mile a minute as my ears start ringing. "Some function? I'm going to have permanent damage? When you say some function, what exactly does that mean?"

Jackson picks up my good hand in his and gives it a little squeeze. It's a small gesture, but it helps me stay grounded. I immediately start breathing in through my nose, trying to regulate my breathing.

Dr. Littleton offers me a sympathetic smile and a gentle pat on my leg.

"Like I said, the injury was substantial, and even though we were able to get in quickly to do repairs, there is no way to tell to what extent the damage is lasting. But I have to be honest with you; complete, full function is not expected with this type of injury. Recovery will require patience and resolve on the part of the patient. It'll be a long road of rehabilitation to gain small, incremental steps forward."

She gets to her feet.

"Now, for at least the next couple of days you'll be our guest, and I want you to focus on resting. I'll be by regularly to check on you, and we should have a better idea of what we have to work with once the swelling goes down a little."

With that she leaves, the nurse scrambling after her muttering something about pain medication. My eyes find Jackson, whose fingers I've been crushing with my left hand. Despite his encouraging smile for me, his eyes are solemn. He looks exhausted and concerned.

He knows—probably better than most—this is the end of my career.

What irony that it should come at the hands of a man whose arrest over a decade ago helped me launch it.

I'm not ready to contemplate the full implications, so I distract myself by asking Jackson, "Do you know how I got here?"

Still holding my hand, he pulls up a rolling stool, sits

down, and starts talking. By the end of it I realize how incredibly lucky I've been.

For starters, if Jackson's mother hadn't insisted on coming, no one would've known where to look for me. I don't even want to think what could've happened to her if she hadn't gotten out of the car and managed to hide.

Next Laine, whose only reason for not killing me right away was to use me as bait for Vallard, and that bullet he intended to end me with never even got fired.

And then Ben...my God. So full of himself as he wasted time taunting me and boasting about his powers of deception. Long enough for Jackson to get there and get a bead on that son of a bitch before he was able to kill me.

I escaped a bullet in my head, not once, but twice. So, yeah, suddenly the damage to my shoulder feels lucky compared to the alternative.

When I'm moved from recovery to a regular hospital room a little later, I'm able to thank Alex and Jonas in person. They apparently drove Jackson straight to Kalispell yesterday afternoon and have been here, waiting with him, ever since.

Realizing that gives me a lump in my throat I have trouble swallowing down. Especially since, by Alex's account, they weren't the only ones in the waiting room.

"JD and Janey drove up last night when they heard," she shares. "They stayed most of the night, waiting to find out if you came through surgery okay. Janey had a full schedule today but they'll be back for a visit tonight."

"Feds got here earlier too," Jonas adds. "Your boss, Bellinger, and Wilcox. They're itching to talk to you, but Jackson's out there holding them off so we could have a quick visit first. I need to get Alex home."

His wife clearly resents that comment as she grunts and plants an elbow in his gut.

"You were yawning pretty hard yourself, old man," she grumbles.

"Well, it wasn't me who thought it was a good idea to go chasing down a violent offender," he mutters back.

The two of them are pretty cute; despite the bickering, their love for each other is written on their faces.

"Thank you." I reach out my hand at Alex and she grabs it in hers. "If you hadn't been there..."

She waves me off with her other hand. "We don't do *what-ifs*. They're a waste of time."

"Still," I insist. "I'm thankful. To both of you," I add, including Jonas with a look.

"It's what family does," he returns, putting a hand on his wife's shoulder. "But we should head out."

"We'll be back though," Alex adds. "You make sure you get some rest."

They haven't been gone a minute when Jackson returns. He walks right up to the bed and leans over me, cupping my face in his hands.

"I hear you were holding off my boss out there."

"Hmm," he grumbles. "They're chomping at the bit, but I told them I needed to make sure you were up for it."

I don't get a chance to answer when he kisses me, slow and sweet, before resting his forehead against mine.

"What was that for?" I whisper.

"That was my way of telling you I love you."

He covers my mouth with his fingers before I can get a word out.

"I spent way too many hours yesterday evening and through the night imagining the worst possible outcomes, and the one thing foremost on my mind was I would never have had a chance to tell you that. Hard to believe, just a couple of years ago, I was ready to throw in the towel. That would've been a tragedy, because I'd never have known there was someone out there perfect for me. I didn't want to wait any longer."

I grab hold of his wrist.

"Jackson..."

"You're it for me, Stephanie. You're my person."

# Twenty-Seven

*STEPHANIE*

"He's awake?"

Jackson leans in to buckle me up. Turns out that's not so easy to do with only one functioning arm.

"Yeah, but I don't think he's talking yet. He may not be able to."

Wouldn't be surprising, given Laine had brain matter leaking from the hole in his head, but I would want to be the one to poke around what's left of it. So many questions remain, some of which I'm not sure I want the answers to.

Maybe it's best if opening his eyes is all the progress he makes for now. At least until I have a chance to find answers to a few of my questions on my own.

I'm lost in thought as Jackson rounds his truck, which now has four brand-new tires, and gets behind the wheel.

I'm heading home. Not my apartment here in Kalispell, but back to High Meadow where—as Alex so sternly pointed out—I can be properly looked after while I recover.

Not that I had any real desire to go back to my cramped apartment, where I'd be staring out my window at the self-storage facility across the road all day. I'd be crawling up the walls in no time. The view at the ranch is much nicer, and you can't beat the company.

I glance over at Jackson, who has barely left my side since I was brought in five days ago. I've had a surprising number of visitors over the course of those days, but Jackson has been the one constant. Even when Bellinger and Wilcox stopped by to question me and indicated they wanted to talk to me alone, Jackson wouldn't budge. He grabbed my hand demonstratively, sat down on the stool beside my bed, and stared them down until they gave up their attempts.

I spoke to them a few times this past week, first going over the order of events, and after that trying to help fill in gaps that remain. It's a weird experience, being on this side of an investigation. I got an earful from Bellinger, who was pissed I'd meddled in an active investigation, when I was technically on leave. Even worse, I got my partner in trouble. Wilcox ended up admitting he'd been the one to run that trace on the cell phone for me, and that didn't go over well at all.

Bellinger had steam coming out of his ears, and if I hadn't been lying in a hospital bed, I'm pretty sure he'd have fired me on the spot. I'm frankly surprised he hasn't done it yet, although that may change after he finds out what I've been holding back.

I know it's wrong to keep potentially important information to the case from him, but this is a loose end I'm determined to resolve myself. Unfortunately, it's going to have to wait until I'm back on my feet, because this is not something I can handle with just a phone call.

"You're quiet," Jackson observes, placing a hand on my knee. "Are you hurting?"

"Not really."

That's to say, it isn't bad, considering I've passed on anything stronger than ibuprofen these past two days. The pain medication they had me on worked wonders on the pain, but it also made my mind sluggish—as if I was under the influence—which I didn't like so much. It's the kind of drug that could easily develop into a habit, which is why I stopped taking them.

What was pure fire before has settled into more of a gnawing ache that runs all the way down to my fingertips which, by the way, I was able to move a little yesterday when the physical therapist came by. Progress will come in small increments, I was told. Sadly, patience is not my strong suit.

Luckily, it's an arm, and not a leg. I can walk fine, and I'm sure with a day or two recovering back at Jackson's cabin, I'll be able to get some things done. Like officially quit my job before anyone has a chance to fire me. I also need to find another place to live; I don't want to continue living in Kalispell, or keep mooching off Jackson. But most of all, I need to make a little trip. Unfortunately, since I can't drive myself, I'll need Jackson's help with all of those.

"Hey, have you ever been to Michigan?"

Jackson turns his head and grins at me. "Yeah, I've been to Michigan. Why?"

I let my eyes drift out the windshield.

"I'm thinking of paying my father a quick visit in the next week or so. Would you be able to come?"

His face immediately turns to thunder.

"You're kidding, right? The man couldn't even bother to call you while you were laid up in the hospital and yet you want to visit *him*?"

Calling my father had been Bellinger's doing. I didn't know he'd talked to him until he mentioned it the first time they questioned me. I wasn't expecting to hear from him. I imagine he was probably annoyed his daily routine was interrupted. After Mom died, the only other person he cared about was my brother, and after David passed away, I swear my dad's heart atrophied completely.

Any contact—which was limited to very sporadic phone calls—was initiated by me. Jackson got progressively more upset when there was nothing, no note, no flowers, and no call, coming from my father.

"Look, I'm fine. Like I told you, I'm used to it. I grew up with a dad who barely acknowledged my existence and, over the years, I've grown calluses on my soul. I simply don't have any expectations. It doesn't bother me anymore."

He throws me a dubious look.

"I call bullshit."

"No, honestly," I insist. "It's easier this way. Occasionally, I'll call him to alleviate my own sense of guilt and duty, but other than that, I'm fine with this distance."

Except, this time I want to see him face-to-face. I want to watch his expression when I ask him about his involvement with those bank robberies.

My father may well be the only one left who has all the answers.

*Jackson*

"We'll be fine here, Ma."

From the stubborn set of my mother's mouth, I can tell she's not happy with my response.

She and Ama, who is back from her family visit, went ahead and made up a guest room in the main house for Stephanie. My name wasn't mentioned, but since I'm not about to let her sleep alone when she's within throwing distance, that would've meant both of us in the same house as my parents.

Why, when we have a cabin with some privacy and a lock on the door just steps away? We've just spent five days in a hospital room with a constant flow of people in and out.

I want some time alone with her. Slow the rest of the world down so we can catch up. No way we can do that with my mother or Ama hovering around all the time.

"What if something happens when you're out on a search?" Ma persists.

"Then she has a phone, or she can use her two healthy legs and one arm. She's not helpless."

"Leave them, Alex," Jonas urges her as he walks up behind her, dropping a kiss on her cheek. "Let those kids catch their breath."

"At least let me pack you up some food," Ama offers.

Since that's what I came in for in the first place, I agree to that.

"Oh fine," Ma finally gives in. "But you'd better make sure my number is programmed in her phone, just in case."

Again, an easy concession on my part, since I did as much already when I picked up a new cell phone for Stephanie yesterday. Apparently, her old one ended up at the bottom of a rain barrel.

It seems to appease my mother, who walks away with

what she perceives to be a win. If I want any peace in the coming days, I'm not about to disavow her of that illusion.

Jonas claps me on the shoulder, while Ama starts filling up containers from the pans she has going on the stove.

"She's rattled," he explains. "Has had bad dreams every night since it happened. Your ma is a tough cookie, but she walked in on a brutally violent scene, the kind of which she'd never been exposed to before. Not like you, me, and even Stephanie, in her line of work. The reality it could've easily been one of her loved ones lying in a pool of blood hit home hard. Be patient with her, and if she's a little invasive, it's only because she needs to reassure herself you're both okay."

I've been so busy looking out for Stephanie, it didn't even occur to me that what played out five days ago must've left its imprint on my mother as well.

"*Shit*. I didn't think of that," I admit.

He gives my shoulder a squeeze before dropping his hand.

"You don't have to. I did, which is my job. Yours is looking after your woman, which I'm glad to see you doing."

It's funny, I can almost hear Thomas in those words. I miss him. Every time I walk up the porch steps now, my eyes are drawn to the empty rocking chair.

When Jonas turns to follow my mother out of the kitchen, I call after him.

"Hey, Dad...you gonna be around after dinner for a drink and a stogie on the porch tonight?"

All I get is a grunt and a nod before he disappears down the hallway, but when I turn to Ama, I catch her dabbing the corner of her eyes with a tea towel.

"Onions," she blurts out when she catches me looking.

I grin at her to let her know I'm not buying it. *Onions, my foot.*

"Whatever," she grumbles. "Take your food and get outta my kitchen."

She shoves a stack of containers in my hands. I lean in to kiss her cheek.

"Thanks, Ama. You're the best."

~

"Oh my God, that feels good."

Bending down I drop a kiss on her lips. Her eyes blink open.

"I'm serious. You are so good at this; it could be a post-retirement career for you. Instead of handing out carts and welcoming customers at Walmart, you could work part time at a salon as a hair washer. I'm serious; you'd rake in major tips with those agile fingers of yours."

I scrunch my nose and continue to work the conditioner in her hair.

"I'll pass. No desire to put these 'agile fingers' anywhere but on you."

Her eyes drift shut again as a smile spreads on her lips.

She'd crashed hard after dinner last night. I remember that, feeling pretty good in the hospital, but getting knocked back on your ass once you get home. This morning I was cooking bacon for some breakfast sandwiches I could bring her in bed, when she came stumbling out of the bedroom, demanding coffee.

Over breakfast she complained about feeling grungy. Since she still isn't allowed to get that shoulder wet until after her checkup with Dr. Littleton next Wednesday showers are still out. The harvest site on her leg had healed nicely, but the larger incision on the back of her shoulder was still oozing a little. So bath it is, and since she only has one working arm at the moment, I offered to give her a hand.

We're in the bathroom and she's sitting on a kitchen chair leaning back against the vanity, with her head tilted back in the sink. It was the best way we could think of to keep that shoulder dry while I wash her hair. I've got the tub filling for her bath after.

I'm trying to remind my dick she's injured, fresh out of the hospital, but there is too much stimulation. Those little pleasure sounds she makes, the slick slide of her wet hair through my fingers, the scent of her shampoo, the fact my crotch is almost in her face. None of it helps me stave off my body's natural response. It doesn't help knowing that as soon as I'm done rinsing her hair, she'll be getting naked to get in the tub, where I'm supposed to help her bathe.

I'm fairly disciplined, a result of my training, but there's a limit to how much of this kind of temptation a man can resist.

I wrap her hair up in a towel and help her to her feet. Then I grab the kitchen chair, which is in the way in the small space, and flee to the kitchen. While I finish up the last dregs of coffee in my cup, I force my mind back to my conversation with Jonas on the porch last night.

He'd already been out there, rocking in Thomas's chair, sipping a bourbon, and staring out at the view by the time I joined him. He was reminiscing at first, about growing up on his father's ranch in Texas, and how disappointed his dad had been when he chose to enlist instead of staying to work the ranch. Then he turned the focus on the future, voicing a desire to take my mother traveling and show her some of the world he'd discovered during his career in the armed forces.

At some point, he asked me point-blank whether ranching was something I could see myself growing old doing, and I had to be honest with him. It isn't. I mean, I don't mind the work, not at all, but I'm not passionate about it, not like I am about search and rescue, the High Mountain Trackers. I shared with him that's the part of my job that makes me feel alive and fulfilled in a way I didn't think was possible even two years ago. He seemed to appreciate...

"Jackson?"

I instantly forget my train of thought at the sound of her voice. Setting down my mug, I return to the bathroom, poking my head inside. My mouth immediately turns dry at the sight of her. She's virtually naked, save for the T-shirt she's got her head and right arm tangled up in.

"I tried to get it over my head before pulling it off my bad arm, but it got stuck on the hair towel."

My blood instantly rushes south as she pulls ineffectively at the stretchy fabric, making her tits bounce.

I brush her hand away and take over, finding the edge of her shirt and carefully peeling it off her. She loses her hair towel in the process, and her damp hair comes tumbling down her shoulders, the ends brushing her pink nipples.

With a pained groan, I turn my back and pinch the bridge of my nose. I don't know if I'll be able to muster the fortitude to put my hands on her and not make love to her body. Almost immediately, I feel the pressure of her hand in the middle of my back.

"Get in the tub with me."

"Hotshot, that's not a good—"

"Please?"

*Jesus*, I'm weak.

Already I'm tugging at my own shirt. I'm a fucking marshmallow in her hands.

I can feel her eyes on my back as I quickly strip, removing my prosthesis last, before turning to face her. Her eyes slide down my body and it feels like a caress, sending a shiver down my spine. Then she fixes them on my cock as she bites her bottom lip, and a drop of precum leaks from the crown.

"You first," she insists.

"You're injured," I try in a last-ditch attempt to be a gentleman, knowing it's already way past too late.

She stubbornly shakes her head. "Only my shoulder. Every other part of me is just fine."

"I don't want to hurt you."

"Then let me do the work. Get in the tub, Jackson."

There isn't a man, alive or dead, who could say no to that. Not one.

I slide down in the warm water and hold out my hand to help Stephanie in. She sinks down with a knee on either side of me, and I can't resist closing my mouth around one of her pink nipples hovering in front of my face. My arms slide around her, holding her in place with the tip of my cock poised at her entrance, while I feast on her breasts.

"Kiss me," she orders, as she curls her fingers in my hair and pulls my head back.

Then she immediately covers my mouth with hers as she lets her body sink down, stealing every last ounce of my breath.

I'm pinned down in a slippery tub, helpless against the slow, delicious torture she subjects me to. Her beautiful hazel eyes lock on mine as she has me groaning, nearly pleading for relief. When it comes, I band my arms around her, fusing her to my body as I buck my release up into her.

"You are a fucking dream, Hotshot," I mumble against the soft swell of her breasts where I've pressed my face. "I honestly don't know what I did to deserve you."

She urges my head back and smiles down at me.

"You didn't have to *do* anything. No sales gimmicks needed. Being you turns out to be exactly right for me."

I lift my face to give her a kiss, when I notice her wincing.

"Are you okay? Did I hurt you?"

She shakes her head. "Just a cramp, I need to stand up."

I help her to her feet and, standing up as well, use the hand-held shower and a bar of soap to get both of us cleaned up.

When I wrap her in my biggest towel a few minutes later, she turns around in my arms, placing her hand in the middle of my chest.

"There was a time in my life I promised myself I would never say these words again to another man. Never make myself that vulnerable again. But I didn't know you then. I've never experienced someone who is as strong, as capable, as protective, and even bossy, but at the same time kind, caring, and gentle. I wouldn't have believed it possible."

She smiles a little as her eyes convey the message before her lips do.

"I love you back, Jackson Hart."

# Twenty-Eight



Stephanie


"Easy with that stress ball."

Jackson reaches over and plucks it from my hand.

"She said five minutes, three times a day. You've been working that thing nonstop since we took off."

Working that thing? I can barely make a dent in the squishy material

"But I can do more," I protest, trying to get the ball back but he tucks it out of reach in his jeans pocket.

I could make a dive for it, but an action like that might be misconstrued by the passengers sitting around us. I'll get it back once we've picked up our rental car. Annoyed, I turn my head to look out the window, not that there's much to see, whatever part of the country we're currently flying over, it's pretty much clouded over.

"Trust me," he urges in a low voice, leaning in to me. "You overwork that arm now; you could do damage that'll set you right back. I've been there and it sucks. Just stick to

301

the plan the PT laid out this morning and learn to be patient. It'll get you much further in the end."

I wish I could cross my arms in defiance, but that's a bit of a challenge when one of them is in a sling. At least I've been given the all-clear and can look forward to a shower at the hotel tonight.

We caught a flight into Grand Rapids, but since we'll be arriving fairly late, we're booked at a hotel not too far from the airport. We'll pick up our rental, crash for the night at the hotel, and drive up to Traverse City first thing in the morning. It's only a two-and-a-half-hour drive.

I hope to find my father home. To be honest, I have no idea how he gets through his days, but I do know he still lives in the old house. Not a surprise, he's probably too stubborn to give it up, but I'd prefer to spend as little time as possible there. My last eight or so years living there erased any lingering good memories from when Mom was still alive. The house could burn down and I wouldn't blink.

I'm not sure how he'll react when he sees me, and part of me is scared of what I may find out, but it's better to know than to wonder.

"I can hear you thinking again."

I turn my head to find Jackson smiling.

"I just don't like not knowing what to expect," I admit. "And I hate that Vallard is still messing with my head from beyond the grave."

I told Jackson about the references Ben made to my father's involvement a few days ago, when I was looking at flights. To his credit, he didn't once tell me I should've shared that information with Bellinger. Instead, he seemed to understand my need to confront my father face-to-face.

"Can't tell you what to expect, but be prepared to find out the worst. Whether or not he decides to share with you,

you'll know either way. And—if I can put my two cents' worth in—I think he's up to his eyeballs. It would explain why he's steering completely clear of you right now."

I have a hard time admitting I've had those thoughts myself. Because even if he doesn't care much for me, he cares about appearances and his reputation with the Bureau.

"Could be."

"So what is the plan? If he's home, if he's willing to talk, and if he admits having even had some minor involvement with this, what do you want to do?"

I've thought about this. A lot. So far I've justified leaving my father's name out of things because I conveniently hung on to the idea Ben was playing games with me. However, once I have confirmation, I have no choice but to report it to Bellinger. I know my career may already be over, and he may be my father, but I'm not willing to give up my honor or my integrity for him.

"If that is the case, I'm giving him twenty-four hours to do the right thing. If he hasn't turned himself in by that time, I will share what I know with Bellinger."

"Will you get in trouble?" he asks, slipping his hand in mine.

"Probably. Hell, they may even draw into question whether or not I had any involvement with these crimes myself, but so be it. They won't find anything on me, and at least I'll know, for once and for all, my father doesn't give a single fuck about me."

I'm pissed I'm still shedding a tear at that deep ache of rejection I thought I'd left behind me. But my use of profanity has drawn the attention of the elderly woman sitting on Jackson's other side. She leans forward and pins me with a disapproving glare.

"Keep your vulgar language to yourself," she hisses.

Jackson doesn't hesitate to swing around at her and block her view of me, responding in a calm, but dead-serious voice.

"Respectfully, mind your own fucking business... *Ma'am*," he adds with emphasis, before turning his back on her.

When he turns back to me, I'm struggling to hold back my laughter. I can hear the woman's disgruntled mumblings behind him.

"Diplomacy is not your forte, but at least you were polite, I'll give you that."

∼

"No."

I take in a deep breath, trying to keep my cool, as we pull into my old neighborhood in Traverse City.

"He may be more forthcoming if—"

"No. I'm not going to let you walk in there alone," he insists.

"You wouldn't insist if I was a guy," I fire back at him.

He shrugs.

"No, I wouldn't. And not because they have a dick, but because I'm not in-*fucking*-love with a guy. How could you even ask me to sit this one out after what we went through less than two weeks ago?"

I already had my mouth open to fire off the next retort but quickly shut it and swallow my words. I'm being a hypocrite; if the roles were reversed, I likely wouldn't let him go in alone either.

"Okay."

His head pivots around at my rather abrupt capitulation

to an argument we've been waging off and on since we left Grand Rapids earlier.

"Seriously?"

It's my turn to shrug, and I do it with a smirk. "What can I say? You finally made a solid point."

He doesn't seem amused at my attempt to lighten the mood.

A moment later I don't think it's funny anymore either, as he pulls up in front of my old house.

What once was a source of pride, a facade of respectability and standing, has become an eyesore. A lawn that is so badly overgrown, you can barely see what used to be perfectly trimmed boxwood hedges my father meticulously maintained. Paint is peeling from the columns of the porch and off the window frames. The porch deck is buckling with moisture and rot. Even the mailbox beside the front door is hanging lopsided, held up by only one screw.

The place looks abandoned, and for a brief moment I wonder if perhaps he's no longer here after all. But then I notice his old Mercury Grand Marquis, still parked in front of the garage, although it looks like it hasn't moved from there in a while, with weeds sprouting up around the tires.

"Wow. Someone doesn't like yard work," Jackson observes. "Is that normal?"

I shake my head and am about to say no, but then I reconsider. I haven't been back here in over a decade. Who knows what constitutes normal anymore?

"I couldn't really tell you."

~

*Jackson*

. . .

I can feel the heavy anticipation coming off Stephanie in waves as we approach the house.

I'd like to hold her hand, give her some physical support, but I know better than to touch her. I'm sure it's taking all her resolve and strength to hold her head high like that and walk straight up to that door. I'll just hang back and be prepared to do damage control as needed.

The only thing that doesn't sit well with me is the fact I ended up not being straightforward with Jonas and my mother about our reason for coming here. Not that I had to lie outright, but staying purposely vague about the reason for the visit felt deceitful nonetheless.

Stephanie tries the doorbell first, but when that doesn't work, resorts to knocking on the door.

A voice booms from inside.

*"Jesus Christ, Mabel! The door's open like it always is!"*

Stephanie throws me a look over her shoulder—maybe to reassure herself I'm still here—before pushing open the door and entering the house.

I was prepared for bad odors and decay in here too, but other than a mild musty smell and faded wallpaper, the interior of the house looks neat as a pin.

*"Mabel?"*

At the back of the house a wheelchair rolls into view, the stooped figure of a man staring down the hallway at us. Half his face droops and his clothes hang off his body.

Stephanie inhales sharply and steps back into my body. I place a hand on her hip to steady her.

"Dad?"

From what I heard of her father, I'd pictured him strong and unyielding, not this wisp of a man a stiff wind could blow away. His voice still holds power when he recognizes his daughter.

"What the hell are *you* doing here?"

Stephanie visibly collects herself before addressing her father.

"I wanted to see you."

The man makes a dismissive noise and fixes his one visible eye on me.

"And who are you?"

"That's Jackson Hart, Dad. My partner," she responds before I can.

Interesting she chose the term partner instead of boyfriend, even though it can mean the same. I have a sneaky suspicion she's well aware her father may be more likely to interpret the term as professional partner rather than romantic one. But, despite her father's obvious failing health, his mind proves to still be sharp.

"Doesn't look like a federal agent to me."

"I never said he was," Stephanie grudgingly admits.

The old man harrumphs, and abruptly turns his wheelchair, disappearing out of sight. I follow Stephanie down the hallway to what turns out to be a kitchen. Her dad is at the kitchen table, a newspaper spread out in front of him.

"You had a stroke. Why didn't you tell me?" she asks him.

"Coffee in the pot is old. Mabel should be here any minute, she can make fresh," he rumbles, ignoring her question, and not looking away from his daily news.

"Who's Mabel?" Stephanie changes direction as she opens a cupboard and pulls down two cups.

Clearly not much has changed since she lived here. I lean a shoulder against the doorpost, determined to remain in the background.

"Cleaning lady. What are you doing here?"

Man, this guy is something else. My fingers curl in my

pockets at the way he addresses Stephanie. It's gonna be hard to keep my tongue.

Stephanie ignores his sharp question and pours us each a cup from the thermos on the kitchen counter.

"I assume you heard about Ben Vallard?" she asks with her back still turned to him.

I'm watching him though, and his reaction to hearing that name is as if someone slapped him across the face. Even his voice suddenly sounds deflated.

"Yeah. He's dead."

Stephanie hands me a cup and I catch her father turning his rheumy eyes on us.

"Did you kill him?"

For a moment I'm a little uneasy, not entirely sure who the question was directed at, but Stephanie responds.

"Does it matter? He tried to kill me."

I'm shocked the man doesn't even look surprised, he just nods.

"Did he do that?" he gestures at the sling she is wearing.

"No," she clarifies as she moves back to the counter, picks up her cup, and leans a hip against the edge. "That was Mitchel Laine."

No visible reaction from her father. He either doesn't know the name or isn't at all surprised to hear it. My vote is on the latter.

"Do you remember him, Daddy? Mitchel? Did you know he survived?"

The man has ice in his veins, the way he looks at his daughter.

"Heard he's a vegetable."

Stephanie nods, taking a sip of the black tar her father calls coffee without flinching. The woman is pure steel.

"We thought so until this morning when he woke up. It's looking like he might be talking soon."

A slight exaggeration but one that has the desired effect as the remaining blood drains from the old man's face.

"It'll be interesting to find out what he has to say," she adds as an extra push.

Her father bites.

"He's a criminal. It'll be nothing but lies."

"Maybe," Stephanie indulges him. "But he had plenty to say before he tried to use me as leverage with Ben. Of course, you and I both know that didn't go very far, since I never was more to Ben than a plaything. You knew that, right, Daddy?"

She's relentless as she pushes him. I can only imagine she'd be a force to reckon with in the interrogation room.

"Anyway," she continues, swirling around the dregs in the bottom of her cup before pinning her father with a look. "Ben ended up talking plenty himself before he was taken out. Boasted, actually. So eager to show me how superior he was. But he wasn't careful enough, was he? No. Guess he wasn't quite the FBI agent you both imagined him to be. His first mistake was underestimating me. His last mistake was leaving two witnesses behind. Did you honestly think you were safe, Dad?"

She expertly rattles the old man, who is now almost purple in the face, clutching the armrests of his wheelchair with gnarled, bloodless fingers.

"He was like a son to me. Looked out for me after David died and left me with hospital bills that would've put me on the street had he not intervened. That's more than I can say for you," he snarls. "You were worthless then, and you're worthless now."

I push away from the doorpost at his spineless verbal

assault, but a sharp headshake from Stephanie stops me in my tracks.

"Good to know I'm worthless to you, Daddy. It makes this next part so much easier."

She carefully sets her cup in the sink and walks over to the kitchen table, planting her left hand on the surface as she leans down in his face.

"You have twenty-four hours to turn yourself in. Consider it my final gift to you. If you haven't turned yourself in by noon tomorrow, I will do it for you."

With that she turns on her heel and walks toward me, her face an impassive mask. Yet I see the tiny muscle ticking at the corner of her mouth, she's barely holding it together.

The old man cackles at her back as he decides to try and bully her one last time.

"You? Your word against mine? You were a failure from the start. Do you have any idea of the connections I still have in the Bureau?"

My presence is ignored. Not that I care much about that, I'm too busy focusing on Stephanie's face to gauge the impact of his words as she approaches.

She stops right in front of me and shoves her left hand into the opening of her sling, pulling out the phone I never saw her tuck in there. Clever woman, she was recording this entire conversation.

With a faint smile for me she turns around one last time, holding up her phone for her father to see.

"Word of warning, Daddy," she cautions him in a calm, but deadly voice. "Do not make the mistake of underestimating me again."

# Twenty-Nine

STEPHANIE

I'm drained, the last couple of weeks have been hell.

Trying to clean up forty-plus years of living from a house you turned your back on is a painful experience. Not to mention frustrating, when you have to do it with one arm because the other one is useless. Of course, with everything going on, I haven't really kept up with my PT or my exercises.

I got the call from the Traverse City police department the morning after Jackson and I returned home. We'd gone straight to the airport when we left my father's house and crashed at my apartment in Kalispell because the plane got in late. We never even made it back to the ranch.

Jackson said he wasn't really surprised my father chose to blow his brains out. According to reports, he probably did so shortly after we left. His cleaning lady found him.

I was mostly angry. It felt like the ultimate betrayal, final confirmation I meant nothing to him. Not that I needed it, it was pretty clear to me already.

My first stop after receiving that call was the office, where I had to sit down with my boss and my partner to fill them in on my father's involvement with Ben Vallard and Mitchel Laine. Jackson wasn't happy to be told he had to wait outside, but there wasn't a whole lot he could do about it. Apparently, he spent his time calling the ranch and making arrangements, because by the time I walked out of the office several hours later, he already had taken the rest of the week off, had flights to Michigan arranged, a hotel booked in Traverse City, and had sourced a funeral home for us to talk to.

Of course it wasn't as simple as arranging a funeral, we had to wait for an autopsy first, and then it took the FBI three days to go over the house with a fine-tooth comb before we were allowed in to dig through his paperwork to see if he'd left any instructions.

I hadn't realized there was a small part of me still craving for some kind of affirmation from my father, until I found an old shoebox in the back of the closet in my old bedroom, which my father had used for storage after I left home. The box was filled with old drawings, silly elementary school awards, snapshots, report cards, water safety certification, a second-place medal my team won in a soccer tournament. A collection of mementos, little milestones of a young twelve-year-old's life.

Nothing was added to the box after my mother died. Not a single piece of paper, no photographs, no ribbons or medals or accolades. The box was tucked away on a dusty shelf, like my father's heart, after Mom passed away. With her gone, our family ceased to exist.

I've been walking around with a raw ache in my chest,

but I still haven't cried. Not after burying my father next to her, as per his wishes, or the long days following, sorting through a house holding many mixed memories.

Jackson stayed and helped until we buried my father, but then he had to get back to the ranch. He would've stayed longer if I hadn't told him to go. He seemed to understand I needed to finish this by myself.

It's been a purging of sorts, trying to get the house ready to put on the market. With every tangible piece of my history passing through my hands—deciding what was worth holding on to and what could be discarded—I felt myself grow lighter. Cleansed and hollowed where the shadowed parts of my soul used to be.

But I still haven't cried.

Until I catch sight of Jackson, standing by the baggage carousel inside the terminal, waiting for me.

My knees buckle and hit the floor, every single emotion I've tucked away these past weeks washing over me at once. I barely notice the concerned looks or kind offers to help. I'm falling apart on the floor in the middle of the damn airport.

Strong hands slip under my arms and hoist me up, and my face is pressed against a clean cotton shirt, smelling of detergent and Jackson.

"Let it out, baby. I've got you," he mumbles with his lips pressed against the shell of my ear.

Somehow, we end up on a row of seats against the wall of the baggage area, with me curled up on Jackson's lap, my face shoved in the crook of his neck, as I bawl until my eyeballs are raw and my head is pounding.

"Ready to go home?" he asks as I mop my face with the hem of my shirt.

I'm a fucking disaster, but you'd never know, seeing the way Jackson looks at me with love in his eyes.

"So ready."

He lifts me off his lap, takes my left hand in his, and walks us over to the carousel to collect my bag. I should be mortified at the spectacle I just put on in public, but I don't care.

I'm too busy filling that hollow feeling in my soul with all the goodness Jackson gives me.

～

*Jackson*

Man, I'm glad she's home.

She was an absolute mess at the airport, but I'm not surprised.

Stephanie bottles shit up, and there was a lot of it, both stuff she carried with her from her childhood, but also this last fresh wave of crap landing on her shoulders.

We both lost a parent at twelve, but the comparison ends there, because I ended up with a mother who focused all her love on me, working her butt off to make sure I had a good life. Stephanie, on the other hand, was mostly ignored by her father in favor of her brother. Then her brother died as well, and now that cowardly piece of shit of a father blew his brains out on his kitchen table and basically left the mess he made of his life for her to clean up.

Yeah, she was a mess, but it's been a crazy few weeks for her.

We haven't been sitting around twiddling our thumbs back at the ranch either.

I'm not sure what crawled up my stepfather's backside, but he's been cracking the whip on us. Aside from the normal workings of the ranch, and the search-and-rescue callouts, he's been having us work down some kind of honey-do list. Replacing older sections of fencing, painting the barn and the rest of the outbuildings, fixing the roof and the gutters, and putting in several new windows at the house. It's been all-hands-on-deck all the damn time.

I've asked him a few times if he was planning to sell or something, but he just shakes his head. It's been frustrating, so when he caught me alone after the welcome-home dinner Ama and my mother put together for Stephanie, and asked if I'd join him on the porch for a chat later, I said yes.

Now, looking down at Stephanie asleep in my bed, where she crashed hard when we got back to the cabin, I regret agreeing to it. I'd much rather strip down, crawl under the covers, and gather her in my arms.

Instead, I press a kiss on the side of her head and exit the bedroom, gently pulling the door shut. Then I grab my phone and make my way over to the main house, where I can already see Jonas rocking in the old man's chair.

*Damn.*

When I walk up the steps he pulls the side table out in front of him and grabs what looks like blueprints from the bench beside him.

"What's that?"

"Pull up a chair," he orders me instead of answering.

He perches the reading glasses he finally conceded to on his nose and rolls out the drawings. I recognize the barn and the breeding shed on the other side of it. New is the building on the other side of the corral across the driveway from the cabins.

"What is that?"

"Equipment storage, offices."

Annoyed I'm still trying to drag information from him, my tone is a little sharp when I prompt him.

"For?"

He looks at me over his readers with one raised eyebrow. I almost laugh, despite my mother's efforts to soften him up, the man is still very much commander of his troops.

"Both the ranch and the search and rescue. We're moving them out of the house."

"Why?"

He ignores my question and flips the top drawing aside to reveal another one. This one shows the view of the front of what looks to be a single level house.

"We're gonna break ground on the office building next week. It's gonna be loud and messy for a while, but it should go up pretty fast." He taps a finger on the image of the house. "This will take longer."

Then he points over to the hill where we buried Thomas last month.

"It's going over there."

"You're building another house?"

Before he answers, he pours us both a bourbon from the bottle he has sitting on the floor next to him. Then he clinks my glass with his and takes a sip.

"Hurts your mother to go up the stairs. Her arthritis isn't getting better with age, and my knees aren't the best anymore either. We'll have a bedroom, bathroom, laundry, everything on the same level. Plus, I can still see everything that goes on here, even if I'm no longer involved."

I almost choke on the mouthful of bourbon I was just swallowing down.

"No longer involved? What are you saying? Are you sick?"

"Fuck no, but I think it's time I hung up my hat. Your

318

mother and I aren't getting any younger and like I told you a while ago, I'd like to take her traveling a bit before we're both too old to enjoy it."

My mouth is already open with the next question, even as I process the shock at Jonas's announcement, but he already has his hand up to cut me off.

"You're like a damn three-year-old with your questions, you know that? Give a man a chance to explain, for chrissakes," he grumbles.

I mimic zipping my lips, which earns me a roll of his eyes.

"Effective as soon as the office building is done, I'm handing the breeding program and the running of the ranch over to Dan. Bo is gonna help him out for a year or two until he's ready to call it a day."

I'm trying hard not to show my reaction. As much as I couldn't see myself living out my days as a rancher, I'm surprised at how much it hurts to see it all passed on to Dan. We're brothers in every way but blood, and Jonas is a father figure in both our lives, but it still feels like a letdown.

"The ranch has been his dream, ever since he came working here when he was still wet behind the ears. Trying to learn the ropes while also looking after his mother, who was already very sick at the time. He turned out to be a natural, as if he was born to it."

I nod in agreement. He's right, Dan could run this ranch in his sleep. Other than my mother, who is a bit of a horse whisperer, Dan has a special talent with the animals, and the ranch hands respect him.

"He's moving into the house then?"

Jonas shakes his head as he offers me a cigar.

"He's already living in his dream house. That's why I'm

moving the offices to the new building." He lights his before handing me the lighter. "The house is yours."

I freeze, the light inches away from the end of my cigar. "Sorry?"

"The house is yours," he repeats. "I don't know if it's your dream house or not, but you can turn it into whatever you want it to be. You've got Stephanie, you're settled in, you need a house."

His head disappears in a cloud of smoke as he takes a draw from his cigar and sits back in his chair, rocking gently.

"I don't know what to say," I finally manage.

He shrugs. "I picked Dan to run the ranch and carry on the family tradition for my father, but I'm handing you my house and *my* legacy; the High Mountain Trackers. That was my passion as much as you told me it's yours."

I'm too emotional to speak, so I stay silent and listen as he continues.

"I wasn't blessed with kids, but I can't tell you how grateful I am to your mother for giving me a chance at fatherhood. Son, you are mine in every way but blood and I love you. I could die happy and grateful tomorrow, secure in knowing my heart's work is looked after."

"I don't know what to say," I struggle to share.

"Nothing to say," Ma says from the doorway.

I don't know how long she's been standing there, but long enough to have a few tears tracking down her face.

"Besides," she adds as she steps out on the porch and makes her way over to Jonas, perching a hip on his armrest. "It's pure selfishness on this man's part. He wants to keep you close so he'll have a front-row seat when you make him a grandfather."

Jonas lets out a boom of laughter, squeezing Ma's hip.

"I think your memory is starting to go, woman. I

distinctly recall you're the one who brought up the prox-imity to possible grandkids more than once when we were discussing the future."

"Are you saying you don't want any?" My mother turns it around on him, catching him by surprise.

"Well, no. That's not what I said. Of course I'm—"

But Ma won't let him finish and smirks triumphantly as she cuts him off.

"Exactly. Just like I said."

I toss back my drink and get to my feet.

"Both of you are jumping the gun, but I'll leave you two to fight it out. I'm going to check on Stephanie."

Ma smiles at me. "You do that, honey."

I lean in to give her a kiss, and then find myself bending over to kiss Jonas's weathered cheek as well.

"Thanks, Dad. I love you too."

# Thirty



"Back already?"

I look up to see Shane Wilcox walking across the parking lot toward me as I step out of the office.

"No, actually."

I stop and shoot a quick apologetic look at Jackson, who is behind the wheel of his truck a couple of parking spots down, waiting for me. He has been for the past hour already.

"Just popped in for a visit then?"

I shake my head, sad, because I'm going to miss my partner. Of anyone I've worked with over the years, he made the best partner.

"More like saying goodbye; I just came out of a meeting with Bellinger."

His reaction is instant and his outburst is bittersweet.

"That pompous ass fired you?"

It doesn't surprise me he'd jump to that conclusion. My

boss was all but ready to hand me my walking papers when I first informed him I'd withheld important information about my father. He didn't, and instead suspended me pending further investigation. That was over two months ago.

"No, he didn't. I quit," I clarify.

"Is it because of your injury?"

He motions at my arm, which I no longer wear in a sling, but is still pretty useless as arms go.

Yeah, I can see the minute progress, but as I told my physical therapist, at this rate I'll be of retirement age before I get any half-decent function back. Hell, I haven't even mastered the fine motor skills required to pick up a marble with my fingers. A six-month-old baby can do better than me.

"Actually, the decision to leave had already been made before I got shot. Everything that happened after just made that decision easier."

"Wow." Shane runs a hand through his unruly hair. "Well, that sucks for me. It means I have to break in a new partner," he busts my chops.

"You'll live."

"Don't have much of a choice, do I?" he teases, before jumping on a different subject. "By the way, did Bellinger tell you we handed off the case to the federal prosecutor? My prediction is that Laine will plead out. He's already confessed and given us the full story."

It's a miracle the man survived in the first place, but he somehow managed to come out of it with his faculties mostly intact. Physically, he wasn't so lucky and has to contend with a host of problems, not the least of which is the loss of his sight, but I'm hard-pressed to conjure up any sympathy for him.

"Yeah, he did mention that."

I was glad to hear it, because it means I won't be called to testify, which I would rather avoid. I want to move forward and not be pulled back to what I'd rather leave in the past.

According to Bellinger, Laine explained his connection with Ben Vallard—the two had been friends since childhood—and confirmed how my father became involved in their scheme. Dad had already implied it had something to do with my brother's hospital bills. Those bills were paid off in three lump sums. The first one was four months after David died. Each of the payment dates was within days of the first three bank robberies. Circumstantial, and it might not have been enough to convict him in a court of law, but it was clear to everyone my father was guilty.

Still, there was some validation in having Mitchel Laine confirm the course of events, and perhaps a hint of a redeeming factor in knowing my father tried to distance himself after David's bills were paid off. For what it's worth.

"So what are you gonna do now?" Wilcox probes. "What could possibly follow an exciting career as a federal agent?"

"Oh, I don't know. I don't really miss getting called out of bed in the middle of the night, or living off fast food and staying in dingy motel rooms. I'm growing partial to eight hours of sleep, and it turns out I enjoy a future with a little predictability."

Shane grins as he checks over his shoulder where he's clearly spotted Jackson waiting in the truck.

"I'm guessing he's part of that more predictable future?"

"Yes. But also my new job with the High Mountain Trackers."

His eyebrows shoot up. "You? You're joining the team? I didn't even know you could ride."

"I can, but I doubt I'll be riding out much. My job is going to be coordinating the searches, liaising with law enforcement, and managing electronic surveillance and communications."

Jackson looks to be asleep when I return to the truck after finally saying goodbye to Shane, with promises to stay in touch. His seat is tilted back and his hat is covering his face. When I lean over and reach for his hat, my hand is snatched midair.

"Took you long enough," he grumbles, pulling me halfway across the console and onto his lap.

But when he shoves his hat back, I notice humor sparkling in his eyes.

"I deserve at least a kiss for chauffeuring you around and waiting patiently while you take care of shit."

I press a kiss to his jaw.

"You deserve a lot more, but not in the FBI parking lot with twenty cameras aimed at us from different angles."

"Spoilsport."

He drops a kiss on my lips and returns me to my seat before straightening himself behind the wheel.

We drove to Kalispell early this morning to wrap up loose ends. Our first stop was my apartment, where we were able to pack up stuff I wanted to keep—which wasn't much —and load it in the back of the truck. I left most of the furniture, which was pretty sparse to begin with, the bulk of the contents of the kitchen, and my TV behind. The landlord can sell it, or rent the place furnished. I don't really care.

It's not like I'll need any of it. There's no room in Jackson's cabin, and when we eventually move into the big house, I already warned Jackson I want to shop for new furniture.

Our own furniture, preferably family-friendly.

"Do we need to go anywhere else?" Jackson wants to know.

With butterflies in my stomach, I turn to face him and try to guess how he will react to what is to come.

"We have just one more stop to make."

*Jackson*

When she directs me to park in front of a western clothing store, I don't think much of it.

But then she starts dragging me across the street to an entirely different kind of store.

I'm confused.

"Where are you taking me?"

I mean, I can see where she's taking me, it's a standalone building, there really is no mistaking it, but it's not computing right away.

Then my eye catches on a display in the window and it hits home with the impact of a fist in the stomach. Her face betrays her anxiety as I slam on the brakes, standing still in the middle of the sidewalk, staring at her slack-faced.

"You're shitting me..."

It's more of a rhetorical question, since the glimmer in her eyes tells me she is dead serious and terrified. Grabbing a firm hold of her hand, I pull her around the side of the building. I press her back against the brick wall and lean in to her, my nose almost touching hers.

"For real?"

She nods, blinking her eyes as I cup her face in my hands.

"You're sure."

"One-hundred-percent," she whispers, a second before my lips cover hers.

∼

"Need help?"

Ma comes down the porch and walks over, as I drop the tailgate on the truck.

"Wouldn't mind a hand." I look beyond her. "Is Jonas around?"

"He's just gone to check in with the contractor. Do you need him?"

I glance over to the construction site on the other side of the driveway. It still looks a bit messy, but the shell of the building is already up. It went surprisingly fast. I can see Jonas looming over a short guy in a hard hat, maybe five foot six or seven, and my stepfather is clearly unhappy about something.

"What's going on this time?"

This isn't the first run-in between Jonas and the contractors. It's mostly a control thing. If this is a foreboding for how things will be when he retires, we're all in for a rocky ride.

"Oh, I don't even know," Ma says, dismissively gesturing with her hand. "He may have found another uneven spot on the concrete floor, or this time it could be a paint drip on the steel beams. Who the hell knows? If he's not bothering the guys here, he's up on the hill stirring up shit there."

Their new house is starting to take shape already as well, but as predicted, the progress is a little slower.

"You should book a trip. Go on a cruise or something. Get him out of here. He says he wants to travel, show you the world. Tell him you need a break. That man will do anything for you. Dan and I can keep an eye out here."

She shakes her head. "He's never gonna go for it."

I grin at her. "Oh, I think he might."

Glancing back at Jonas, I put my fingers in my mouth and blow. His head swings around at my sharp whistle, and I motion for him to join us. He immediately wanders over.

"You're back," he states the obvious. "Did everything with Stephanie's apartment get sorted?"

I'd used that as an excuse when I sent them a message yesterday to let them know we wouldn't be back until this morning. I wasn't about to share I was taking Stephanie for dinner and then a private night at the Red Lion Hotel to celebrate.

"It did."

I hand him a box of books from the back of the truck and give Ma a basket of bathroom linens to carry inside. I follow behind with the rest of Stephanie's books.

She's already inside, putting on a pot of coffee, and turns around when we file into the cabin. Her eyes find mine right away and I shrug in response to the question I read in them.

"Where do you want these?" Jonas asks.

"If you wouldn't mind putting them under the window in the living room for now? I'll figure out where to put those later."

"If you don't have room here, feel free to find a home for them in the big house," Ma offers. "You may as well, you'll be moving in there soon enough."

"Not if those yahoos keep dragging their asses the way they do," Jonas grumbles. "It'll never get done."

"Maybe they could get some work done if you weren't breathing down their necks all the time," my mother fires back, handing me the opening I need.

"You guys should take a trip," I suggest, shooting a pointed look at Ma to weigh in.

"I wish we could," she chimes in. "The dirt and the constant noise of the construction is starting to get to me. I get headaches, my body is aching, and I haven't been sleeping well either."

As expected, that gets my stepfather's attention.

"You should see the doctor."

"I don't need to see a doctor; I need to get away from here for a bit."

"I promise, I'll take you wherever you want to go *after* construction is finished," he returns. "We'll have all the time in the world to travel."

While the two of them are hashing it out, I've made my way over to Stephanie and drape an arm over her shoulders.

"Actually," I interject. "I would strongly suggest using what's left of this summer to get any traveling you were hoping to do out of the way, because there's no way you'll be able to get Ma away from the ranch after March of next year, and you may not wanna go either."

Stephanie snuggles into my side, putting her hand on my chest. She knows where I'm going with this.

"Why the hell not?" Jonas demands to know.

"Because you're both going to want to stick around for the arrival of your first grandchild."

## *Epilogue*

*ALEX*

"Is that them?"

Ama almost shoves me out the front door to get a look at the approaching vehicle.

"Yes, it is, and back off," I snap. "It's my turn now."

Several months ago, Ama got to welcome her gorgeous first granddaughter, Sage, home and I'm not proud to admit I've been green with envy. But I'm damned well going to make sure I'll be the first to greet my brand-new grandson.

Jackson sent pictures last night after he was born, and that little sweetie reminds me so much of his father when he was a baby, it made me cry. Or maybe that was because I so badly wanted to hold that little one, but my son and his wife had requested no visits in the hospital so they could have a chance to connect with their child before introducing him to everyone else.

So yeah, no one—not even Ama—is going to get in the way of my first meeting with my grandson.

I can't believe I'm a grandmother, despite wearing a T-shirt identifying me as Nana with big letters on my chest. Jonas has one that says, Pops. I had to make him wear it, which he grudgingly did. Of course as soon as the guys got here, they've been teasing him, earning me his dirty glares.

I don't care. Stephanie had those shirts made for us and I happen to think it's cute, so Jonas will just have to get over his badass self.

When the truck pulls up right in front, the butterflies that have been dallying about in my stomach since I woke up this morning suddenly explode into a wild frenzy, making me mildly nauseated. I feel like a teenager on prom night, waiting for her date.

I watch as Jackson gets out, rounds the hood to the passenger side, and helps Stephanie out of the vehicle first. Then he ducks in to the back seat and reappears with a baby carrier in his hand. As they climb up the steps to the porch, Jackson glances up and catches sight of me, his face splitting into a wide grin.

*My God, look at my boy. A father.*

"I'll leave you to it," Ama graciously announces as she backs away from the door.

But she is quickly replaced by Jonas, who stands behind me and places a steadying hand on my shoulder as Jackson walks up.

"Let's go into the office," I hear my husband suggest behind me, but I hardly register it.

I'm too busy falling in love with the little sleeping face peeking out between the blanket and the knit beanie covering his head. I let myself get hustled into the old office at the front of the house, where Jackson is already unbuckling the baby with great care.

"Oh, give him to me, already," I blurt out, wiggling my fingers impatiently.

The moment my son places that little bundle in my arms, my butterflies disappear and I feel something in my chest shift into place with a click. Like the final piece of a puzzle filling the last empty spot I didn't realize was there.

I am whole.

~

*Jonas*

This place is a goddamn gong show.

There are bodies everywhere, kids running around, everyone talking and laughing, babies crying.

It's mayhem, and I fucking love it.

My eyes find my wife, who is more beautiful today than I have ever seen her. Beaming with happiness, pure love shining from her eyes, she is stunning.

I found a quiet spot in the corner of the living room, from where I have a view of the entire open space. If this were summer, we'd all be outside for a cookout, but it's cold and it's snowing a little, so everyone is congregated in the house.

Everybody is here. Fletch and Nella dropped by with their son, Hunter, who is a solemn fourteen-year-old but already almost as tall as his father. Sully and Pippa showed up with Carmi, a rambunctious teenager who is currently chasing after Aspen, Dan and Sloane's girl, while their boy, Sammy, is sitting in the high chair, being fed cake by Ama.

Lucy and Bo came to welcome the new addition as well. Bo is still looking pissed because Jackson made Lucy cry—

which is a rarity— when he asked her to be the baby's godmother. Appropriate, since Lucy is like a cross between a sister and an aunt to Jackson. Bo will get over it, Lucy will make sure of that.

Hayley, Wolff and Jillian's twelve-year-old foster daughter, is sitting quietly on a stool in the kitchen, observing everything that goes on around her from under her eyelashes. She'll get used to the boisterous crowd and her place in it, eventually. She doesn't know yet her foster parents have put the wheels in motion to legally adopt her.

Of course, JD and Janey are here with their little girl, Sage, who is currently being burped by Grandpa James. God, the boys and I had some fun ribbing him about becoming a grandfather, right up until we found out I would be joining his ranks shortly after. Now the other guys tease us both.

Before today I'd snap at them, but now I just smile at their antics. Let them laugh, I don't give a rat's ass. Nothing they can say is going to put a damper on the high I'm on. I fucking love being Pops to this little nugget.

"How is he doing?"

Jackson comes over to check on his son. I look down at the tiny human in my arms.

"Yeah, he's fine. Still sleeping. But I'm pretty sure he just shit his diaper."

Jackson grins. "No time like the present to get your hands dirty, Pops," he teases.

"Oh no," I scoff, shaking my head. "You won't get me changing diapers. That's a parent's job, he's all yours."

I reluctantly release my grandson to his father's care.

*Bruce Jonas Hart.* BJ in short.

I about lost my shit when Stephanie announced it.

Named for Jackson's father and for me. Thought my fucking heart was going to explode.

*Jesus.* A new life, named after me.

I don't know if Jackson and Stephanie realize what they've given me.

When Jackson disappears with BJ, I get to my feet and catch Bo's eye, nudging my head to the front of the house. Fletch already caught on and is moving in the same direction, and I see James handing his granddaughter off to her mother. I'm not sure where Sully is, but he'll figure it out.

Shrugging on my winter coat, I check the inside pocket for the cigars I packed in there when we left our place earlier, and step outside.

"Figured you'd find your way out here shortly," Sully says, already perched on the railing.

The other three file out behind me, James with a bottle of bourbon.

"Forget the glasses?"

"Nah, figure we can drink it like we used to," he suggests.

There were only a few occasions I can remember we'd actually have a nice bottle of liquor to share after an assignment—often times it was some cheap local booze with an alcohol level high enough to strip paint off walls. But those celebrations were just as important as the hard and dirty work we did every day, shoulder to shoulder in building this brotherhood we forged.

A brotherhood that still feels as strong as it was almost a lifetime ago.

I hand out cigars while James breaks the seal on the bourbon and passes it around.

This is what I wanted, all those years ago when I aged out and discovered I missed that brotherhood so fiercely, I had to find a way to get it back. And I did, with the ranch and High Mountain Trackers. That's all I wanted.

But what I didn't bank on was that each of us would find a way to make that life even better, and richer, when we let love in.

"We were so sure we had the world by the balls back then," I suggest. "If our former selves could see us now—married, a fucking house full of kids, and now the start of a third generation—we'd have laughed so hard."

Everyone nods in agreement, but it's Bo who responds.

"We were fucking tools."

SHUTTER SPEED

FREEZE FRAME

IDEAL IMAGE

**Portland, ME, Series:**

FROM DUST

CRUEL WATER

THROUGH FIRE

STILL AIR

LuLLaY (a Christmas novella)

**Cedar Tree Series:**

SLIM TO NONE

HUNDRED TO ONE

AGAINST ME

CLEAN LINES

UPPER HAND

LIKE ARROWS

HEAD START

**Standalones:**

WHEN HOPE ENDS

VICTIM OF CIRCUMSTANCE

BONUS KISSES

SECONDS

SNOWBOUND

*About the Author*

USA Today bestselling author Freya Barker loves writing about ordinary people with extraordinary stories. With 60+ titles to her name, Freya inspires with her stories about 'real' people, perhaps less than perfect, each struggling to find their own slice of happy.

Freya has her hands full with a retired husband, a needy pup, and a growing gaggle of grandbabies, but she continues to spin story after story with an endless supply of bruised and dented characters, vying for attention!

Recipient of the ReadFREE.ly 2019 Best Book We've Read All Year Award for "Covering Ollie, the 2015 RomCon "Reader's Choice" Award for Best First Book, "Slim To None", Finalist for the 2017 Kindle Book Award with "From Dust", and Finalist for the 2020 Kindle Book Award with "When Hope Ends", Freya spins story after story with an endless supply of bruised and dented characters, vying for attention!

www.freyabarker.com